THE EDUCATION OF
ASA PAXTON

The Education of Asa Paxton is the first book
in the Haint Blue Series.

Praise for *The Education of Asa Paxton*

"Gary Minder is a fine storyteller and a sensitive student of the human condition. This is as powerful a debut novel as you are likely to read, written with a deep sense of character and place. Bravo!"

—Frye Gaillard, author of *Go South to Freedom* and co-author of
The Southernization of America: A Story of Democracy in the Balance

"Take me somewhere I've never been: 1930s Alabama, authentic and vibrant. Let me step inside the skin of a young transplant struggling to find his place in a culture at once treacherous and inviting, populated with colorful characters who ride the rails, swing hammers, wrestle pigs, defy the odds, and move through this sharply imagined world like believable humans. Mission accomplished."

—Lila Quintero Weaver, author of *My Year in the Middle*
and *Dark Room: A Memoir in Black and White*

"Gary Minder has created an excellent overview of life in 1930s South. He has a gift for creating believable characters and on-point dialogue. I was left wanting much more, and the ending intimates a sequel might soon be in hand."

—TK Cassidy, author of *Whoodah Thunket and the Girls*

"First-time author Gary Minder has created a tender coming-of-age story set against a well-researched backdrop of deep-south segregation. He writes with vivid clarity and sensitivity, confirming that even in the darkest eras of human existence, there are those whose lives serve as beacons of conscience."

—Carolyn Breckinridge, author of *Kaleidoscope Jane & Other Stories,*
Tuscaloosa Moon, and *Tuscaloosa Boneyard*

The Education of Asa Paxton

A Novel

Gary S. Minder

RubyeGay Publishing
Tuscaloosa, Alabama

The Education of Asa Paxton is the conjuring of characters and events out of the soul of the Heart of Dixie. This is a work of fiction. Unless otherwise indicated, all the names, characters, businesses, places, events, and incidents in this book are either the product of the author's imagination or used in a fictitious manner. Any resemblance to actual persons, living or dead, or actual events is purely coincidental.

Cover design by Diana L. Sharples
Interior design by Rebecca Todd Minder

For my children, who make the world a better place.

"Today is the oldest you've ever been, and the youngest you'll ever be again."

—ELEANOR ROOSEVELT

Acknowledgments

I simply have no words to describe my deep gratitude toward my wife Rebecca. She introduced me to characters, helped me research and learn more about all things Southern, edited multiple drafts of the manuscript, designed the interior, and encouraged me every step of the way. Thanks to the folks at Cotton and Gin for their keen eye and solid suggestions. A special thank you to my friends at the Tuscaloosa Writers and Illustrators Guild (TWIG) for providing a safe space to share my writing. I have countless friends and acquaintances who have continually encouraged me, read ongoing drafts, and helped me better understand details of The Depression, nuances like slang, and settings like clothing. Although originally written as a legacy project for my children, I hope *The Education of Asa Paxton* is one that many will enjoy.

The following pages include tobacco and alcohol use and language. Racism, rape, and incest are discussed in the dialogue. This novel is appropriate for adult and mature young adult readers.

In the Heart of Dixie, some things are better left unsaid.

CONTENTS

PART ONE

CHAPTER ONE
THE BURGHOFF

Uncle Clem burst into his tiny apartment and declared the end of SOS and fried bologna for Mom, Dad, and me. "It's gonna be caviar and steak from now on, thanks to Clemont Forrest Paxton." "SOS" wasn't how he said it. Every twelve-year-old in Chicago knew SOS was crass street talk for chipped beef on toast. I didn't dare unpack or even utter those three letters in the presence of Mom or Dad. Unlike me, Uncle Clem didn't hesitate to let the "S-word" fly.

Mom's hand slapped the tabletop. "Clem. The boy, for Pete's sake."

My uncle always made a dramatic entrance, usually laced with profanity. He flashed me a devilish grin. "What about the boy?"

I was "the boy." I was always "the boy," not Asa when Uncle Clem shot off at the mouth. Wondering how the drama would play out, I backed up between the stove and radiator to avoid the crossfire.

"For crying out loud, Clem. We use the proper language in this household—chipped beef on toast."

Dad scolding his brother was bold, considering we took refuge in my uncle's apartment after Dad lost his job and our brownstone flat when the stock market crashed three years earlier in '29.

"Aw, loosen up, Hank. Your Coopers are riding up in all the wrong spots. Big brother has come through for you and yours ... thank you very much."

Dad and Uncle Clem had a long-standing dispute over which twin was the elder. Grandma and Grandpa Paxton said they came out so quickly they were mixed up when issuing birth certificates. They didn't distinguish the birth order. Mom believed my grandparents knew who was older. She felt they made up the ruse to prevent the elder, by only a minute or two, from feeling a sense of authority or birthright. That the twins would disagree on the matter for the rest of their lives hadn't crossed my grandparents' minds. Dad's body language was stiff. He didn't want to rehash what Mom sarcastically called their "age-old feud." He was more interested in how Uncle Clem had come through for us.

"I have great news. Elliot Drumpf killed himself."

"Who?" my parents asked in unison.

"I've told you Drumpf's story. Remember? My first project for Robinson was in Blue Rock, Alabama. I walked in on Robinson's switchyard manager, Drumpf, banging his so-called secretary, Vulva. She wasn't on Robinson's payroll."

Dad looked like he had stepped on a tack. Mom came halfway up from her chair and looked at me for a reaction before laying into my uncle. "Clem! Vulva? For Pete's sake!"

Uncle Clem laughed. "I know. Only in Alabama would someone name their daughter Vulva."

What Uncle Clem meant by "banging Drumpf's secretary" and why the name Vulva riled Mom was beyond my innocence. I first imagined a hammer involved. That didn't make sense. I thought of bangers and mash, a frequent dinner in our home. That wasn't right either—but oh how close I was. Had I been a few years older, I'd have made the connection of Drumpf, a banger sausage on top of Vulva, a warm serving of mashed potatoes. I was seventeen when Uncle Clem's crude remark surfaced from the depths of my mind and finally made sense. The timing of my eureka moment could not have been more disruptive.

"I just left a meeting with Robinson," Uncle Clem revealed. "He was squawl'n because Drumpf screwed him. Robinson never saw it coming. Drumpf falsified loan documents at a savings and loan in Alabama, pretending to have the authority to mortgage a house down the tracks from the Blue Rock rail yard. The loan was in the company's name, which passed credit muster. Drumpf had all the correspondence from the bank sent to the switchyard office. All this took place shortly after he was hired in twenty-one. Back then, bankers played loosey-goosey with their depositors' money. Bank should've asked more questions."

I didn't understand all the talk about banks and correspondence or what it meant to be screwed by Drumpf. I did understand what he meant by squawl'n. It was the type of lingo Uncle Clem used.

A head roll accompanied Mom's heavy sigh. Uncle Clem ignored her. Dad appeared more interested than Mom. "Drumpf made payments for years. We think his plan was to sign the deed over from the company to his name once he paid off the loan. The Chicago office didn't know Robinson Holdings had a mortgage on a house in Alabama. When the market crashed, Robinson cut everyone's pay rather than lay people off. Drumpf couldn't keep up with the loan payments. It finally snatched him in the ass last month after the bank traced legitimate ownership to the head office. Robinson ordered him to Chicago to unravel the mess and can him. With the house payment and Vulva sixty days late, Drumpf took the easy way out."

I knew what he meant about being late on the house payment. It was like being put out of our brownstone flat when Dad lost his job. It wasn't until I was older that I understood what he meant about Vulva being sixty days late.

"Story is, Drumpf took a jug of bourbon halfway out on the Tennessee River train trestle, sat down, and drank till he blacked out. The next train through was the evening non-stop freight from Memphis to Decatur. I bet that train blew through him like grits through a midget."

"What's grits?" I asked my uncle.

"It's like Cream of Wheat. Except they eat grits in the South, and they don't put sugar or milk over them."

"Grits through a midget," I laughed.

Dad growled at me. "That's nothing to laugh about, Asa. A man took his own life. As for you, Clem, we have a small person at church who I doubt would like that type of language."

I could see Mom was wound tighter than a full thread bobbin. Her fingernail drumming ceased. "I don't know why you're telling us all of this. It's time Asa went to play in the stairwell with his friends."

"Hold on, Dory. This concerns your boy, too."

"Please let me stay. Please?"

Mom and Dad gave each other "the look." They had an innate ability to agree on decisions where I was concerned without speaking. Mom shot Uncle Clem a nasty glare. "Asa can stay, but no more vulgarity or violence."

"Dorothy Paxton, you know I don't mean any harm."

"Don't give me that phony, innocent business. Get to the point."

"I've made the deal of the century for you all. Robinson needs someone to run the switchyard in Blue Rock. The job's yours for the taking, Hank."

Mom scoffed, "Blue Rock, Alabama? Out of the question."

"Hear me out, Hank. I told Robinson you're the man for the job. Told him you're smarter than me and can fix anything." Uncle Clem's crazy eyes grew wilder than usual. "Then I started negotiating. I told Robinson the only way you'd move your family is if he paid you enough to take over the payments on the house he inherited from Drumpf's fraud. You'd get the equity already on the loan and the deed when paid off. Once Robinson thought about it, he realized it made business sense. He'd get a trustworthy manager without the headaches of a legal battle over the house with the bank. You know how bankers are these days. They want to rub the dirt off of every red cent."

"What's the catch?" Dad asked.

"It's Alabama," Mom spat.

I wasn't uncomfortable living in Uncle Clem's apartment, but an entire house in a town with a warmer climate, I was ready to start packing. Dad went to his thinking spot—the frosty kitchen window.

"It's out of the question. Hank ... tell him it's out of the question."

Dad stared into the dingy window's wintry abyss—the who, what, where, and when didn't concern him. I was pretty sure he was thinking of the bottom line. My parents never argued in front of me. I could always tell when they were biting their tongue until they could battle it out in private. Things were teetering toward a closed door "discussion" between my folks.

After a tense silence, Dad asked, "What's the pay?"

"Don't know."

"See," Mom said, sounding snotty, like know-it-all Stacy Carter from my fifth-grade class.

Uncle Clem laid dead-pan eyes on Mom while addressing Dad, "I don't know the pay, Hank. You'll have to work it out with Robinson, Hank. He wants to meet you tomorrow morning, Hank. This ain't no pig in a poke, Hank. He's always been fair to my crew and me. Besides, you have any better prospects? You own a house? You have your own apartment? You even got a pot to piss in, Henry Oliver Paxton? You're dang lucky I've earned Robinson's trust over the years, Hank."

The expression on Mom's face—I'd never seen it before. In one fell swoop, Uncle Clem put a lid on Mom and made clear my parents' lack of options.

Uncle Clem crouched to my eye level. "Now then, Hank, Dory, since I just got paid, something you all wouldn't know about, I'd like to take my nephew to dinner at The Berghoff. What are you two having? Shit on a shingle? Again?"

I tried, unsuccessfully, not to laugh.

I'd never been to a fancy restaurant. If I had, I couldn't remember the occasion. Since The Crash, dining out was not an option. I'd also never been out and about with Uncle Clem. He was always a brief stop coming from somewhere and on his way to somewhere else. Thanks to my uncle, we had it better than many Chicagoans. Fortunately, Uncle Clem was away on the tracks with his crew for weeks or months at a time. His job freed up space for Mom, Dad, and me. Every once in a while, I'd wake up to him snoring on the other bed in our shared room, having arrived while I was asleep. He'd be gone before I got home from school. In my mind, the apartment hardly seemed like it was my Uncle's.

"Here. Hold my hand," Uncle Clem ordered when we hit the sidewalk. I scanned the street, hoping none of my buddies were watching. I didn't need Uncle Clem's hand-holding. Kids my age had free reign of the neighborhood. Parents wanted us out of the building, or at least in the stairwell for relief from tight quarters. They knew we couldn't get far since there was no money to ride the L.

The Berghoff overwhelmed this twelve-year-old. A glowing three-story sign affixed to the side of the building was a fitting welcome to the ornate-wood-paneled dining room and bar. Uncle Clem pointed out the exact stools Grandpa, Dad, and he sat on when Grandpa took them for their first beer at eighteen. That's when I realized this was more than going out to eat. Uncle Clem was introducing me to a family tradition. I looked over the German menu and found an item I felt comfortable pronouncing. "What's blutwurst?"

"You don't want that. It's blood sausage. I think you'd like their signature dish. The wiener schnitzel with spaetzle and creamed spinach."

I'd never heard of wiener schnitzel or spaetzle, and creamed spinach sounded about as appetizing as shit on a shingle. Nevertheless, I put my trust in Uncle Clem. He spared me the tongue twister by ordering for both of us and, with a wink, ordered me a large root beer.

We talked the entire evening. I had more questions than he had answers about Blue Rock proper. He did, however, have story after story about the South. He described the world's first self-serve grocery store named Piggly Wiggly. I remained skeptical about a store actually called Piggly Wiggly until I saw one for myself. He talked of his experience in Winona, Mississippi, putting his gandy dancer crew together. Uncle Clem showed me a different side that night. He spoke deliberately and sounded more like Dad than the gritty, wild-eyed man I had come to expect. Looking back, I realize he was preparing me for the culture shock of the Deep South. "Your dad is gonna take that job."

"I don't know about that. When Mom puts her foot—"

"She'll come around. Your mom has good reason to be concerned. She'll make the best of it." With that, he abruptly changed the subject. "Let's stop by the Union League Club on the way home. It makes The Berghoff look like a street-corner hotdog stand."

After the warm apple strudel topped with ice cream, we headed to a stately gray-stone and red-brick building a block out of the way on West Jackson. The doorman greeted my uncle like an old pal. "Hey there, Clem. Who's your little friend?"

"Hi, Ian. This here's my nephew, Asa."

Ian gave me a genuine smile and a warm handshake. "Like King Asa from the Bible?"

"Yeah … um, I mean, yes, sir."

"That's a fine name, laddie."

I followed Uncle Clem's starry eyes up past the imposing gray stone-work of the first five club levels, past the red brick guest room floors, all the way to the eighteenth-story crown of the building. "Asa, for better or for worse, this is where my life changed." It would take six years before I understood what he meant.

Everything my uncle told me that evening whittled down to one sharp point. My life was about to change.

CHAPTER TWO
NORTHERN PRESBYTERIANS

The Southern accent I began developing in my twelfth year never fully harmonized with the Tennessee Valley drawl. If a conversation with a new acquaintance went further than "yes, ma'am" or "no, ma'am," I was dismissively or sometimes suspiciously identified as "ain't from 'round here," "carpetbagger," or "a Yankee." Only once was I called a Yankee in a flattering tone. Otherwise, I was *persona non grata*, or "welcome as an outhouse breeze," as one old son of the South said to me. Damned be the locals as far as I was concerned. My lack of Confederate pedigree can't deny the plain fact my adolescent years spent in scenic northwest Alabama gave me the right to call Blue Rock my hometown.

Our sudden move south from Chicago in 1933 was a blessed escape from our family's financial struggles. I was too young to understand why the move to the Heart of Dixie caused my parents so much consternation. While they were packing our few belongings, Dad uncharacteristically raised his voice at Mom. "I won't pander to those Southern degenerates and their goddamn Jim Crow. They have no right to call themselves Christians." I didn't know at the time what Dad meant by Southern degenerates or who Jim Crow was. When pink blotches developed on his neck and he took the Lord's name in vain, I knew better than to ask questions.

Mom's response was swift and stern. "Hank, the boy heard you. For Pete's sake, don't talk like your brother."

I found Uncle Clem amusing. Mom found him to be quite vulgar. She once told me Uncle Clem wasn't always boorish and boundaryless. When she first met him, he was innocent and unassuming. Mom explained, or complained, how years of living out of boxcars, fraternizing with train engineers, ship deckhands and hobos from New Orleans to Norfolk had taken a toll on my uncle's sense of decorum.

The Uncle Clem I knew was nothing like the two pictures in the apartment of him and Dad. One hung on the wall in the tiny kitchen next to a sepia photograph of Grandma and Grandpa Paxton. The two handsome teens in suits were unmistakably twins. The other sat in a tabletop frame on the dresser in the bedroom Uncle Clem and I shared. Baby-faced toddlers in matching sailor outfits were a mirror image. Over the years, Dad's physical appearance barely changed. Over the same period, Uncle Clem's appearance and demeanor changed dramatically.

My uncle could best be described by the vocation that molded him. Not only was his vocabulary filthy, there was no daily bath in his line of work. His face was weathered and rutted like an old railroad tie. His voice was as rough as a track bed of jagged granite. Yet, unlike his mouth, his character and spirit were as clean and smooth as a well-traveled steel rail. His resemblance to Dad was still there if you looked closely, though a stranger never would identify him as my father's identical twin.

Dad's blasphemous pronouncement about Southern Christians and Jim Crow seemed to go against what little I understood of our family's Christian faith. It shook me when he said, "goddamn." My parents were stoic Northern Presbyterians with a deep sense of acceptance, forgiveness, and social justice, as declared in worship every Sunday. Following announcements, the congregation recited the church's mission statement to begin worship. "Celebrating Christ's universal love, we seek to promote justice, embrace kindness, and walk humbly with God." I memorized the mission statement before I learned the Lord's Prayer or the Doxology. In my mind, Dad was out on a limb regarding Southern Christians and the fellow named Jim Crow.

Family lore traced our bloodline to Richard Warren, a Puritan separatist listed on the 1620 Mayflower passenger manifest. Warren traveled alone and miraculously survived the first winter. His wife and five daughters left England three years later to join him. Five years after that, he was put in the ground at aptly named Burial Hill in Plymouth, Massachusetts. Though his life was cut short, his seed had been planted, for which I am eternally grateful. At some point, a female Warren married a Presbyterian Paxton, thus adding a new branch to the Mayflower family tree. When the Civil War created a moral chasm in the Church and the Southern Presbyterian Church formed, Grandma and Grandpa Paxton became founding members of the Northern Presbyterian Church. Conforming to Presbyterian conventions, Dad was a buttoned-up man. Even when he didn't work for weeks because of The Depression, he kept a stiff upper lip. Every meal began with giving thanks for what little we had. At least a penny was held back for the plate on Sunday. I'd never heard him curse, let alone take the Lord's name in vain. Not long after our move to Alabama, I understood why Dad's steadfast religious convictions were at odds with most of our new neighbors. Altar calls, tent revivals, and baptism by submersion in a muddy river were not part of our spiritual traditions. Southern churches' acceptance of Black Codes and Jim Crow was not on our moral compass. Thankfully, God's grace provided a few righteous Southerners who were my family's salvation.

Our move was both hasty and ten years in the making thanks to Uncle Clem's relationship with his industrialist boss, JR Robinson. I found it hard to imagine my uncle's life, riding the rails with six Mississippi Negroes and a white Louisiana Cajun. Over time, I wove together a few threads from the tales Uncle Clem and his employees told while they visited. Still, there were details of my uncle's life I was not allowed to know.

CHAPTER THREE

1922

C lemont Paxton cut his gandy dancing teeth managing the underground miniature rail system for the Chicago Tunnel Company. While Chicago's elevated train, commonly known as the L, moved people above ground, the compact underground rails moved products, refuse, and mail and provided cool tunnel air to theaters and offices above ground.

In the spring of 1922, Clem received an invitation to lunch at the Union League Club of Chicago as a guest of JR Robinson. Clem passed the gilded entrance of the club many times over the years. He never imagined he would be a guest and didn't know why he'd been invited.

"May I help you?" asked the doorman, dressed in a red velvet tailcoat, shoulder epaulets, and a feather-plumed top hat.

"I'm here to see Mister JR Robinson. His secretary sent me a lunch invitation." Clem's unbuttoned raincoat revealed a crisp white shirt and red tie. He hadn't been to a formal event in several years. At the last minute, he discovered he'd outgrown his only suit jacket.

"Sir, you're not permitted in the main dining room without a jacket," the doorman said as he gauged Clem's frame. "I'll save you trouble with the maître d. We keep a variety of jacket sizes on hand."

Clem was guided to the cloakroom at the secondary entrance on Federal Street. "May I take your raincoat?" the bob-haired attendant asked.

"Yes, thank you."

"Penny, Mister Paxton is going to need a jacket. He's having lunch in the main dining room."

"What size do you wear?" Penny asked.

Clem looked at his arms and midsection. "No idea."

"I was thinking thirty-eight long," the doorman suggested.

Penny disappeared among the racks of overcoats and raincoats. The doorman whispered from the side of his mouth, "Penny's an aspiring flapper by night."

Penny reappeared with a black suit jacket bearing the club's golden crest on the breast pocket. "Give this a try," she said.

The doorman pulled the sleeves of Clem's shirt to expose a little of the white cuff. He turned Clem around and brushed the jacket's shoulders, arms, and back. Penny eyed Clem from head to toe. "You missed your calling, Ian. You should've been a haberdasher."

Ian looked Clem over. "Well done, young man." He extended his arm with the palm of his hand turned upward, "Follow those stairs to the second floor." Clem took two steps forward, stopped, reached into his pocket, and turned back to Ian. "That's kind of you, sir. This is a private club. We don't accept tips."

"Right." Clem started into the lobby, stopped again, and turned back to Penny. "Do I need a ticket for my raincoat?"

"No, sir. Your coat is hanging in the club's jacket spot. We'll trade them out after lunch."

"Right."

Clem took in the club's expansive lobby. A Persian rug partially covered marble floors. Artist's canvases framed with elaborate molding added depth to the dark wood-paneled walls. The coffered ceiling glistened from a silver-leaf pattern. An enormous bouquet filled an urn added life to the space. Ornate wrought-iron balusters supporting a polished-brass banister trimmed the wide marble stairway. Ascending the stairs, Clem stopped halfway, filled his lungs and slowly exhaled.

A tall, thin, lefthanded maître d standing at his podium made notations in a reservation book. Clem waited patiently. The maître d eventually glanced up. Below a large-bony nose, his upper lip and thin pencil mustache quivered at the sight of the gold-crested blazer borrowed from the cloakroom. *Not a member. Doesn't even own a jacket.* Ignoring Clem, he returned to his notating.

"I'm here to meet with Mister JR Robinson."

The maître d snapped to attention. "Oh, yes sir, Mister Paxton, sir. We've been expecting you. Right this way."

The maître d wove between the tables with an unusual gait. His hips twisted slightly, his shoulders and head bent to one side. Clem glanced at patrons' meals, hoping to decipher what to order. One diner was delicately carving some sort of small bird. Another was having a go at what appeared to be a whole trout stuffed with creamed onions. The fancy accompaniments in, on, and around the meats concerned him. He was out of his culinary element.

In the back corner of the dining room, a square table with two place settings arranged at right angles from each other provided a view of the entire room. The maître d coughed gently. Broadsheets of the Wall Street Journal folded, revealing a short, stocky, mustached, middle-aged gentleman. "Mister Robinson. I'd like to introduce Mister Paxton." Clem was unaware the maître d's order of introduction was proper etiquette. Robinson rose and shook Clem's hand firmly.

"Have a seat, Mister Paxton."

"Please, call me Clem."

"Very well then, Clem. I imagine you're wondering why you're here."

"Yes, sir."

"Let's order first. Then we can talk about what's on my mind. I'm having the steak frites. It's wonderful. They serve the filet with a hollandaise sauce. The fries are perfectly crisp. Order whatever you like."

"Sounds good to me," Clem said without looking at the menu. Steak with fries sounded simple enough, although he wasn't sure about the sauce.

A waiter appeared and stood stiffly with his hands behind his back. "May I take your order, or would you like more time?"

Robinson looked at Clem with a snicker. "I'll have the steak frites, medium rare, and a glass of Bordeaux."

"Perhaps your usual, sir, soda water with lemon." The waiter turned and leaned slightly toward Clem. "And you, sir?"

"I'll have the same, except I'd like a glass of milk."

"Excellent, sir." The waiter collected the menus and backed away from the table.

"I miss a glass of wine with my meal or a scotch with my after-dinner cigar. These damn politicians with their self-righteous alcohol prohibition."

"Yes, sir."

"So, Clem, I've had my eye on you the past couple of years. I've asked around about your family, work habits, and temperament. I've been told, early in your career, you caught wind of a labor leader trying to organize a union with the boys you manage underground. Story is you deftly negotiated a raise for your workers. The union walked away empty-handed."

Clem paused momentarily to formulate his response. "Yes, sir. It kept my workers happy and the union out of our hair."

"Risky strategy. They could have unionized even after a raise."

Clem picked up his polished knife and examined his eyes in the reflection, contemplating what to say next. "Yes, sir. It may have been risky, but let me tell you my management philosophy. Assuming this is an interview?"

Robinson smiled approvingly. "Go on."

"I have no problem with unions if it's what the workers want. However, I have a problem with union-busting thugs. I don't believe in squeezing as much out of a man for as little pay as possible. If you hire good people, pay them fairly, and treat them with respect, they will do what they are hired to do. They'll stick with you and save time and money in the long run, Mister Robinson."

"Please, call me JR."

"JR, you ask any business running products underground. They'll tell you there are no light fingers on my crew. So far, I've avoided moving whiskey for the Mob or paying bribes for police protection."

"I like your management philosophy. Hopefully, you'll be interested in the opportunity."

"I've topped out underground. I'd be foolish not to keep my options open."

"I need one confirmation before we go any further. I understand you're single with a twin brother here in Chicago. Parents up near Evanston, correct?"

"Yes, sir. I don't like the idea of being tied down. Perhaps one day ... if

I meet the right gal."

"Perfect. Let me explain what I have in mind. I've been expanding my businesses. I own companies in several industries, mostly in the Midwest and the Southeast. They all fall under Robinson Holdings. I'm the majority stockholder in all the companies except for my stake in railroads. An issue recently brought several of my businesses to a standstill. A shipment of cotton and coal bound for one of my textile mills was delayed for days due to maintenance issues on the rail line they were traveling." Robinson leaned forward to emphasize his point. "It cost me a pretty penny. The owner of the railroad was a little too comfortable and didn't put a priority on the repairs. I can't have a slowdown in production. I'm investing in rail lines for leverage."

"I'm guessing you have me here to talk about rail work?"

Robinson's hand banged the tabletop. "Exactly. You'd be away from home most of the year. That's why I asked about your marital status."

Clem leaned toward Robinson with his elbows on the table and his hands clasped together. "Tell me more about the job."

"If we agree to do business, you'll assemble a crew of gandy dancers as my hot-shot repair crew. If there is trouble on a line affecting my business, you fix it, and fix it fast."

"Sounds like a lot of hurry up and wait for a problem."

"It's more than the occasional track problem. You and your crew will also be one of my profit centers, albeit a small revenue stream. I'll contract you out to businesses when you're not working on a breakdown or routine maintenance. Every new factory, warehouse, and grain silo needs a side track to access the main routes."

The server interrupted the conversation with an entrée in each hand. Robinson picked up his fork and steak knife and rubbed them together as if to sharpen the blade. Clem thought better of attempting the strange ritual he was witnessing. Robinson jabbed a crisp potato fry with his fork and swooped it through the creamy hollandaise covering his steak. Clem followed suit with a potato fry, and the discussion continued through the meal.

"I wouldn't know where to start with assembling a traveling crew."

"It's up to you, but I have a suggestion. I'd go south. Mississippi or Alabama. Hire a group of Negroes. We'll pay them fairly. If you treat them right, they'll be loyal and work hard."

"That's an interesting angle."

"If you decided on that route, beware of the white people down there. They still think Negroes are less than human and they have divine dominion over them. Let them think your crew works at sharecropper wages and conditions."

Clem expressed several other concerns as the two men dined. Robinson assuaged each situation. He had a plan for everything—including Clem's training.

The waiter appeared with a tray of dessert selections and offered coffee. "I'll pass. Have whatever you'd like, Clem."

"No, thank you. The steak and holiday sauce was delicious and filling."

A grin tightened Robinson's lips. He retrieved a folded sheet of paper from his breast pocket and handed it to Clem. "There's my offer. I believe it's fair, given you and your crew will be away from home most of the year. No feather-pillow hotels and fancy restaurants. It'll be boxcars, fire pits, and canned beans."

Clem held the offer for several seconds while he composed himself. Once he unfolded the paper, he examined it as if it were a hand in a high-stakes poker game. There were two line items. One labeled "Supervisor" with a figure Clem would have never expected. The second, marked "Crew X 7," was equally shocking. Maintaining his poker face, Clem asked, "May I keep this?"

"Depends. Are you still interested?"

"I'm interested," Clem replied with the slightest of smiles.

"Come by my office tomorrow. I'll introduce you to some of my people."

Lunch was over. Clem returned the borrowed jacket and left the club on cloud nine. If everything worked out, his income would more than triple, and he'd be working for who appeared to be a fair man.

CHAPTER FOUR
WINONA, MISSISSIPPI

Over three months, Clemont Paxton learned the ins and outs of Robinson Holdings. He adapted his experience with the two-foot-wide rail lines under the heart of Chicago to the skills necessary to manage full-sized tracks. More importantly, he learned how to read the rail routes and freight schedules covering the eastern half of the United States. "Time to sink or swim," Robinson told Clem during what would be their last weekly lunch meeting.

Clem took Robinson's advice of hiring a crew of Negroes in the South. He could have booked a room on the company dime aboard the full-service Panama Limited departing Chicago's stately Union Station en route to New Orleans. Instead, he hopped a boxcar on a dead-heading freight train traveling the same line from the Grant Park industrial railyard. With a rucksack, a bedroll, and an aluminum tube filled with rail maps and schedules, Clemont Paxton left behind his tiny apartment and his predictable life. He was on his way toward an uncertain future with the excitement of a young greenhorn on a new adventure.

The boxcar jolted back and forth as the locomotive departed. Eventually, the jerking gave way to gentle rocking from side to side. Chicago's skyline faded into the twilight as the Brooks locomotive ushered its boxcars south through the plains of Illinois. Lights from distant farmhouses dotted the landscape, the farthest of which became one with the star-scape of the crescent-moon night.

Clem's excitement eventually succumbed to heavy eyes, rhythmic track seams, and the train's sway. Every so often, he was woken by the jolt of the train slowing to pass through a small town. Matches illuminated Clem's pocket watch, first at 12:30 a.m. Again, at 1:55 a.m. After a 3:10 a.m. awakening, he closed the boxcar doors and fell into a deep, peaceful sleep.

Clem woke to sunbeams flowing through small gaps in the boxcar walls. Particles of dust danced in illuminated wisps of coal smoke above his face. He took a moment to shake off the sleep before crawling to the east door of the car. With a yank, Clem slid the door wide open. Bright sunshine set an embankment of iron-rich-red soil ablaze, shocking Clem's morning eyes. He quickly shut the door and retreated to the west side of the car. He slid the door open cautiously, revealing a neighborhood of uniform streets and well-maintained homes. The train passed through a deserted downtown and diverted west onto a parallel track, moving away from a passenger rail station.

A "Winona, Mississippi" sign dangled above the passenger platform. Clem recognized the name from his studies and concluded he was in Central Mississippi. Clear of the tracks dedicated to the passenger station, the two sets became one, passing several small industrial businesses and warehouses. Tufts of cotton clung to buildings' common brick exteriors. Exiting town, the line paralleled a stand of trees, separated from the tracks by a poorly maintained dirt road.

Looking south in the distance, Clem could make out a clearing. The train came upon a small community of narrow, wooden homes with rusted tin roofs. Houses were either unpainted or covered with sad, cracked, and faded whitewash. At their base, the wood-clad boards were stained a pale red from rain-splattered iron-rich soil. Unlike Winona proper, there was not a single blade of grass.

The neighborhood was eerily quiet. Not a soul in plain sight. The only signs of life were chickens scratching about, several makeshift pens

holding hogs, and a mule tied to a wooden post. Based on his under-
standing of the South, Clem assumed the community was the Negro section of segregated Winona. The type of community he planned to prospect in for laborers. There was no time to hesitate. Clem grabbed his
belongings. With butterflies in his stomach, he leaped from the train.

In the distance, the faint sound of a piano and a man's voice broke
through the silent air. He realized Sunday worship services explained
the stillness of Winona and the segregated outlier community. He wove
his way on the dirt paths, tracking the buzz of the gospel worship. The
source was a simple but pristine church. Unlike the whitewashed homes
in the community, the church's clapboards boasted a thick coat of white
paint. Two wooden steps, the width of the building, led to a wide-shallow
porch. A simple wooden cross hung on the A-frame section between the
church's main entrance and the pitched roof line. Double doors propped
open against the outer walls welcomed in the fresh air.

A piano struck chords in time with the preacher's booming cadence.
From a distance, Clem couldn't make out the worship leader's words,
though he was generously filled with The Spirit. Clem approached
the church from a wide angle to avoid the line of sight from the pulpit. He took up a position at the outside edge of the doorway. From the
porch, he could hear the message clearly and see half of the congregation seated on the left side of the church. Men, women, and children in
their Sunday best filled the backless pews. It was a steamy Mississippi
morning, and the preacher appeared to have been at it a good spell.
Women fanned themselves. Men wiped their faces and the backs of
their necks with handkerchiefs. After bouncing around Bible passages,
the preacher proclaimed, "I'll let the Apostle Matthew bring it all home."
His long pause created the desired effect. There were dramatic "amens,"
calls of "go'n wit it," and "preach, brotha" from the congregation.

The preacher belted out Matthew 5:5. "Blessed are the meek, for
they shall inherit the earth." In a more subdued tone, he said, "Let me
break it down. On Friday, the white man from the South don't hide his
hate, and the white man from the North don't keep his promise. Forty
acres and a mule means we think you a fool. But now don't y'all lose
faith. Sunday's a-comin'."

His volume would build with each conviction, then tail off toward the end. The congregation would echo, "Sunday's a-comin'."

"On Friday, the white man from the South cheat the black man out of government, and the white man in the North let it happen. Don't lose faith. Sunday's a-comin'. On Friday, the white man in the North says you free, but don't come up here. The South is where you got to be. Don't lose faith. Sunday's a-comin'. On Friday, the white man from the South says you is a sharecropper now and in debt to me. Don't lose faith, y'all. Sunday's a-comin'."

The preacher forearmed the beads of sweat above his eyes. "Psalm 37:7 tells us, 'Be still before the Lord and wait patiently for Him; do not fret when people succeed in their ways when they carry out their wicked schemes.'"

With a quiver in his voice, the preacher saved his most damning conviction for last. "The white man hang our sisters and brothers like Jesus on the cross, 'cep'm from a rope and a tree." The preacher closed his Bible, grasped each side of the pulpit, and stood silent with his eyes closed and face toward the church rafters. Clem peeked his head in and out of the doorway. He remained undetected. Once the congregation ceased their vocal expressions, the preacher continued. "All these crimes may be a heavy burden for our people but we know what Jesus knew as he hung on the cross that Good Friday so long ago." With a deep breath, his voice erupted with all the guttural strength he could muster. "That's OK. Cause Sunday's a-comin'. And on the third day, come Sunday, Jesus knew he gonna win. And come someday, the meek shall inherit the earth."

The pianist crashed down on the out-of-tune keys. The congregation leaped to their feet, clapping and dancing in a frenzied rhythm to the music. Some congregants broke out in song while others proclaimed joyful, "amen," "praise the Lord," and other shouts of jubilation.

Clem peeked inside and saw the preacher dancing his way from the pulpit down the center aisle. He jerked his head back from the doorway. The preacher's convictions of the white man had Clem unsettled about his circumstances. He was on the wrong side of town. The train was long gone. The angry preacher was headed his way. And he was as white as a KKK robe.

Crossing the sanctuary, the preacher took the customary place to greet the congregants as they exited the church. He looked up and saw

Clem standing across the doorway. His eyes widened. His jaw slacked. His Bible hit the ground. The preacher's voice cracked, "Who are you?"

Before Clem could respond, a large older woman with a young boy in tow crossed the threshold to greet the pastor. She didn't see Clem. The young boy did. With youthful innocence, the boy asked, "Is you the white man from the North, or is you the white man from the South?"

The older woman turned, looked wide-eyed at Clem. Her head lashed back to the preacher, and without saying a word, she grabbed the little boy by the forearm and hurried off.

Clem stepped into the doorway, picked up the Bible with his left hand and offered his right hand. Instead of accepting the handshake, the preacher nervously surveyed the surroundings. The congregation went from a raucous, joyful exodus toward the front door, into murmurs and an about-face at the sight of a white man. Other than the pianist, every man, woman, and child hurried to a side exit.

"Who sent you? Who's you whit?" the preacher asked.

"No one sent me. I work for Robinson Holdings out of Chicago. I'm here looking for a handful of workers."

"You's here lookin' fo some niggahs?"

"No, sir. I was raised not to use that term. I'm looking for seven strong men to work on the railroads."

The preacher's cadence, posture, and dialect changed as if he flipped a switch. "So you're looking for some Negro men you can work hard, pay poorly, and take advantage of, is that it?" He reached over to Clem's hip and grabbed his Bible.

"No, sir. I am not. I can pay a group of Negro men more money than they can make in the South. That'll keep them loyal and on the job. As a man of God in this community, you might have some influence over a few strapping young men who could use a good-paying job. Perhaps you'd be willing to help me?"

The man of God rubbed the salt and pepper stubble on his face. "What did you say your name was?" the preacher asked, extending his right hand.

"Clem Paxton."

"My name is Thomas Freeman. Everyone calls me Preacher. How about we step inside and talk?" Preacher yelled across the sanctuary to the pianist organizing sheet music. "Sam, this here is Clem Paxton from Chicago. You go on home. We're gonna stay here and talk a while."

"OK, Pop," the pianist replied and exited the side door.

After an hour-long conversation, which included more than one mention of the wage offer, Preacher agreed to help Clem. "It would be best if I talk to the folks I have in mind first."

"Sounds good although I have two caveats. It's been suggested while in the South, there is always the impression my crew works at no better than sharecropper conditions and wages. I don't care for that notion and mean no disrespect."

"That was good advice. White folks around here don't take kindly to any Negro success."

"One more thing. I have an assignment in Blue Rock, Alabama. It's not urgent, but the sooner we can put this together and head out, the better. In the meantime, can you suggest a place to bed down?"

"There's a motor lodge in town. White folks only, of course. Miz Hattie works there, cooking and cleaning. She says it's really nice. The room comes with supper and breakfast. Follow the tracks back into town. It's across from the courthouse."

"So, what's the next step?"

"I'll explain everything we talked about to some folks this afternoon. Meet me here at nine o'clock tomorrow morning. I'll take you around. I hope you know what you're getting yourself into."

The two men parted ways. Clem would have felt he had a successful morning had Preacher not questioned what he was getting into. Not a soul was in sight as Clem traced his steps back to the tracks and dirt road to the white side of town.

The Negro side of town had been a culture shock. The motor lodge was Clem's second culture shock of the day. Winona Inn Motor Lodge may have been "real nice" by Miz Hattie's standards, however, the small-town establishment was a far cry from the Chicago hotels Clem was familiar with. At one time, it was a large house or perhaps a plantation Master's home. The relic survived the Union Army's fiery march through the South. The dingy-whitewashed two-story wooden struc-ture rested on a stacked brick foundation. Clem felt a sensation of being off balance as he stepped across the creaky sloped porch.

The proprietor, doubling as the front desk clerk, greeted Clem out of the corner of his eye rather than looking him straight on. "How you?"

"I'm well, thank you. I'd like a room for a night or two."

The clerk looked over Clem's shoulder at the rucksack and metal tube. "Well, which is it? One night or two?"

"Let's start with one night."

"Ya look like some kinda wunderer. We don't want no trouble."

Clem couldn't understand what the clerk said in his thick accent. "What do you mean by wunderer?"

"Wunderer. Like a hobo."

Clem answered the question with his wad of folding money. The clerk turned the guest book to Clem. "Aight then. Sign here. What brings you to Winona anyhow?"

Clem side-stepped the question. "What time is dinner?"

"Fie. In yonder room."

Clem kept the purpose of his visit close to the vest and attributed the reception to his Midwestern accent, wanderer-style luggage, and bed-roll. After the awkward exchange, Clem spent the afternoon holed up in his room, studying his maps and freight schedules until five o'clock.

Dinner was a low-brow affair. The waitress called the night's meal "to-day's meat-and-three plate" before asking, "Whachoo wanna drank—sweet tea, water or arrah-see?"

There was no choice in the matter of the "plate." Clem was served a stiff country-fried steak swimming in white gravy, purple-hull peas, collards, and a triangle-shaped piece of dry cornbread. A small bowl of banana pudding for dessert was served along with the "plate." Clem was no stranger to banana pudding. However, this was his introduction to the incarnation with a layer of vanilla-flavored cookies. The meat-and-three served as sustenance. Banana pudding was an enjoyable treat, making the meal worthwhile.

Exhausted from the day's events, Clem sat in the rocking chair by the window in his room. He watched the sun slowly settle behind the mas-sive domed courthouse guarded by a limestone soldier "Honoring The

Confederacy, President Jefferson Davis And The Soldiers Who Fought For States' Rights." The back-and-forth rocking did little to soothe Clem, nagged by Robinson's warning to beware of the Southern whites and Preacher's ominous comment about what Clem was "getting into."

CHAPTER FIVE
GANDY DANCERS

Wafts of hickory smoke, sizzling fatty sausage, and an orchestra of birdsong woke Clem. The extensive repertoire of a male mockingbird staking out his territory rose above the common flock. Clem's pocket watch read seven o'clock. Plenty of time to lounge and listen to the mockingbird chirp his way through various calls before a brief pause, followed by a repeat performance.

After splashing water in his face from the clay pitcher and basin in his room, Clem stopped at the communal lavatory on his way to breakfast. The tough country-fried steak was in the way of his morning constitution, allowing only fluid relief.

Breakfast was a serve-yourself undertaking consisting of a large pot of sausage gravy kept warm on a hot plate flanked by a pile of biscuits. The gravy was either the same recipe as the previous night's chicken-fried steak gravy or leftovers with sausage added for heartiness. Next to the biscuits sat a large bowl of unidentifiable, pale-green semi-gelatinous carnage. "Excuse me. What is this?" Clem asked the lady ahead of him in line.

"Sweet-pickled watermelon rind," the woman answered in a thick drawl.

Clem scooped out a small portion to give it a go, ensuring the watermelon avoided contact with the rest of the breakfast. He wolfed down his biscuits and gravy. A bite-sized chunk of the pickled watermelon was a cautionary sample. The combination of texture and flavor was unlike anything he had ever experienced. Firm and slimy with a sweet and tangy tickle of his tongue. It was refreshing. Pleasantly surprised, he finished the portion and returned to the buffet for another larger portion. He discovered a short time later the sweet and succulent rind had the added effect of a laxative.

Clem visited the lavatory a second time for a long and strenuous evacuation of his bowels. Afterward, he secured his belongings in his room and locked the door. On the way out, he stopped at the front desk to pay for a second night. With a spring in his step from his successful lavatory visit, he headed back to the Negro enclave.

A day made all the difference when Clem entered Preacher's neighborhood. On this day, people went about their business. Clem's arrival was met with either a pleasant stare or a smile. A wave from a teenage girl having her hair braided on a front porch let Clem know he was welcome. Word of his good intentions had obviously filtered throughout the community. Preacher rose from the church steps and brushed the dust from his backside. "Good morning. I wasn't sure if you'd be back."

"Good morning. What do you mean, 'wasn't sure I'd be back'?"

Preacher accepted Clem's outstretched hand. "Our conversation yesterday sounded too good to be true."

"I'm committed now. I've got to make it work. Do you have some prospects for me?"

"I do indeed. I have to warn you, though. There's some skepticism. Maybe suspicion is a better word. White folks don't show up out of nowhere offering jobs with that kind of pay down Mississippi way."

"How will I know if they're good workers?"

Preacher gave Clem a disgusted glare. "Have you already forgotten where you are? This is Mississippi, son. The only work around here for Negro folk is hard work, back-breaking work. I thought that's why you came here."

"I'm sorry. You're right. Let's move on."

Preacher led Clem to a shack three doors down from the church. It mimicked every other shotgun shack in sight, tidy but in need of repairs. The house could've used a new front porch. Several floor-boards were missing, the rest weathered and uneven. Clem eyed curi-ously a clear mason jar filled with water and pink granite pebbles hung by a string in the center of the open doorway.

"It's to ward off flies," Preacher told Clem.

Bright sunshine outside and the lack of natural light inside muted ev-erything between the front and back doors. From the porch, Clem made out a simple furniture arrangement. A ragged settee and side table near the front of the shack served as a living room. A potbelly heating and cooking stove was strategically centered in the middle of the struc-ture for maximum efficiency. To the left of the stove, a dining table with bench seating made the house a home. The right side of the stove pro-vided a clear path to the back door. A double bed butted up to the outer wall of a room at the back left side of the house.

"Mack? Miz Edna? Y'all in there?" Preacher yelled.

A woman with a strong voice hollered back, "You got the white man whit you, Preacha?"

"Yes, ma'am."

"Well, c'mon."

The woman waddled across the floor to meet Preacher and Clem next to the settee. "So you want to take my Mack away? Whatchoo think? You think we need some kinda white savior?" Edna scolded, inching closer to Clem. "We don't need no white savior." She continued her tirade, be-coming louder and more animated. "Y'all think you better than us. All y'all wanna do is take advantage. Let me tell you some—"

Clem had enough. "Miz Edna, I doubt you'd harangue me if I were a white landowner from Winona paying your Mack sharecropper wages to pick cotton. I'd wager you'd be more worried about what they might do to you and your Mack if you let loose your tongue on them like you are with me."

Clem followed Edna's eyes to Preacher, who had backed into the cor-ner of the room. Preacher's right arm was bent at his elbow, with his fist over his mouth. Clem could see the smirk under Preacher's hand as he gave Miz Edna a gentle, disapproving nod.

"Humph." She turned and stormed toward the back door, mumbling under her breath while at the same time repeatedly yelling, "Mack, get yo two-faced black ass out here."

A tall, slender figure stumbled through a side bedroom or bathroom door. His hands fumbled with a rope serving as a belt around his baggy pants. Preacher yelled with laughter, "Miz Edna, let him finish his mornin' business." Miz Edna ignored Preacher. She was on Mack's heels, heading back to the front of the shack.

Clem stretched his hand out to introduce himself. Miz Edna stepped in front of Mack. "You gonna give him work clothes?"

Clem didn't notice Miz Edna's pointer finger inches from his chin. He was fixated on Mack's vitiligo-divided face. Beginning at Mack's left temple, a distinct separation of dark and light skin angled halfway across his nose, and past the right side of his lips and chin, ending at the shirt collar. Two dime-sized light dots stood out on the dark half of his face. One dark spot contrasted the white cheek.

"I said, is you gonna give him work clothes?"

"Uh, yes, ma'am."

"And work boots?"

"Yes, ma'am," Clem said, hearing without listening to what Miz Edna demanded. "What happened to your face?" Clem asked.

Miz Edna did the answering. "God didn't know if he should be black or white. Whachoo care? He can swing a hammer."

Clem snapped out of his stare and reached around Miz Edna's large body to shake Mack's hand. "My hand gots it, too."

"Makes no difference to me," Clem said, giving a long, accepting handshake.

After several minutes of finalizing details, Preacher and Clem left. Once they rounded the side of a neighbor's house, Preacher fell out in laughter. "It doesn't matter. Black or white, that man needs a savior from his woman."

"You should've warned me about her. And his face." Preacher kept on laughing. "And speaking of two-faced, what's your story? You go from speaking Mississippi Negro to Northern English like flipping a light switch."

Preacher stopped in the middle of the dirt road, stared at the ground, and contemplated his response. "What do you know about Reconstruction?" Preacher asked.

"What's Reconstruction?"

"That's what I thought." After a long pause, he looked Clem in the eye and went on. "The simple answer about my speech. My parents were born into slavery, but they secretly educated themselves. After the Civil War, during Reconstruction, my father became a state representative. He was a skilled orator but never lost his ability to relate to Negro Mississippians. My father insisted my communication be respected by both white people and Negroes. The whole Reconstruction plan didn't work out well for us Negroes. Maybe I'll explain it to you one day. We don't have time now."

Preacher continued down the dirt road. Clem followed silently, stupefied. Preacher was a more complicated man than he assumed.

Clem was led to a wooded area at the edge of the community. A pig trail wove between large, heavily canopied trees. Cool night-time air lingered in the shade. Morning dew remained thick on moss-covered tree trunks. Large glistening spider webs stretched from tree branch to tree branch. After a short stretch, a roadless shanty neighborhood emerged. The scent of damp smoke and moist-iron-rich soil filled the air. Windowless shacks were cobbled together with scrap metal, discarded furniture, and an occasional row of clapboards and shingles. Clem looked around the squalid shanty town in shock. "This is unreal."

"What? Didn't you know people lived like this? There are twin brothers who grew up in this slum. They could use a break in life. They could use your jobs."

"Twins? How exciting. Guess what, Preacher? I'm a twin."

"There's another like you? Lord help us."

"My brother and I have much in common, but we're also very different. He's settled down in Chicago with a wife and one-year-old boy."

Preacher pointed to a large magnolia tree skirted at its lower third. "Twins' place. They're clever using the magnolia for an extra layer of shelter. It keeps most of its leaves year-round."

A mashup of wood, tin, and shingles encompassed the bottom of the tree. Animal skins were skillfully stitched together and fastened around the trunk below the first layer of leafy branches. The hides were pulled tight and fastened to materials making up the dwelling's outer walls. Their home was neither a shack nor a teepee—it was both.

"What are their names?"

"Jesse and Jacob Charlochee. Everyone calls them both Twin. They're always together, and you can't tell them apart. It's easier to address them as one person."

"Any surprises, like Miz Edna and Mack?"

"I don't think so. They don't say much but understand the job. This is just a formality."

"Twin," Preacher hollered.

Two men emerged from the structure. Their ragged outfits were almost as identical as their rugged faces. They had strong-sharp jawlines and bony-narrow noses with wise deep-set eyes. The twins' only distinguishable difference was in their newsboy hats. One was a houndstooth pattern, the other an Irish tweed.

As predicted, the conversation was one-sided. Clem rambled while the twins replied in grunts. Arrangements were made, and the twins ducked back into their place.

"That was awkward," Clem said.

"Of course it was. Their upbringing wasn't like yours or mine. They're half Creek Indian."

"I don't understand. Half Creek Indian?"

"Of course you don't understand. You've spent your whole life within the Chicago city limits. Right?"

"Pretty much."

"The twin's father was a Creek Indian. Their mother was a young slave he purchased. They're half Indian and half Negro. Somehow, they ended up in Mississippi instead of Alabama or Oklahoma."

Clem was dumbfounded. He grabbed Preacher by the arm and stopped him on the trail. "You're telling me Indians had Negro slaves?"

"You have entered a strange and complicated world, Mister Clem Paxton. Come on. Let's go see Miz Frida and Tiny." Clem silently trailed Preacher, trying to make sense of Indians owning slaves. He had never given much thought about slaves nor Indians, much less whether one owned the other.

They came upon a large single-story home at the west edge of the community. The age-old brown batten board house was a stain on a background of lily-white cotton sewn all the way to a creek watering a stand of meandering trees.

"Back in slave days, this house was the overseer's quarters. After the war, Miz Frida squatted it."

"After the Civil War? How old is Miz Frida?"

"Old. No one knows how old. When the Union Army came through, they burned down the big house and ran off all the white folks. Miz Frida has lived there ever since."

Preacher pointed to an Osage Orange wood post protruding from the ground on the side of the house. Its decades-old iron restraining ring remained in the hardest of wood, as if slavery would exist into the next millennia. "I think Miz Frida feels like she paid for the house on that whipping post."

"My god."

"Tiny is her grandbaby. Her daughter died giving birth."

"What happened to Tiny's father?"

"He went North. Said he wasn't really free in the South. Miz Frida wouldn't let him take Tiny. Haven't heard from him since."

"Is she going to let me take him for my crew? Does he need her permission?"

"He's a grown man now. He's not very educated. He has a lot of common sense, though. A hard worker, too. He wouldn't leave Frida without her blessing. Miz Frida wants to meet you before she decides to give it or not."

Clem started toward the porch. Preacher grabbed him by the arm. "Now hold up, son. You best treat Miz Frida with the utmost respect and reverence. She can hardly see and barely walk or talk. An overseer once choked her so hard it messed up her voice box. She's had a hard life."

"I understand. I can only imagine what this woman has seen and been through."

Preacher rapped hard on the screen door. The front door was propped open with a straight view of the glowing white cotton outside the open back door.

"Miz Frida," Preacher yelled, "It's me, Preacher, and Mister Paxton we done talked about yesterday. We's comin' in."

Miz Frida sat in the light of an open window overlooking the whipping post. Her back to the door, she moved gently back and forth in a rocking chair. Her arm raised from under a shawl and gave a weak wave, accepting her guests.

Preacher stopped Clem from proceeding any farther than just inside the screen door. He went to the old woman and leaned his ear close to her mouth. Preacher's head nodded, taking in her words. Clem could barely hear her strained voice.

Preacher stood upright and waved Clem over. Miz Frida inched her way to the edge of her chair, grabbed Preacher's arm, and pulled herself up. Her shawl fell from her shoulders into the rocking chair. She wore a loose, full-length skirt and a white shirt with thin shoulder straps. The shirt covered only her breasts and the lower half of her torso. Light from the window exposed long-ridged scars from the top of each shoulder, crisscrossing down her back. In a raspy voice, Miz Frida ordered Clem, "Come close. Come into the light."

Clem stepped into the beam of light, a couple of feet from Miz Frida.

"Closer."

Clem took another step. Miz Frida grabbed Clem's shirt and pulled him in—inches from her. "Let me have a look."

Staring up at Clem's face, she cupped his jaws with her cotton-picking-gnarled fingers. Slowly, she rotated both her head and Clem's head. Miz Frida's large-milky cataract pupils were surrounded by dark rings. "You's young." Her swollen knuckles moved over Clem's cheekbones to his eyes, which reflexively closed. Clem stood stiffly.

"You's belly churn'n, I can tell. But you's strong-willed to come down to Mississippi."

Her hand slid down each side of his nose to his mouth. Cracked thumb skin gently pressed the middle of his lips, then moved to each side of his mouth before dropping to his chin. She pinched Clem's chin bone with her thumbs and forefingers. "I can tell you's a good boy. A kind boy to take a chance on us. I trusts you."

Clem felt a numbness emanating from his chest and climbing up his spine, first to the nape of his neck, then through his skull to the back of his eyes. He couldn't hold back the tears. Clemont Paxton was overcome with a feeling of both honor and unworthiness in Miz Frida's presence. He felt insignificant compared to the former slave.

Frida lovingly wiped Clem's cheeks. "Preacha. Go fetch Tiny from out back."

While Preacher collected Tiny, Miz Frida imparted her sage advice. She took Clem by the hands. "Boy, when life give you the bullwhip, and at some time it do, you gots to be strong and carry on."

"Yes, ma'am. Thank you, ma'am."

The whine and slap of the rear screen door grabbed Clem's attention. Preacher's average frame was a shadow in the doorway against the bright cotton field. The screen door opened and shut again. Preacher's frame was overtaken by an enormous figure blotting out all but a ghostly white cotton hue around the massive silhouette. The figure continued to grow as he walked toward the front room.

"This here's Tiny. Tiny, this here's Mister Paxton."

In front of Clem stood a man with legs the size of Clem's midsection. He was barrel-chested with a slender waist. Each muscular arm was thicker than one of Clem's legs. His broad shoulders barely distinguished his neck from a round and baby-faced head. Instinct took over Clem's stunned state. He reached out to shake Tiny's hand. Tiny looked for approval from his grandmother. After a nod from Miz Frida, Tiny gently engulfed Clem's hand.

"Mimi told me I could goes wit'choo and have a real job working on the train tracks."

"Yes, sir," said Clem.

"Mimi promised Preacher and Sam go'n look after me. Keep me safe."

Clem looked at Preacher with confusion. He pursed his lips and shook Clem off. They made arrangements to depart the following day. Miz Frida gingerly hugged Clem goodbye.

One step off the porch, Clem asked, "What did Tiny mean about you and Sam looking after him?"

"I didn't want to cause Miz Frida any concern back there. Sam and I are the last two prospects I have to offer for your crew ... or, I should say, require. Miz Edna, the twins, and Miz Frida would only agree to the job if I were part of the crew. I'm not going anywhere without Sam. That makes six of the seven spots you need to fill."

"How old are you?"

"I'm young enough to put in an honest day's work. I'm old enough to know you need me more than I need you."

"You're being awfully presumptuous."

"I presume you've only worked with Italian and Irish men up in Chi-cago. You're not ready to drag a bunch of Negroes up and down railroad tracks and through Jim Crow towns in the South. You suffer from the no-table disadvantage of youth and naivete."

Clem's jaw clenched. His face grew red. Much to his chagrin, he knew Preacher was right. Over the course of a day and a half, Clem realized what he had gotten himself into.

Clem huffed out an angry sigh before laughing it all off. "All right. It's a deal. If nothing else, you can carry water for Tiny."

CHAPTER SIX
ETIENNE BOUCHER

C lem and his new hires hopped a northbound freight train from the outskirts of Winona. They disembarked in the Memphis railyard at noon and ventured into downtown. Clem was on a mission to collect provisions. The crew's focus was sustenance. White faces, including those of two police officers on foot patrol, eyed the Negro men on Clem's heels. A motley crew, they looked suspicious and unsuitable for high street. Preacher was in Clem's ear. "We've got to find the Negro side of town. And quick."

"I agree. Over there," Clem nodded toward a group of Negro women at a bus stop. "You go talk to them. Find out where we can buy some work clothes and lunch. We'll hang back."

Preacher's conversation with the women was brief. "Sorry, Clem. I'm empty-handed about the clothes. They said no white store owner would let a group like us in. It's three buses to get to a store on the Negro side of town."

"That's not helpful."

"They were nervous talking to me. One suggested ordering from the Sears catalog. Said we can get lunch from the kitchen door in the alley behind Buster's Diner down the street."

"This is absurd."

"Welcome to the Negro world, Boss," Mack said.

"Sorry, guys. We'll have to work in the clothes on our backs until we get a Sears shipment delivered to Blue Rock."

Clem swatted flies buzzing the trash cans next to Buster's kitchen door. He yelled through the screen to a Negro washing dishes. "Excuse me, sir. I'd like to order some food."

The sudbuster was taken aback. "Excuse me, Suh?"

"We'd like to place an order." The man disappeared and reappeared with a white waitress. Looking over the menu, Clem was out of his element. The waitress impatiently tapped a pencil on her order pad from behind the screen door. "Why don't you come inside and eat? We have one open seat at the counter," the waitress eventually offered Clem.

"No thank—"

Preacher stepped in before Clem could finish his sentence. He reverted to a tongue the waitress would expect and accept. "Mista Boss, suh. Maybe I's could hep with the order."

"Yes, Preacher. Thank you."

Preacher removed his hat, hung his head low, and despite being several inches taller than the waitress, gave the appearance of looking up to her. "Can we's have enough fried chicken for seven? A double order, please. A mess of rice and gravy and seven bottles of arrah-see?"

The waitress scribbled on her order pad, turned to Clem, and said in an ugly tone, "You're gonna have to pay in advance. Eight dollars and seventy-five cents."

Clem, determined to get the best of the woman, pulled a wad of cash from his pocket and counted out eight dollars and the seventy-five cents from his loose change. "Here's for the food. Please, hold on a moment." He counted out three more dollars and handed them to the waitress. "This is for you. We like to tip our servers well."

The waitress gave Clem a long, nasty glare before calling out to the kitchen staff. "Order in for a bunch of niggers out back."

Once the waitress was out of sight, Preacher grabbed Clem by the back of his collar. "What's wrong with you? You want us all to get a beating, or worse?"

"That's right," Mack said. "You best start calling us boy, too."

In a rare moment of vocal input, the twins added their two cents. "White folk get lynched for helpin' Negroes round here. So you best start actin' like we ya boys when we're round other white folks, or you might end up swingin' from a tree with the rest of us."

"Uh-huh," the other twin agreed. The twins had barely spoken two words since Clem met them, which made their input all the more significant. Clem had been warned. Until then, he hadn't taken seriously how deadly traveling the South with a crew of Negroes could be. The twins' graphic pronouncement was what he needed to hear.

Once the food arrived, the crew retreated from the bustling shops back to the relative safety of the railyard. Starving, they ran the last stretch, bounding over tracks, ties, and awkward mounds of granite rock beds. Tiny was ahead of the rest. Sam was a few steps behind. Tiny leaped into the boxcar next to the car they had traveled in. As soon as he got on his feet, he jumped back out while Sam was climbing in. Sam immediately took a few steps backward with hands raised.

"Mister Clem," Sam screamed. "You better get a hurry along." Clem bringing up the rear, double-timed the rest of the way.

A tall, skinny white boy appeared from the inside corner of the boxcar. In his shaking hand, a fish-cleaning knife held Sam at bay. One side of the blade was jagged for scaling. The fileting edge was curved and tapered to a point—a fishmonger's tool, capable of murder. The boy's voice trembled, "Yaw niggers be stayin' way from *moi.*"

"Easy now. Nobody's going to come at you," Clem said in a calming voice. "Put the knife down."

Sam slowly inched to the door and jumped out of the boxcar. The boy turned to Clem, revealing a battered face. One eye was swollen shut. His lips were fat, dry, and cracked with crusty-dried blood on the edges. He had a plum-sized knot on his forehead and finger imprinted bruises on his neck and arms. Preacher stepped toward the boxcar door and spoke in a fatherly tone. "Who did this to you, son?"

The boy bent over and commenced sobbing. He could barely get the words out. "Mon père," he said, gasping to speak and breathe.

"Put the knife down," Clem ordered firmly. "I'm coming up there. We won't hurt you."

The knife hit the boxcar floor. Clem climbed in, kicked the blade out of reach, and dropped to one knee beside the doubled over boy. "Take a breath. My name's Clem. This is Preacher." The boy took a couple of short-staggered breaths before a controlled, deep inhale. Hiccups set in.

Preacher climbed aboard. "What's your name, son?"

"Etienne Bou—" A hiccup interrupted.

"Come again?" Clem asked.

The boy held one finger to his face, signaling an inevitable hiccup. As soon as the hiccup passed, he quickly blurted out his name before another hiccup could strike. "Etienne. Etienne Boucher."

Calming the boy with humor, Preacher joked, "Sobbin' done gave you the hiccups." Another hiccup quelled the boy's weak laugh. "I doubt you're French-Canadian. Cajun?"

In a thick accent the boy replied, "Cajun. From Lusiana, ya."

"Where are you headed?" Clem asked.

"I don't know. Don't care. Anywhere way from *mon père*."

"Where's your mother?" Clem asked.

"Might be run off. Might be dead. Père beat her, too. One day she gone."

"Sam. Fetch me our water jug," Preacher ordered.

Clem discharged everyone else. "You all take the food to the other car and start eating." Sam hustled back with the water and made a bee-line to lunch. "We're going to clean you up, young man. Stay put while Preacher and I talk for a minute."

Preacher and Clem hopped from the boxcar and strolled out of the boy's earshot. Tiny emerged from the other car with a paper bag and set it in the doorway of Etienne's car. The crew had cut into each of their portions to feed the boy.

"Merci," Etienne thanked Tiny before bare-handing the sloppy rice and gravy into his mouth.

"Well, shit," Preacher said.

"I know. I wish we hadn't come across him."

"I see they shared their food with the boy. Or gave him your portion," Preacher poked.

"I've lost my appetite," Clem said. "I wish he hadn't threatened Tiny and Sam. It took some grace for the crew to share their food."

"We can't leave him here, Clem. He's too old for an orphanage and clearly can't take care of himself. He'll either end up dead or a sodomite's bitch in the state pen. I'm glad you, not me, are the boss of this undertaking."

Clem bristled at Preacher's assessment. "I need to think." Clem turned and walked away.

Preacher sat in the doorway of the makeshift dining car eating his lunch. He watched Clem pace back and forth, talking to himself. He was organizing his thoughts through slight hand movements. After several minutes, Clem returned to his crew. "Everyone gather around. We've got a situation with the boy. Preacher and I talked about his prospects. If we leave him on his own, his chances aren't good. You all know I have seven spots to fill on this crew. I propose we take him in. At first, for no pay. Only food, clothes, security, and guidance. If things work out, he can become the paid seventh hand once he can carry his load. Now, this isn't a democracy, but given the near-constant proximity we'll have to each other, I'll let you all decide. Any discussion?"

"What you mean, any discussion?" Mack asked.

"He means do you have anything good or bad to say about it," Preacher explained.

"He called us niggers. I ain't his nigger," Mack said.

"He had a knife on me and Tiny," Sam added.

"That's right," Tiny agreed.

"Twin?" Clem asked.

"Don't care. We here to make money," one twin replied. His brother nodded in agreement.

"If I make the offer to the boy and insist, now's the time he has an epiphany about the equality of all men in God's eyes, and he agrees, can you accept him?" Clem asked.

"What all that mean?" Mack asked.

"It means Clem will have a come-to-Jesus with the boy about calling us niggers and thinkin' he's better than us," Preacher said and added his two cents. "Clem. It's hard to change a white man's heart."

"I understand the concerns, but he's still only a boy. A product of his environment. Maybe his heart can change while working with us."

"What all that mean?" Mack asked again.

"The boy's a heathen. He needs to be washed clean by a river baptism," Preacher said.

"Oh, I get it."

"I think we all would be OK with giving the boy a chance," Preacher said. The rest of the crew nodded in agreement.

Clem returned to the boy. He wet his handkerchief, dabbed the cool water on the swollen eye, and peppered the boy with facts in the form of questions. "Son, you have any money?"

"Naw."

"You have a way of making money?"

"Naw."

"You have any prospects?"

"Naw."

Clem moved the cool, wet cloth to Etienne's lips. The crusty blood took several rough passes to clean, causing Etienne to flinch. The cuts on the corner of his mouth had opened from his attack on the chicken, rice, and gravy. "Don't open your mouth too wide for a few days."

"Yah, Suh."

"So all you've got is a busted-up face and a fishing knife you pulled on my crew who you called niggers."

"I was scared. Dey all come runnin' up on *moi* in rumpled cloads like day a bunch of hobo. I'm sorry. Dey kindly shared day food whit *moi*."

"I want you to listen carefully."

"Yah, Suh."

"We're a railroad track crew. We travel around fixing rail lines and laying new sections of track. This afternoon, we're moving on to a small town in Alabama. If I left you here with nothing but a full stomach and a clean face, my mother, father, and God would never forgive me. You have a choice. I'll put you on a train back to New Orleans. You can show the police there what your father did to you … let them sort it out. Or, you can come with us. I'll feed you, I'll clothe you, and you'll work alongside my crew for free. I'll pay you once you're strong enough to pull your weight."

"I do dat," Etienne said eagerly.

"It's not that simple. Why did you call my crew niggers?"

"Don't know."

"If you don't know why you do something, you probably shouldn't do it."

"Yah, Suh."

"Never again?"

"Yah, Suh. I promise."

"You're going to have to earn their respect."

"Yah, Suh."

"It's settled then. Our train should be through here soon. You stick close to the group. We're not stowaways like you. We have full authority to ride freight trains."

Clem and his employees disembarked at the Blue Rock switching yard late afternoon.

"That must be our project," Clem said, pointing to a pile of rocks, rails, and creosote-soaked ties delivered by a supply train. "You all go take an inventory. I'll introduce myself to the yard manager."

The manager's office and a water tower were positioned between two sets of tracks. A simple structure above the ground on a steel I-beam frame aligned the office windows approximately even with the cab windows of locomotives. Water, sewage lines, and a boiler were visible under the building. A short staircase paralleling the tracks rose a few feet to the office door. Clem's employer, JR Robinson, owned stock in the rail lines and switchyard. Clem didn't think it necessary to knock. He walked in on Elliot Drumpf, the manager, lying buck-naked on his back and tied to the base of a radiator. Gyrating on top of him, a woman wearing only a train engineer's hat wailed, "toot-toot, toot-toot," while the yard manager grunted out chugging sounds.

PART TWO

CHAPTER SEVEN
1933

Under overcast skies and with frozen breath, Mom, Dad, and I boarded the Panama Limited departing Chicago's Union Station. Glorious sunshine and sweater weather greeted us in Corinth, Mississippi—a welcome change from the Chicago winter. Uncle Clem traveled ahead from Chicago after Dad was hired. He left the switchyard's pickup in Corinth on his way to meet his crew in Memphis. Corinth and Blue Rock were less than an hour apart as the crow flies. Driving to our new home was a two-hour slog through the Tennessee Valley.

It took only a few bumpy and tense miles in the cramped front seat of the pickup for Mom and Dad to admit I was right from the get-go. Once in the open air of the truck bed, my senses took in the wonder of the Deep South. Winter-barren trees and dormant undergrowth provided a leafy-brown carpeted view deep into the backwoods of Mississippi and Alabama. Strange-contorted trees wrapped their exposed roots around moss-covered boulders like veins clinging to a life-giving heart. Streams cascaded down rocky hillsides, carrying leaves as tiny as Mom's measuring spoons and as broad as the business end of a large spade shovel. Many of the leaves and twigs gathered at the water's edge while others floated out of sight. All would eventually decay, nourishing the land and, ultimately, the Tennessee River. From the truck bed, the twisting, turning, bumpy roads felt like the rides at Chicago's Riverview Amusement Park.

My excitement about the move to Blue Rock was more for the change of scenery than what the town offered. Despite Dad's disdain for Southern Christians and Jim Crow, I wondered, but didn't dare ask, if Mom and Dad felt any excitement about the move. They obviously felt some awe when we came to the Shoals Creek bridge at the east edge of Blue Rock. The pickup pulled over and my parents got out. "Oh my," Mom gushed. "How beautiful."

My father's eyes were filled with wonderment. "This sure beats the Chicago River," Dad said. To the southwest, the Tennessee River babbled and sparkled under the mid-afternoon sun. In the sky above, a murmuration of starlings, numbering in the hundreds, possibly thousands, shape-shifted in graceful harmony, swooping up, down, back and forth across the face of the low winter sun. To the north, the Shoals Creek tributary was rimmed by cattails and other grasses. River rocks anchored green lily shoots, anticipating their spring bloom. Egrets plodded about the water in search of a meal. A pair of monogamous red-tailed hawks worked diligently, repairing damage to their previous year's nest. Transporting me back in time, a Great Blue Heron, resembling a library book pterodactyl, floated overhead.

I was drawn to the middle of the substantial motor bridge resembling an inverted train track. Thick wooden ties were supported underneath by steel I-beams. Secured to the crossties, end-to-end wooden planks separated at the average width of a vehicle traversed the length of the bridge. Arched-steel trusses and guard rails were the design of a competent engineer. Paralleling the vehicle crossing, a short wooden trestle serviced rail traffic. I leaned over the railing and spat into the deep churning confluence of the tributary and river. Looking west, a long wooden train trestle crossed the river. The same trestle Elliot Drumpf stumbled across to end his life less than a month before. I heard Uncle Clem's voice whisper in my mind, "Grits through a midget." I no longer found my uncle's morbid description of Drumpf's demise humorous.

Somehow, Dad got lost trying to find our new home. Getting lost in Blue Rock was no easy feat. "For crying out loud," Dad barked after passing Calvary Baptist Church for the third time in ten minutes. "For crying out loud" is how Dad expressed himself when he was frustrated, which frequently evoked a smirk from Mom, as long as she was not involved in whatever was frustrating him. Her smirk usually added to Dad's irritation.

"For Pete's sake, Hank. Pull over and ask someone for directions," Mom sighed. "For Pete's sake" is what Mom said when frustrated. Mom's "for Pete's sake" also covered disappointment and disgust at Dad's stupid jokes.

From my perspective, all the turns, backtracking, and dead-end roads were no waste of time. They gave me the lay of the land. After passing the Town Hall, doubling as the Sheriff's Office, and passing the public school for a second time, we stopped at Smalley's Grocery. "Nope," Dad said before I could jump from the truck to explore the store with him. He was on a mission. He was in the store less than a minute before storming out. Mocking the storekeeper's accent and choice of words, Dad said to Mom, "It's over yonder."

We headed back past Town Hall a third time and passed Calvary Baptist Church a fourth time. After one right turn, then a left at a stretch of vacant land, in less than a minute from Smalley's, there it was, home. Had Dad been more patient three times prior and followed the road up to the ninety-degree corner for the last turn, he would have seen our house. Instead, when all he saw was a wide-open stretch of land before the sharp curve, he got frustrated, said, "For crying out loud," and turned around. When Mom realized how close we had come to our street, she said, "For Pete's sake."

I hadn't inquired about the particulars of the house during my dinner with my uncle at The Berghoff. My new home and surroundings were a bit of a surprise. In Chicago, the houses and apartment buildings were tightly arranged, with little to no open space between them. Only one house across from ours occupied the dead-end street. On the west side of our property, a cleared patch buffered a wooded area. Two rutted patches the width of a vehicle chassis paralleled the east side of the house. To the right of the makeshift driveway, a stretch of vacant land intersected the Shoals Creek motor bridge and train trestle.

The two-story batten board and metal roofed house was symmetrical. Four centered stairs led directly to the front door. A waist-high railing supported by wooden spindles framed the porch. Windows flanked each side of the front door. The pitched roof was broken up by two windowed dormers above the porch overlooking the front yard. I couldn't wait to explore. Pea gravel flew from the soles of my shoes as I reduced the four porch steps into two. "Key's supposed to be under the doormat," Dad shouted.

The smell of charred wood lingered throughout the main floor of the cool-damp abandoned house. The inside was as efficient as the outside. To the left of the front door, the dining room table provided seating for four. To the right, a couch and rocking chair identified the living room. A staircase in the hallway at the center of the home rose to the second floor. The main bedroom, bathroom, and kitchen occupied the rear of the first floor. Upstairs, two bedrooms lacked furniture. The small bathroom lacked toiletries.

The absence of any personal items in the entire house gave me a chill. There was no shaving kit, clothes, paperwork, or family pictures—no evidence of Drumpf's existence. By the time Mom made it inside, I had explored the whole place. I found her in the living room, examining the furniture, the fireplace, and dust on the windowsill. "This place could use a feminine touch."

"Where's Dad?"

"He went straight to the backyard. Your uncle said there was a surprise for him back there."

I bolted out the kitchen door and found Dad in the driver's seat of a burgundy convertible. Two railroad ties had replaced the crippled vehicle's wheels. Winter-barren wisteria vines wove their way around the car. Dried thistle made climbing into the passenger side a prickly task. "This is exciting. It's a Citroen C-5 Cabriolet," Dad said. He handed me a note Uncle Clem left on the car seat. *Twit left you a Frenchy. It doesn't run. Robinson need not know of its existence. Wheels are in the pole barn.* The note was signed, *Big Brother.*

"Does this mean we get to keep it?"

"Our mortgage with Robinson says we're buying this place, lock, stock, and barrel. I'll have to figure out why it won't crank. It's French. Getting parts could be an issue."

After examining the car's details, I headed to the pole barn at the back of the property near the train tracks. The large structure had no door. Stored inside were lawn implements I knew I would one day have the displeasure of using. A wooden workbench shelved mason jars containing nails, screws, and other oddball items. The only exciting feature of the outbuilding was a second-floor loft accessed by a homemade wooden ladder. I imagined the perch as my hideout or maybe a clubhouse if I made some friends. It was almost as good as a treehouse.

Dad summoned me from the kitchen door, bearing a hatchet and an assignment. "Go into that patch of woods and gather up any dead branches. If they're long or too big, cut them. And be careful." Wielding a hatchet in the woods would be a grand adventure for a city boy. However, I wanted to investigate more of the surroundings. I also had three dollars and eighty-five cents Uncle Clem gave me, a fortune at the time, burning a hole in my pocket—change from our bill at The Berghoff. Sheer willpower kept me from spending it on candy and comic books in Chicago. I knew I'd be glad I saved it when I got to Alabama. "But Dad, I wanted to explore the neighborhood."

"There's no coal in the basement for the furnace. We'll have to make do with the kitchen stove and fireplace for heat until we get a coal delivery."

There was no point in arguing. If I satisfied Dad quickly, there might still be winter daylight left for a quick run to Smalley's Grocery. Heading towards the woods, the house across the street caught my eye. A figure watched me from a downstairs window. I couldn't make out if it was a man or a woman. Whichever, they made me uncomfortable. Adding to my discomfort, I came across a burn barrel. I could make out masculine buttons and thick zippers clinging to scraps of blackened clothing. Two metal photo frames held the charred and contorted remains of Drumpf's memory. I imagined the soot-covered straight-edge razor was Drumpf's final act of self-respect—a clean shave. My mind's eye saw a faceless man burning all evidence of his existence before his drunken death march onto the long train trestle. To ease my morbid thoughts, I convinced myself Uncle Clem did the burning to give my family and the home a fresh start.

After collecting enough wood to make it through the night, Dad released me, pending Mom's approval. Mom discharged me after delivering a stern safety lecture. Thankfully, it was brief.

Smalley's Grocery was neither a big nor a bustling store. A single pump out front under a tall orange Gulf sign provided the town's sole source of petrol. The dusty railingless porch, inches off the ground, featured a wooden bench for lazy day loitering. On each side of the front door, matching screened windows were striped with steel bars for security. The pitched roof hid behind a boxy facade bearing the black hand-painted name Smalley Grocery. Below the moniker, rusty tin signage covered whitewashed wood siding. I recognized Marlboro, Winston, and, of course, the bottle-shaped Coca-Cola sign. There were other products I'd never heard of. An Indian Chief in feather regalia advertised Red Man chewing tobacco. The five-cent Moon Pie marshmallow treat looked interesting.

Pinned above the door handle, a handwritten note warned, *Vernon, Don't you come home drunk again!* It was signed, *Rubye*. The spelling of the author's name vexed me. Was it a Southern spelling?

A bell rigged above the door announced my arrival. Inside, to the right by the window, sat three old white men in a circle of four mismatched chairs. In the middle of the circle rested a nearly full spittoon. A line of projectiles that had fallen short created distinct trails to the base of each chair. Two of the men barely glanced at me. The third man slurred, "Holler at me when you done knowed whatchoo wont."

All three had a cheek full of chewing tobacco. Between the bulging mouths, spitting sounds, and funny accents, I couldn't make out what they were discussing.

The treats I came for were secured in a glass case under the register near the front door. I wanted to assess everything Smalley's offered before making my purchase. The store appeared to be organized with shoplifters in mind. Large burlap sacks of onions, nuts, flour, and tubs of lard filled the patron's side. Smaller, more expensive items were kept behind the shopkeeper's counter. A large jar of pickled pig's feet on the counter jumped out at me. I had never seen such a thing. Uncle Clem tried to describe them to me at The Berghoff. He scrunched his four fingers on one hand together with his thumb tucked against his palm. Crazy Uncle Clem's contorted fingers were a pretty accurate depiction. The feet were pale pink and looked awfully soft and fleshy, like they couldn't possibly support a large animal.

My fixation on the pig's feet was interrupted by the jingle of the bell above the door. An old white man, missing half of one leg, struggled in on crutches with the note in his mouth. He didn't appear to be drunk. He was skinny and frail. His raggedy homemade crutches and un-hemmed half-pant leg reminded me of the destitute Great War amputees and other maimed unfortunates I had seen lined up for free soup in Chicago.

"Whatchoo-no-good, Vernon?" one man asked.

"Aw, ain't nothin' to it," Vernon replied. The note fell to the floor. He tried to bend down. Unsuccessful, he quickly gave up. He didn't need to reread it. The message was clear. A grunt accompanied Vernon's struggle into the empty chair. As he sat down, his frayed pant leg hiked up, exposing the mutilated leg's nub. The shopkeeper handed Vernon a rope of chewing tobacco. Vernon tore off a chunk with his long yellow teeth and began to break it down to a manageable consistency.

Between the pink pigs' feet floating in the giant pickle jar, all the spitting and nattering, and the addition of an old one-legged man, I felt uneasy, out of place, and ready to skedaddle. "Excuse me, sir, may I please have a pack of Wrigley's?"

All four men stopped their yakking and looked up at me. "Where you from, boy?" asked one man.

My Chicago accent gave me away. I didn't respond. The storekeeper made his way behind the counter and retrieved the gum with his tobacco-stained, dirty-fingernailed hands. I dropped a nickel on the counter and reached for my purchase. The storekeeper pulled the gum back. "Your pa was in here earlier askin' for directions to the Drumpf place, wern't he?"

"Yes, sir." Uncle Clem told me addressing the men and women with sir and ma'am was especially important in the South. I was glad right then that I hadn't forgotten.

"Heard y'all were comin' from Chicago. Your pa's gonna take over the switchyard," the storekeeper said, sliding the gum to me. His tone was not welcoming. I didn't respond.

"Your pa is brothers with that Clem who come through town two or three time a year," the amputee yelled across the room. Tobacco-browned saliva ran down his chin. He'd yet to work his chew into complete submission. Once again, I didn't respond. The door opened, the bell rang, and a tall, sturdy man wearing a beige shirt and matching beige slacks entered the store.

"Howdy, Sheriff," the storekeeper said.

The sheriff noticed me before acknowledging the other three men in the store. "Well, hello, young fella," the sheriff chirped with a genuine smile. "Who are you?"

Before I could respond, one of the seated men answered rudely, "I surmised he's the nephew of that nigger-lovin' Clem Paxton that come through town from time to time."

The sheriff's hands clenched, and his smile turned into a frown. "Clarence, why do you have to be so ugly?"

"Fact is, times like these, those niggers and that Cajun have jobs that should be goin' to white folk. Now they done brought a carpetbagger down to run the switchyard," Clarence said. The amputee and other nameless man nodded in agreement.

The sheriff squatted to my eye level. "Don't you mind them. What's your name, son?"

"Asa. Asa Alan Paxton."

"Asa? Like the king from the Bible?"

"Yes, sir."

"That's a fine name."

I took it as a good omen when the sheriff used the exact words as the friendly Union League Club doorman a week earlier. "Thank you, sir."

"I see you got some Wrigley gum. I visited Chicago back in twenty-eight. Saw the Cubs play and visited the Wrigley Building by the river."

"My Dad used to take me to see the Cubs play. But then he lost his job."

"I know, son. Times are tough, but you'll be OK now that your pa got the job at the switchyard."

"Yes, sir. Would you like a stick of gum?"

"Thank you, but no. You share it with someone your own age. Tell your parents Deputy Taylor says welcome to Blue Rock."

"Yes, sir."

I left Smalley's with mixed feelings. Deputy Taylor was friendly. I wasn't sure about the storekeeper. The other three old men scared me. Before I climbed the porch stairs to my new home, I glanced at the house across the street. The moment my eyes reached an illuminated figure in an upstairs window, the stalker disappeared and the light went out.

Mom and Dad had gotten to work while I was at Smalley's. The house was warm from the fireplace and the stove in the kitchen. They rearranged the living room furniture to take advantage of the hearth. Mom made a bed for me on the sofa. Crackers and salami Mom packed for the trip was our dinner. "Where all did you go?" Mom asked at the dinner table.

"Smalley's Grocery."

There was a long silence, broken only by the crunching in our mouths. "And?" Mom asked.

"And what?"

"Oh, for Pete's sake, Hank. It's like pulling teeth."

Dad jumped in. "What's the store like? Was it busy? What kind of stuff was on the shelves? Was the storekeeper polite?"

"You saw what was in the store and talked to the storekeeper when you went in for directions. You can tell Mom about it." I wasn't trying to be smart-mouthed. I just never understood why Mom and Dad always wanted me to talk about stuff at the dinner table.

"It's called a pleasant conversation. Besides, I didn't look around. I got directions and got out of there."

"I can tell the teenage years are going to be a joy," Mom complained.

"OK, OK. First, the storekeeper was sitting with two old men. They were chewing and spitting tobacco. Then an old, one-legged man on crutches came in, sat down, and started chewing and spitting. There was a big jar of pickled pigs feet on the counter. They had the usual stuff. I asked for a pack of Wrigley's, and one of the men asked where I was from. They knew Uncle Clem and figured out he was my uncle and that Dad was taking over the switchyard. Called Dad a carpet-some-thing. One man said Uncle Clem was a nigger-lover, but the deputy had come in, and he told him to stop being ugly. The deputy was really nice to me but didn't want the stick of gum I offered him. His name was Dep-uty Sheriff Taylor, I think. He told me to tell you, 'Welcome to Blue Rock.' Then I came home." I hoped my report would satisfy Dad's request for a pleasant dinner conversation. No such luck.

"Where did you get the money for the gum?" Mom asked.

"Uncle Clem gave me the change from the check at The Berghoff."

"Did you thank him?" Mom asked.

I gave Mom a testy stare. She should know better. I knew how to say "please" and "thank you."

"Tell me about—" Mom started to say. I was saved by the approaching sound of the first train through Blue Rock since our arrival. We rushed from the table to the kitchen door. The locomotive's bright headlamp and powerful sound approached our house. The engine's sound dropped to a lower pitch after it passed. Boxcars and coal cars were barely visible in the early winter dusk. Once again, grits through a midget came to mind. I remembered Uncle Clem said the train that did in Drumpf was the evening non-stop from Memphis to Decatur. It must have been the same train. After several minutes, the caboose, glowing from the crow's nest windows and red tail lamps, passed the house and disappeared over the Shoals Creek trestle.

"I was worried it would be much louder," Mom said. "I can live with this."

"You and Asa will probably get to where you don't even notice the trains," Dad predicted. "I'll probably notice every single one."

I spent the rest of the evening poking at the wood in the fireplace before climbing under the blankets on the couch. I laid in my makeshift bed, spooked by the figure in the windows across the street. Another train passed through the switchyard, calming my fear. I would grow to love the sound of locomotives, the rhythm of steel wheels on track seams, and engineers' signature pull on their whistle.

CHAPTER EIGHT
BRUNSWICK STEW

A chill had settled in the house when I woke in the middle of the night. I'd been dreaming about the figure watching me from the windows across the street. It must have been three o'clock when the evil stalker crept into my slumber because three a.m. is when they are most potent. A few red embers, kindling, several thick knotted branches, and my huff and puff brought the fireplace back to life. The efficient kitchen stove needed only a bit more wood to put out heat until sunrise.

I didn't know if the cold, my dream, or Dad's snoring through my parents' open bedroom door woke me, but I was determined to go back to sleep. Mom and Dad had each other to keep warm. I shut them off from the heat sources and shut myself off from Dad's log sawing.

At sunrise, a crack of rifle fire echoed from the woods behind the pole barn. Dad made it to the kitchen door before me. "What do you think that was?" I asked.

"I'm guessing a hunter. They hunt in places like this."

Mom yelled from bed, "Maybe you shouldn't be near the door or windows."

Here we go. Mom's gonna have me holed up in the house all day as if there was a gangster gunfight going on in the streets. Or in this case, the woods out back. Fortunately, the mystery was quickly solved. A gruff-looking man emerged from behind our property with a rifle strapped over his left shoulder. A limp juvenile deer was wrapped around the back of his neck and shoulders. His right hand gripped the rear hooves. His left hand held the front hooves. He glanced at Dad and me and veered east of our property. Once the man passed, I could see the tender face of the deer. Its lifeless head bounced off the rifle barrel and the man's back with every step. It was such an innocent-looking victim. Dad noticed the tear rolling down my cheek. He squatted down to wipe it away. "It's OK to be sad for the deer. It's one of God's beautiful creations, but that's the way of the world. The deer will probably feed that man's family for the rest of the winter." I didn't realize the incident foreshadowed my future in the rural South.

Dad kept me close the rest of the day. There was much to do. We gathered wood for the present and felled three trees with a two-man cross-cutting saw Dad found in the barn to dry for the future. Dad taught me how to clean and maintain the coal furnace in the basement. We stacked dozens of Drumpf's empty bourbon jugs in the basement's corner. Dad said there must be some use for them but cautioned me, "No one needs to know about these empty jugs."

"Yes, sir." I knew what Dad meant—Prohibition.

Despite being Sunday, we dedicated the afternoon to working at the switchyard. I cleaned the office and bathroom while Dad made phone calls. He had to get some trains back on schedule. The rail traffic that required a switch in direction had been delayed until Dad arrived. I felt proud listening to my father's orchestration on the phone. He sounded so important. "Don't you worry, Travis, I'll be waiting to switch your train northbound," and "I hear your concern, Junkin. Your train will be first," Dad said in his confident and reassuring voice. His phone conversations continued until he called it a day.

Cool and crisp air settled over Blue Rock by the time we headed home. We strolled the tracks instead of weaving through the neighborhoods. A beautiful winter sunset on our backsides created long, faint shadows stepping ahead of us. In the distance, the cozy glow of our new home looked like a Rockwell cover of the Saturday Evening Post. Wafts of smoke seeped from the fireplace chimney, and the stovepipe protruding from the side of the kitchen. "Do you smell that?" I asked from the corner of our property. It was more than smoke. Dad didn't answer. He smiled and got a head start, running toward the back door.

Mom was at the stove stirring a cast iron Dutch oven. She announced in a sing-songy voice, "We had visitors today. They brought us dinner."

"Who visited?" Dad asked.

"Deputy Sheriff Taylor and his wife, Gay Lynn."

"What's in the pot?" I asked.

"Gay Lynn called it Brunswick Stew. They brought warm cornbread, too. Gay Lynn said she thought we could use a proper Sunday dinner. She said, 'Y'all need to put some South in your mouth.' Isn't that a cute expression?"

The pot was filled with a variety of beans, corn, meat, potatoes, and stewed tomatoes. The aroma of the savory stew on the wood-fired stove and the sweet smell of cornbread was more than a meal—it was comforting. A feeling I didn't recall ever having in Chicago. A feeling that didn't come from shit on a shingle.

As Dad gave the dinner blessing, I realized it was the first Sunday I could remember we didn't go to church. After dinner, we all retired to the living room. Dad moved back and forth in the rocking chair with his eyes closed next to the fireplace. I climbed under my blankets on the couch. Mom sat at my feet with her Bible. It took only one day for Mom and Dad to turn the cold, damp house into a warm, cozy home.

My day had been filled with mixed emotions. The early morning hunter and innocent doe. Proud feelings of listening to Dad work the telephone. The comforting meal delivered by Blue Rock's finest. However, the entire weekend, I was haunted by a figure in the windows across the street and the dread of what Monday would bring.

CHAPTER NINE
THE MISFIT CLIQUE

Mom heated the leftover brunswick stew for breakfast. I was too nervous to eat. Starting a new school midway through the year had me worried. I would be more of an outsider than if enrolled at the beginning of the year, where I might blend into the excitement all kids feel on the first day of school. As luck would have it, a pudgy, strawberry-blonde, freckled boy about my age was leaving the house across the street with books belted together. "How you?" the boy yelled in a thick accent from his porch.

Was he the stalker? "I'm fine, thank you. I'm starting school today."

"Wanna walk with me?"

"Sure. My name's Asa. Asa Paxton. I moved here from Chicago."

The boy's thumb flew backward over his shoulder toward the front of his house. "I've been watching you and your folks all weekend from yonder windows." Relief coursed through my veins—*stalker mystery solved.*

"Name's Richard Aycock. Everyone calls me Itchy on account of my skin." He pulled up his shirt sleeve, exposing a red-flaky patch of skin on his forearm. "Sometimes it's worse, usually in the summer. Don't worry. Doc says folks can't catch it from me."

"Does it hurt?"

"Naw. Just itches like crazy. Doc says scratching makes it worse. There's a balm that helps. My folks don't have money for it right now."

We set out for school. Itchy turned down an alleyway I didn't think was the right way. "We're gonna cut through Shanks' yard. He walks to school with me, too."

Shanks, a funny-looking fella, sat on a stack of books at the back stoop of his house. He was thin and gangly with ears that were not only big, they protruded from his head more than anyone I'd ever seen. His hands were unusually wide with long unkempt fingernails. He had the biggest feet I'd ever seen. Behind pale lips were painfully crooked teeth. He reminded me of the vampire Nosferatu on the movie poster in the box office window of the abandoned movie theater on Foster Avenue back in Chicago.

"This here's Asa from Chicago. He moved into Drunkard Drumpf's house this weekend." Apparently, Drumpf's love of Kentucky bourbon was no secret to Itchy, his friend, and probably the whole town.

"Name's Shane, Shane Biddle. Everyone calls me Shanks."

"Why do they call you that?"

"I got big muscles below my knees. You can't see them cause of my britches, but they're big. When I was five, my grandpa said I had man shanks. He called me Shanks once, and it stuck. Said they're extra strong from carrying around my big feet. I'm the fastest swimmer in Blue Rock 'cause of my big feet and hands. I can hear better than most folks on account of my big ears. I can hear a flyin' cockroach ruttin' in a pile of leaves or under loose tree bark."

Just like that, I made two friends and established the Blue Rock Misfit Clique—me with my Chicago accent, an itchy redhead, and a boy named Shanks with feet and ears like a kangaroo. None of us would ever win a popularity contest.

Before moving to Blue Rock, I expected my education to progress through the proud three-story, brick-and-stone-facade middle and high school back in Chicago. Instead, I got a dingy-clapboard building, a rusted tin roof, and a cast-iron school bell mounted to a post.

A week earlier, Mom sent a telegram to Blue Rock Elementary, registering me for class. Miz Montgomery had my books on an empty desk in the front row directly across from her desk.

"Class, we have a new student today. His name is Asa Paxton. He is from Chicago. Y'all make him feel welcome at lunch and recess."

I thought Miz Montgomery sure was nice ordering the class to make me feel welcome. That is, until she said, "Now open y'all's reader book to chapter twelve. Asa is going to read the first two pages aloud."

Geez. Miz Montgomery isn't very nice making me read aloud, it being my first day and all. I opened my book and quickly surveyed the text. At that moment, I thanked the good lord for the witches of Ravenswood Elementary in Chicago—they had taught me well. The text was large and double-spaced between lines. Chapter twelve reminded me of the books we read in third grade. I made the reading look easy.

My nervous stomach had passed by lunchtime. The salami on crackers Mom packed hit the spot. There weren't enough chairs around my table for all the kids who wanted to sit with me. It wasn't a matter of popularity. It was a matter of curiosity. By the time lunch was over, my novelty had worn off with my sixth-grade classmates. Itchy, Shanks, and I were left alone at recess after lunch to shoot marbles in the dirt.

Penmanship exercises came after recess. There was no amount of preparation from Ravenswood Elementary that could help me in that subject. The last class of the day was math. Like every other subject in Miz Montgomery's class besides penmanship, I was way ahead of the curve.

While I was at school, Mom and Dad went shopping in Muscle Shoals. Dad's boss gave him an advance on his first paycheck. Bare minimums were on the list. They bought enough food to hold us over until payday. There was one extravagance. A brand-new mattress for me. No bed frame, though a mattress on the floor in my upstairs bedroom was a step toward normalcy and privacy.

CHAPTER TEN
$\mathcal{S}$IT–N–$\mathcal{S}$PIT $\mathcal{C}$LUB

I quickly learned Blue Rock was nothing more than a pitiful town kissed by the seductive waters of the Tennessee River. Located on the west side of Alabama's Lauderdale County, the river separated Lauderdale from Colbert County to the south and Mississippi's Tishomingo County to the west. In a futile attempt to evade the Gulf of Mexico, the river made a defiant northward bend only to be gobbled up by the Ohio River, which in turn succumbed to the pull of the Mighty Mississippi.

Traversing the Tennessee River, a long-wooden train trestle connected Blue Rock, Alabama, with the much larger town of East Bluff, Mississippi—the same trestle Elliot Drumpf stumbled across to end his life.

East Bluff was a geographical tease—a large town I could see but could not touch. With no auto bridge, the shortest route was over an hour by motor vehicle. There was no passenger rail service. Only hobos used the freight trains to cross the river. The Wilson hydroelectric dam upstream had unpredictable water releases, making boat travel between Blue Rock and East Bluff ill-advised. Over the years, substantial water releases at the dam caught unsuspecting boaters off guard, causing numerous deaths. As a result, the federal government eventually banned ferry service and boat travel on that section of the river. Our town had only one thing going for it—the Wilson Dam electrified Blue Rock.

Dad's switchyard sat on the west side of town with room to reroute north-south trains to east-west routes and vice versa. Several side tracks allowed for the shuffle of locomotives and boxcars. Our new home was approximately two Chicago-sized city blocks from the east edge of the switchyard.

There wasn't much reason to go to Blue Rock unless you were a freight train heading somewhere more important. The town had no significant industries. Its largest employer was the Pottersfield Casket Company. The owner and lone salesman, Hugh Underwood, cornered the simple pinewood casket market from New Orleans to Charlotte by giving kickbacks to unscrupulous city and county officials. He earned the nickname Undertaker Underwood. When the Great Depression hit, Pottersfield Casket Company grew from ten employees to twenty. Otherwise, Blue Rock had only a few storefronts. The one-chair barbershop kept inconsistent hours. Its red-white-and-blue helical pole by the entrance had an electrical short, rendering it spinless and unilluminated. The beauty shop was by appointment only. Otter's Feed and Seed carried farming products, basic hardware, and a repair shop equipped to handle cars, trucks, and farming machinery. And then, there was Smalley's Grocery.

Mom and Dad quickly made peace with the move to Blue Rock. They got to work. "It's an investment," Mom and Dad would say when I complained about their choice of groceries. There was no steak or caviar as Uncle Clem promised when pitching the railyard job. Instead, every penny spent had a purpose. "Use it up, wear it out, make do, or do without," was a frequent saying from Mom and Dad. To save money for supplies to build a chicken coop, we ate grits with a dab of Oleo for breakfast instead of eggs and bacon. To save money for a vegetable garden, dinners included shit on a shingle or fried bologna instead of pork chops and applesauce. We ordered only half a load of coal for the furnace and cut up the felled trees for the wood stove and fireplace to save money heating the house. Dad bought two good fishing poles instead of parts for the broken-down Citroen.

In the spring of 1933, Dad and I built a chicken coop against the west side of the house. The coop's design and proximity to humans kept foxes, coons, and coyotes out. However, we suspected when one of the nests was eggless, a serpent was the thief. On the east side of the barn, we planted a large vegetable garden extending just short of the railroad tracks at the back of our property. Deputy Sheriff Taylor's wife, Gay

Lynn, recommended the location. She said the morning sun will bring the garden to life, and the barn's afternoon shade will keep the sun from scorching the produce to death.

While Mom and Dad made peace with the move to Blue Rock, my initial excitement became tempered. Every time I entered Smalley's, the old men of the Sit-n-Spit Club tried to get at me. They would "Yankee" this and "Yankee" that, loud enough for me to hear. "Nigger-lovin' Clem Paxton" and his gandy dancer crew frequently became the subject of jawing in my presence. Old Man Smalley never partook in the jabs because I was a paying customer, though he never objected to the abuse from the rest of the club.

Shanks and Itchy gave me the lowdown on the other three old farts. Vernon Jackson, the one-legged man, was Shanks' grandpa. He lost his leg to a cottonmouth. The way Grandpa Vernon spun it, he was fishing on the bank of Shoals Creek, minding his own business, when a cottonmouth went out of its way to bite him. Shanks overheard his mama tell a friend Vernon was drunk on 'shine and poked at the snake with a stick until the snake was full up of Vernon's provocation. The poison and infection from the bite would've killed the drunkard had they not cut off part of his leg.

My friends couldn't agree on why Skeeter Lightsey was such a miserable cuss. Shanks said it was because his wife ran off with a traveling salesman soon after they married. Itchy contended Skeeter was a more complicated malcontent. Itchy once heard Sheriff Taylor tell Skeeter he needed to "get over your mommy issues," whatever that meant. Regardless, Itchy and Shanks agreed Skeeter wasn't right in the head.

When I told my buddies how Sheriff Taylor was friendly to me the first time I went into Smalley's and how he told Clarence to stop being ugly, they explained local politics. Clarence Filbert had been Blue Rock's mayor since the beginning of time. He despised Sheriff Taylor, who took every opportunity to get at Clarence. He hated Taylor because, as the mayor put it, "Taylor won't get with the damn program." Itchy said "the program" was several things. Sheriff Taylor's refusal to call Clarence "Mister Mayor," was disrespectful. Making matters worse, everyone in town called Deputy Taylor "Sheriff Taylor," even though he was only a deputy appointed by his older brother, the duly elected sheriff for the whole county. Taylor's older brother worked in Florence, the county seat. He only came around Blue Rock at election time. Policing the town, Deputy Taylor had a soft touch, which Mayor Filbert didn't like. Taylor was tolerant of hobos who passed through town. He handled disputes evenly, regardless of a person's social or economic status. Worst of all, he laid down the law regarding the white townfolk harassing Uncle Clem's Negro crew when they came to work on the switchyard tracks. Blue Rock didn't have any Negroes like other parts of Alabama. There was no daily hate and oppression to be had. When in town, Uncle Clem's crew were tempting targets.

Blue Rock was a racist contradiction of itself. There were whites-only and Negro-only water fountains and bathrooms with no Negroes to use them. Town Hall had an empty bookcase dedicated to nonexistent copies of Negro marriage licenses. The seldom-used jail had one cell for whites and one for Negroes. Never once had the Negro cell been occupied. The residents repeatedly voted for the ineffectual Clarence Filbert as mayor. They voted the elder Taylor in as County Sheriff to keep the younger brother, the fair-minded Taylor, as Blue Rock's deputy. The friction between Taylor and Mayor Filbert was sport for many of the town's persnickety residents.

I was too young to understand my unsettled feelings about Blue Rock when confronted with the signs of racism and ugliness. Uncle Clem tried to prepare me for Jim Crow when he took me to dinner at The Berghoff. My young mind couldn't put all the puzzle pieces together. I eventually resigned myself to ignoring the racist ugliness, with one exception. The first time I heard Itchy use the term "nigger" was the last. It didn't end up in a brawl. I wasn't a fighter, but Itchy knew I was serious. I never heard Shanks say the word. Either Itchy told him not to around me, or maybe, given all the bullying Shanks endured, he was more sensitive to ugliness.

The routine weekdays of school and weekend chores were broken up by the wonder of my first Alabama spring. Daffodil shoots appeared near the end of February. Cherry and Bradford Pear trees came in like Chicago's March lion, covering the Blue Rock streets with white-blossom petals resembling snow. March went out like a lamb with pink and white dogwood trees and fluffy azalea blooms in all colors of a rainbow.

In Chicago, the saying was, "April showers bring May flowers." However, in Blue Rock, May brought Shoals Creek water warm enough to wade through and become one with the abundant aqua life.

The school year ended in June, ushering in long-hot days and only slightly cooler nights. Dad and I spent the morning hours fishing. Afterward, we worked at the switchyard until he cut me loose at lunchtime. Every Friday, Dad would pay me a small sum of money. It was never the same amount for some reason. Dad would always say, "Now you share your good fortune with Itchy and Shanks."

Dad had no affection for my buddies' parents, although he told me it was our Christian responsibility to be an example to my impressionable young friends. My parents constantly corrected Itchy's and Shanks' grammar, enunciation, and pronunciation, except for "ain't and y'all." They provided a definition when they used words they thought the two might not know. "Those boys need a leg up in life," Mom told me.

Summer afternoons were spent swimming. It's how all the Blue Rock boys cooled off. Older girls were forbidden from engaging in such physical exposure. The last time a Blue Rock girl went in the drink was when the preacher submerged them in the name of Jesus. After baptism, they were expected to be chaste Southern Belles.

The Tennessee River watershed offered many swimming holes close to home. Two hands-down favorites were the Mayor Clarence Filbert bridge, bearing metal signs at each end boasting his name and position. The sign was regularly desecrated with graffiti or buckshot holes by rowdy drunkards. Mayor Filbert kept after the road maintenance man about the sign's upkeep or replacement. Adding insult to the mayor's injury, everyone called it Shoals Bridge instead of its official name. The bridge traversed the deep confluence of Shoals Creek and the Tennessee River. Younger boys like me stuck to the vehicle level for an exhilarating fifteen-foot leap. Some high school boys would shimmy on hands and knees up the angled I-beam to the cross beam atop the truss bridge for a thirty-foot drop into the water. The higher jump was only doable on cloudy days or after rain cooled the steel.

The second-best swimming hole was called The Lynchin' Tree. A large water oak hugged the river bank below a steep hill. Someone hung a thick rope from a sturdy branch with a noose-style knot tied at the bottom. A swinger put one foot in the loop while holding the rope above the knot. The noose must have been the creator's morbid joke because they added another knot below the hangman's knot to keep it from cinching down on the passenger's foot. There were a couple of downsides with The Lynchin' Tree. First, only one person could go at a time. If high school boys were present, your turn wasn't guaranteed. Also, there was the risk of injury. Unlike Shoals Bridge, where you couldn't miss the water, The Lynchin' Tree's rope swung over a long stretch of dry, rocky hillside and shallow river before reaching a spot deep enough to let go. Once, Shanks tried to release over the water, but his big ass foot and ankle got tangled up in the rope's bottom. Fortunately, his powerful calf muscles and gangly upper body saved him. As the rope swung back toward the rocky hillside, he bent at the waist and grabbed the rope above the noose seconds before scraping dry land. He must have gone back and forth twenty times before the rope came to a standstill at the edge of the water. It took two high school boys to untangle him. An overweight boy would have been doomed with a broken ankle and a painful hillside collision.

Summer evenings were lazy. Dad sat in his rocker listening to the radio or reading the *Times Daily* out of Florence. Mom claimed the couch with her ever-present novel. After dinner, Itchy and I hung out at our club in the pole barn loft. We talked about our favorite baseball players and other important subjects. I described games at Wrigley Field, Chicago's elevated mass transit system, and the city's beautiful library and museums. Sometimes, we would laugh at the littlest things or nothing at all. We loved laughing with each other. When it was time for Itchy to go home, I went to bed on the miserably hot second floor. I slept spread-eagle naked on the sheets to expose as much bare skin as possible to the open air. At some point, while asleep, I would roll over on my side and pull a sheet over my body.

By the end of August 1933, Mom and Dad's investment strategy began to pay dividends. We had eggs from our hens and garden fresh vegetables. If we had luck on the river, bass, trout, catfish, or crappie blessed our dinner table.

The last Saturday before the start of seventh grade, Mom and Dad went shopping in Muscle Shoals, leaving me home alone for the day.

They needed more than Smalley's Grocery stocked. Uncle Clem and his gandy dancer crew were coming to stay with us for the first time since our move. Dad had requisitioned Uncle Clem and crew to shore up a few tracks around the switchyard. Out-of-line rails caused the train's wheels to shriek. Folks from one end of town to the other complained to Mayor Filbert about the annoying shrill. My parents never strayed far together, leaving me to my own devices. For my birthday a week earlier, my gifts were a compass, one dollar, and a lecture about being old enough to take on more responsibility. Staying home alone must have been one of the new responsibilities. I was more concerned about what other, less-enjoyable burdens might come my way.

Itchy, Shanks, and I were to meet up at my house after we finished our Saturday chores. I promised to share my good fortune and buy treats for a last hurrah before school started on Monday. The only time my friends enjoyed treats was when I bought them. Money was scarce in their home. The eight months I had known Itchy and Shanks had been hard on my cohorts. All three of us went through a growth spurt. I was the only one who had enough food to keep up. Itchy was no longer the short-pudgy redhead I met in January. Even with the lack of regular meals, he grew about five inches. Shirts that once fit left his wrists exposed. His trousers sagged at the waist. The lack of expensive balm and summer exposure worsened his red-flakey skin. Shanks was least fortunate. The inches he grew upward stole what little meat he had on his bones in January. His pants hung low off his midsection, exposing more hip and backbone than was healthy. His skin was pale gray. Dark circles around his eyes made him look deathly ill. His large hands, feet, and ears made him look even more gaunt than when I first met him.

When my buddies arrived at my house at one o'clock, neither had eaten breakfast or lunch. I made them both a bologna sandwich alongside a tall glass of milk. I didn't need permission to feed the boys. Once, at the beginning of the summer school break, Shanks and I had been playing in the club. We broke for a drink of water. In the kitchen, Mom's eye caught Shanks while she washed dishes. She had a look of both horror and sadness at the boy's malnourished frame. "Shane, have you eaten today?" Mom asked.

Shanks hung his head. "No, ma'am."

"You boys, go sit at the kitchen table."

Mom went to the refrigerator and poured a tall glass of milk and water from the sink. Her hands trembled, assembling two smoked liverwurst sandwiches. I had already eaten lunch. Before I could reject the second sandwich, she gave me a subtle, don't you say a word nod. She didn't want Shanks to feel the humiliation of eating alone. She served me the water. Shanks got the milk. His sandwich, I could see, had twice the meat as mine. Mom brushed his dirty hair behind his ears and kissed him on the forehead. She returned to the sink and washed the dishes in a frenetic, shaky way. I knew without seeing her face, Mom was crying. While she was cooking that evening, I overheard her and Dad talking about Shanks. At the dinner table, Mom said the prayer. As far back as I could remember, she had never said the prayer. It wasn't one of Dad's canned versions like "Bless us, oh lord" or a spoken version of "The Doxology." Mom made it up as she went, praying for Itchy and Shanks and better prospects for their parents. After grace, she made an announcement. "We can't feed the entire town, but God help us, we can feed Richard and Shane at least one meal a day."

After my friends finished the bologna sandwiches, we headed to Smalley's. I received the usual welcome from the hateful Sit-n-Spit Club. "I heard your nigger-lovin' uncle's comin' to straighten the tracks next week," the Mayor said.

"What's the story with that C-C-Cajun they drag around?" Skeeter asked with his stutter and uncontrollable twitch that afflicted him from time to time.

There was no point in responding to either of them. But what Vernon, Shanks' one-legged-grandpa said, got to me. "Shanks, don't you dare go round Paxton's house while them niggers are in town."

"Yes, sir," Shanks cowed. What else could he say? It angered me though. The Paxton house had fed Shanks many times, and I was about to pay for his treats ... again. I gave Vernon an angry stare, though I thought it best to keep my mouth shut.

Itchy, and I got a bottle of Dr. Pepper and a Hershey bar. Shanks got his usual—a small bag of roasted peanuts and an RC Cola (I had by this time finally realized what people were talking about when they said "arrah-see cola."). We took our loot to the bench on Smalley's porch.

It didn't take long to shed the ugliness from inside. Shanks stuffed two unshelled peanuts halfway up his nose. It gave Itchy and me a good laugh while Shanks crossed his eyes and kept a straight face for as long as possible. When Shanks finally exploded into laughter, the peanuts shot out of his nose, which made us laugh even harder. Like always, Itchy and I finished our chocolate bar and Dr. Pepper before Shanks finished his soda and nuts. The boy had a routine. First, he shelled a couple of peanuts and dropped them into his RC. He would then take a small sip of soda, allowing the peanuts to slip into his mouth. After he chewed and swallowed, the process was repeated. This took an annoying eternity. I cut our fun short when Mom and Dad passed us with a truck bed full of provisions—an exciting prospect.

There were groceries from Piggly Wiggly and boxes from the Army-Navy Surplus store. Dad first grabbed a long object wrapped in a blanket and secured with string. "What's that?"

When he said, "Not a toy" I knew it was a gun. "Take the boxes to the barn. Once you're done, we'll talk."

I unloaded the pickup and met Dad at the kitchen table. "Asa, this is a second-hand shotgun. It's different from a rifle." Dad's voice was more stoic than his normal steady cadence. His words were deliberate. "A shotgun scatters little pellets called birdshot or bigger pellets called buckshot. This one has a full choke. The choke makes them scatter a little less. It's good for turkey or duck hunting. A rifle fires a single bullet. It's good for deer hunting. Sheriff Taylor told me what to buy."

"Are we going bird hunting?"

"We? No, not you and me, we. Sheriff Taylor and me, we. I've never hunted or shot a gun. Sheriff Taylor is going to teach me. Once I learn to hunt turkey safely, I'll teach you."

"Can I hold it?"

"This one time. Get it out of your system. After that, you're not to touch it until I teach you how to respect it."

The wooden butt of the heavy shotgun was slightly worn. It smelled like spent firecrackers and sewing machine oil. "It's an investment," I said.

Dad laughed and took the gun from me. "It's more than that. It's a tool for both good and evil. You go back to your friends at Smalley's. Tomorrow we've got work to do. Uncle Clem will be here by dinner."

I tossed and turned in bed, kept awake by my excitement over meeting Uncle Clem's crew. The night Uncle Clem and I talked over dinner at The Berghoff began to take on more meaning. His words were calculated. I thought I had more questions about Blue Rock than he had answers. In reality, he was giving me answers to questions about the South I didn't know I had at the time. He also knew there would come a day when his crew would descend upon our home. His goal was to prepare me. The description of his workers was detailed. He painted a picture of Mack's marbled skin, Tiny's enormity, and Sam's gift for music and rhythm. He explained the twins' plight of being both Negro and Indian and not fully accepted as either. Etienne was the pride and joy of the entire crew. They saved the boy's life, and he became the crew's adopted white little brother. Lastly, there was Preacher. Uncle Clem described him as a Renaissance man. Renaissance was a type of word he wouldn't normally use. A word I didn't know. Uncle Clem explained Preacher was more intelligent than most people, including him and Dad.

CHAPTER ELEVEN
SINGING SAM

S unday morning, Mom served me eggs and biscuits with a side of chores. *Build a stone fire ring out back. Roll eleven logs around the pit for seating. Stockpile kindling and split wood for the pit and kitchen stove.*

With the fire pit ready for company, Mom joined me in the backyard to help assemble the sleeping arrangements. My parents purchased eight fold-up cots, cotton rope, and a large roll of mosquito netting from the Army-Navy Surplus Store. We strung the line from a hook on the west corner of the barn, around the T-pole clothesline near the kitchen door, and back to the east corner of the barn. We positioned the cots under the rope and draped a sheet of mosquito netting fastened with a clothespin over each cot. Each makeshift tent included a glass jar repurposed as a vase filled with fresh lavender. The jar's tin jar cap served as a candle holder on the ground next to each bed. I couldn't help but snicker as Mom admired our work. "You know, Mom, it could rain."

"If there's rain, we string one end of the rope inside the back wall of the barn and move the cots inside. Easy-peasy," she said, slapping her hands clean of the rain problem. A few months after the crew's first visit, Dad and I fortified the barn with a sliding door constructed from an abandoned handcar's wheels and a short length of track.

Just when I thought I could ditch Mom to play catch with Itchy, she ordered me into the kitchen to help with dinner. It was hot outside. The kitchen was even hotter. Mom had been baking biscuits, bread, and sugar cookies all morning. On the stovetop, a pot of dried white beans was reconstituted and seasoned with hog jowls for a hearty stew. I was handed a large knife and a basket of our garden's vegetables to chop for the stew. Mom never trusted me with Dad's sharpened kitchen knives before. I realized KP duty was another one of the new responsibilities I was lectured about on my birthday.

Uncle Clem and his crew jumped from the boxcars on the tracks behind our house. The conductor said goodbye to his passengers with a toot of his whistle. It wasn't long after the friendly introductions that Uncle Clem stuck his foot in his mouth. "I'm so hungry I could eat dog shit off a stick."

"Clem," Mom shouted. "The boy, for Pete's sake."

"For crying out loud," Dad barked. Uncle Clem looked at me with a hint of a wicked grin. The row caused the crew to disperse to the cots with their rucksacks and bedrolls.

The tension Uncle Clem's comment created subsided over dinner. Mom, Dad, Preacher, and Sam ate at the dining room table. The twins sat on the edge of the back porch. Mack and Tiny ate leaning against the logs by the fire pit with Uncle Clem. Etienne insisted I eat with him in the Citroen. "I call da driva side," he said.

Except for Etienne, the crew members were just as Uncle Clem described over dinner at The Berghoff. I pictured Etienne as the skinny, frail, bruised, and battered boy Uncle Clem said he first encountered years back. Instead, he stood tall with broad shoulders and muscular arms. His jawline was strong and chiseled, with a dimple in his chin. He wore a constant grin as if he were the happiest man on earth.

Etienne wolfed down his dinner, deposited his plate on the car's back seat, and acted like he was driving the crippled Citroen. He shifted the gears and leaned left and right as he turned the steering wheel into make-believe curves on a make-believe road. He behaved more like a kid than a grown man in his late twenties. "I bet you know da best swimmin' holes. Maybe you take me swimmin' afta you done finished with school, and I finish work tomorrow?"

"You bet, Etienne." I had a new friend.

After dinner, conversations moved from person to person and group to group. Etienne gathered the outside plates and utensils and joined the conversation Mom, Dad, and Sam were having as they cleaned the dishes and kitchen. The twins joined Mack and Sam at the pit and started a small fire. Preacher joined me in the Citroen with questions about school, my friends, and if I enjoyed living in Blue Rock. I knew it would be impolite to tell him about the racism I encountered and how my friends were forbidden to come around when the Negro crew was at my house. So, instead, I painted a pretty picture of swimming holes and the natural beauty Chicago lacked.

My night ended before I was ready. Mom thought the first day of school required extra sleep. I opened my bedroom window overlooking the backyard and listened to our guests from my bed. I couldn't make out what was said around the fire pit, but hearing the voices was comforting. The conversations eventually gave way to Sam's sad-lilting harmonica.

The sun rose to the vocal cords of Sam singing, "This is the Day the Lord Has Made." There was enough time before the school bell to tag along with the crew and watch a few minutes of the team working.

At the switchyard, Sam sang while the crew organized equipment and assessed the task at hand. They moved with purpose, coalescing in a shoulder-to-shoulder team with long-steel gandy bars in hand along a line of rail. Uncle Clem squatted over the track at one end of the crew to survey the misalignment.

"You ready, Sam?" Uncle Clem asked.

"Ready as I'll ever be."

Sam broke out in a rhythmic song about a road to heaven's gate paved with God's grace. The rest of the crew, except Uncle Clem, added the chorus about an earthly railroad track fraught with despair. Gandy Company's steel bars clanked and clamored in rhythm with the song, slowly inching the rail into alignment.

As the week progressed, the high-pitch shrill of steel wheels on rails subsided and disappeared entirely by Friday. All week long, I looked forward to spending the weekend with our guests. To my disappointment, a call came late Friday, ordering the crew to Kentucky immediately. A truck near Paducah attempted to beat a train full of Robinson's coal at a crossing. The result was a mess.

Uncle Clem and his crew's visit to our home in 1933 was the first. It wasn't the last. While much of the country languished in the Great Depression, Robinson exploited business opportunities created by President Roosevelt. Once dam construction began on the Tennessee River, Robinson's rail lines and trains were kept busy throughout the Tennessee Valley—as was the gandy dancer crew and the switchyard.

CHAPTER TWELVE
*P*UBERTY

M ayor Filbert was a poor example of leadership. He was a hateful fat cracker in a seersucker suit with little understanding of good governance. Despite the mayor's objections, progress began to encroach on Blue Rock. In 1935, the Tennessee Valley Authority funded the construction of a motor vehicle bridge connecting Blue Rock, Alabama, with East Bluff, Mississippi. Filbert was more worried about his precious Blue Rock changing than the poverty he governed. He feared Negroes living in and around East Bluff spilling into his territory.

Itchy's and Shanks' dads were hired on at the bridge project, and it showed. The two boys put on much-needed weight. Shanks' skin color went from pale gray to a healthy olive tone. Itchy's face and shoulders became the second front of his war with skin lesions. Mom told him not to pick and gave him a small jar of honey to dab on his worst pimples— an old wives' tale for treating severe acne. It was a magically dreadful age. The time when awkward things popped up. One minute, you're minding your own business in class, the next minute ... surprise! You've got a hard-on for no apparent reason. I said many silent prayers that the teacher wouldn't call me up to the chalkboard in that state. While boys were trying to figure out how to control hormonal phenomenons, girls the same age had a one- to two-year head start on puberty. They understood biological facts boys couldn't fathom.

Itchy's pubescence came with an oddity. Itchy asked at recess, "Can we meet up at the club? I got something to show y'all after school."

"What is it?" Shanks asked.

"I can't talk about it here."

"What's wrong with you?" I complained. "You could have waited until after school to bring it up. Now we're gonna wonder for two hours."

At the club, Itchy paced like Lincoln Park Zoo's caged animals. "Men, you're probably wondering why I've called y'all here today," Itchy said as if addressing a military platoon. Humor was his way of calming his nerves.

"Get on with it," Shanks ordered.

"Give him a minute, Shanks. He's obviously unstrung."

"Have either of you got hair growing, you know, down there and in your pits?" Shanks and I were dumbfounded for a moment. "Hold on, Itchy. You said you wanted to show us something. I don't like where this is headed," Shanks said.

"I'm with Shanks. Keep your britches on."

"I ain't dropping my drawers, but I do gotta show y'all something."

Itchy removed his shirt, exposing his pink torso. He grabbed the back of his head, revealing his armpits. "What do y'all see?" He asked.

"What the hell is that all about?" Shanks asked.

"What? I didn't notice anything."

"Look at his pits. Look closely."

"Oh damn. That's weird." Under one armpit, Itchy had a small tuft of red hair. The other armpit was bare. Halfway down the underside of his bicep was a strawberry blonde tuft.

"Y'all got hair growing in the wrong place like me?" Itchy asked.

"Not so far, but now that I see you, I think I'll keep a close eye on things," I said.

"Mine's all where it's supposed to be ... 'cept when I get a wild hair across my ass," Shanks said, which made me laugh.

"Come on, y'all. This is serious. Folks are gonna make fun of me at the swimmin' holes this summer. What am I gonna do?"

"I suppose you could shave it off the wrong spot," I suggested.

"How's that gonna look if I got hair under one armpit and not the other?"

"Shave 'em both," Shanks said.

"That's no good. While everyone our age is sprout'n pubes, I'll look like a babe in the woods."

"I've got it," I said. "Wear a shirt when you go swimming. If anyone says anything, tell them you burn easily and need to cover up. It's the truth."

"I like it," Itchy said. The problem was solved.

At some point, Itchy's mom caught a glimpse of his displaced hair and took him to see Doc Watson. After examining Itchy's pits and consulting an anatomy book, the doctor determined Itchy must have been born missing some or all of his pectoral muscles on one side, which shifted the hair follicles down the underside of his arm. The doctor couldn't be one hundred percent sure of his diagnosis but felt the matter was nothing to get in a stitch over.

Dad attempted to guide me through the time of change in my life. He never had "the talk" with me but frequently said, "Now that you're becoming a man," followed by some awkward prognostication. He also occupied more of my time with what could be described as adult activities and responsibilities. There was always a reward for a willingness to put my best foot forward. Dad saved enough money to purchase the needed parts for the broken-down Citroen. The repairs were my job, with Dad over my shoulder pointing me in the right direction. My reward was driving lessons and occasional use of the vehicle. At the switchyard, my responsibilities expanded from cleaning to routine maintenance and repairs. I was taught how to lube the switchyard diesel locomotive, the pickup, and the big Leyland truck. Dad called me his "little grease monkey." Unlike the this-and-that-Friday pay I received when I was younger, Dad increased the money and called it "an allowance."

I was introduced to turkey hunting. It took Dad eighteen months from the day he bought the shotgun to solo bag his first turkey. He brought home a couple of kills over those months. They were birds Sheriff Taylor shot and donated. I became a skilled turkey caller but didn't like pulling the trigger. Watching a bird struggle after the hit and the plucking-and-gutting process was most unpleasant. Dad reminded me after every kill that hunting was a valuable skill during hard times.

Fishing was another matter. I felt no remorse when catching, gutting, and fileting a fish. I carried a sharp knife to end its life quickly and mercifully. If a catch was too small to eat, I released it to live another day. The area provided plenty of meal-size bass, catfish, crappie, and trout. I rarely came home empty-handed.

Uncle Clem and his crew's visits became routine. Helping feed the hungry mouths became my routine. I was the hunter, tasked with landing as many fish as possible and hopefully a turkey. Mom was the gatherer, harvesting vegetables from our garden and baking all day. The crew would roll into town and work in the area all day, then return to our house in the evening to eat, relax, and bed down.

The crew was scheduled to arrive the evening of the third Saturday in September 1935 to lay a short temporary track at the Blue Rock to East Bluff motor bridge project. Cranes mounted to flatbed rail cars were used to lift materials into place. There were similar projects at the dams and bridges under construction up and down the Tennessee River.

The crew had been working near Nashville with no timely trains headed to Blue Rock. Dad left early that morning in the company's Leyland truck to collect Uncle Clem and crew. I headed out with the shotgun and fishing rod over my shoulder, a freshly sharpened six-inch pocketknife, and a few feet of cotton rope to hang a turkey for cleaning and string my fish together for transport home. I left the mason jar of old chicken and turkey organs in the refrigerator. Catfish loved the rancid smell of old hearts, livers, and chunks of neck bone. I thought the odor might deter any turkeys from coming close. I hoped to shoot a turkey early, pluck and gut it in the field, and use the organs and bits of neck bone as catfish bait. I had heard a gobbler a few weeks earlier in a wooded area on the outskirts of town. Where there was a gobbler, there would likely be hens. Conveniently, a few hundred yards away was a spot in the river dominated by catfish.

I made turkey calls for what felt like an eternity, sitting in the dirt, my back against a blue lichen-covered boulder. Turkey hunting took patience, frequent changes in the type of call with pauses. The male bird called back only once. I could tell they were close but nervous. Finally, a hen's curiosity got the best of her. She followed the sound of my calls. The male chased after her. I had a clear shot at the hen in the distance.

The gobbler was hidden behind a large oak. I took a deep breath, exhaled halfway to steady myself, then pulled the trigger. As luck would have it, the gobbler stepped from behind the tree and in front of the hen. I hit them both with one shot. The two birds flopped about each other, resembling a cock fight rather than taking their last gasps. I always kept my distance, not wanting to add the stress of a human bearing down on a creature struggling to survive. Down feathers floated gently above the birds before peacefully descending on the limp dead fowl. Once it was over, I said a prayer. I always said a prayer for the deceased. After my first kill, I prayed for forgiveness as I wept.

My good fortune continued at the fishing hole with no remorse or prayers. After all, the disciples were fishermen, and Jesus had his own special powers when it came to fish. Everything I caught was a keeper. When I landed about a ten-pounder, I took it as a sign to count my blessings and call it a day with twelve nice catfish. I gutted the fish and cut the tails and fins off to reduce as much weight as possible. I left the heads on to run the rope through the fish's mouths and gills for transport. Lugging home my fish and fowl was an exhausting chore, even after the cutting, gutting, and cleaning.

I thought Mom would be pleased with my bounty. Instead, she had the house on lockdown. I had to bang on the kitchen door while struggling with the shotgun, fishing pole, and around thirty pounds of meat over my shoulder. I was irritated at first.

The windows over the sink and by the kitchen table were closed and latched. The kitchen was hotter than July from the stove. Mom appeared distracted and nervous. "What is it, Mom? You look worried."

"I wish your father was home."

Mom took the shotgun and folded the barrel open over her knee. "Hand me a couple of shells." Mom loaded the chamber, dropped the other shell into her apron pocket, and ordered me to stay behind her as she cautiously exited the back door. We split the pole barn and garden headed toward the back of the property. Mom slowed as we reached the end of the barn. She nervously looked about. "I've been afraid they're still lurking around. Look," she said, pointing to smoldering remains of a small fire between the train tracks and the back of the barn. "I came across it while working in the garden."

I put my hand over the coals—*no glowing embers.* There was barely any warmth. "It's OK, Mom. No one's tended this for a while."

"It's not only the fire. See that." Mom pointed the gun barrel at the back wall of the barn. A series of large shapes and figures drawn in white chalk against the dark wood depicted a sort of hieroglyphic story. "They took. They. They took some ... some vegetables from this end of the garden."

"I think we're safe. Mom, you need to hand me the gun."

"It really scared me. It looks like some sort of New Orleans voodoo curse," she said, wiping her nose and eyes. The scary novels Mom was always reading had caught up with her.

"Let's go back inside, call Sheriff Taylor, and see what he thinks." If this had happened when I was eleven or twelve, I would have also been scared, only because Mom was scared.

Miz Gay Lynn was operating the switchboard when I called for Sheriff Taylor. I heard her yell, "Wake up, Taylor. A truck full of hogs done tumped over. They're runnin' amok all over town." Miz Gay Lynn laughed so loudly at her joke, I had to pull the receiver away from my ear. "I'll send him directly," she said through staggered breathing.

Mom asked, "Can you please deal with Sheriff Taylor? I don't want him to see me like this. Can you tell him I'm napping?"

"I'll take care of it."

"Everything OK, Asa?" Taylor yelled from his patrol car.

"I think so, sir. I need to show you something out back."

"Where's your ma and pa?"

"Dad went to Nashville to pick up Uncle Clem and company. Mom's inside."

"She OK?"

"She's napping. Something you would know about. Did you corral all them hogs?"

"My Gay Lynn thinks she's sooo funny."

"What do you make of that?" I asked at the back of the barn.

"You had a visit from a hobo, or hobos. Is this the first time you've had this happen?"

"Yes, sir. They took some vegetables, too."

Sheriff Taylor pulled his spectacles from his shirt pocket and honed in on the markings. "I recognize some of these scratchings. It's called war taggin'. It's how hobos communicate. This one on top means to keep quiet. Together, the circle with the arrow and the locomotive says to head that'a way to hop a ride. It's pointing west cause the trains slow down at your pa's switchyard. The hobos can travel north, south, east, and west from the switchyard." Another symbol stirred a chuckle. "This one means the law in town is tolerant. Guess the word's out about me with the hobos."

"Should I be worried?"

"Naw. I don't think so. Just the same, I'll come by later and talk to your pa and Clem. Tell your ma there's nothing to worry about." Without having seen her, he'd sensed Mom was shaken up.

Once the crew arrived, Sheriff Taylor convened a meeting behind the barn. Dad, Uncle Clem, Preacher, and I went over the markings. My inclusion made me feel grown-up. Uncle Clem identified the meanings of the markings Sheriff Taylor didn't recognize. "That one there says you folks are rich."

"They got that all wrong," Dad said.

"It's the Citroen parked beside the house. It's a little flashy and impractical," said Preacher.

Another sign expressed no knowledge of the resident's temperament. At one point, Mack wandered behind the barn to see about the fuss. "That Skinny Sully's tag," he said after a quick look.

"I'm impressed, Mack. How do you know that?" Sheriff Taylor asked.

"Look at the wheels on the train headed to the switchyard. The wheels ain't round. They all S-shaped. He always mark *SS* somewhere in his tag. You know, *SS* for *Skinny Sully*."

"Should we be concerned?" Dad asked.

Uncle Clem, Preacher, and Sheriff Taylor agreed they'd never had a problem with hobos. Mack imparted his grounded wisdom. "You know Skinny Sully's gonna run his mick mouth to other hobos about the barn, the garden, and how every which-away you can go from the switchyard."

"Some of 'em can be a little pushy, knocking on your door," Sheriff Taylor added to Mack's assessment. "They try to strike up a conversation about Jesus to woo some food or money. You want me to run off anyone who comes round?" he asked Dad.

"I can promise you, Mom doesn't want any hobos knocking on the door when she's home alone," I said.

Mack chimed in with a passionate plea on the hobos' behalf. "They just tryin' to get by. Folks been strugglin' since twenty-nine. We been blessed all this time."

"We come across hobos on the tracks all the time with no trouble," Preacher added.

I objected strongly. "We don't need hobos coming around our house. Y'all didn't see Mom. She was mighty shook up."

After listening to everyone's opinion, Dad took a stroll through the garden rows. He plucked a squash blossom, examined it, then folded the flower into his mouth. "No, Taylor, you don't need to run anyone off. Preacher and Mack are right. We are blessed. We can accommodate a few visitors." I felt like I'd been punched in the gut. He didn't see Mom crying. Dad went into the barn and returned with four railroad spikes and a length of cotton rope. He jammed the spikes into the ground with the heel of his boot and strung the rope around each offset head, cornering off a small section at the back of the garden. "Asa, after dinner, I want you to take the whitewash from the barn, the small paintbrush, and my Bible. Paint what it says in Leviticus 23:22 next to the marks on the barn. Under that, write, 'Only take what you need from the roped-off area of the garden and do not approach the house.'"

Preacher recited the scripture from memory. *"When you reap the harvest of your land, moreover, you shall not reap to the very corners of your field nor gather the gleaning of your harvest; you are to leave them for the needy and the alien. I am the Lord your God."*

"Aaay-men," Mack said.

Surprised, Uncle Clem asked, "Well damn, Hank. When did you learn to pull scripture out of your ass like that?"

"While you were learning all manner of vulgarities," Dad responded tersely. An awkward hush ensued. Sheriff Taylor had a look of embarrassment for Uncle Clem.

"Well then," Sheriff Taylor said, breaking the long silence. "I think I'll run along."

Mack slinked off, not wanting any part of a family row.

I said, in an assertiveness I'd never before had with Dad. "I'll do the painting, but you'll have to explain your thinking to Mom. You weren't here. You didn't see her crying." Dad accepted my charge with a respectful nod and headed toward the house.

Preacher put his hand on my shoulder and looked me squarely in the eyes. "Asa, in the Bible, God, Jesus, and the Holy Spirit tell us repeatedly to fear not, do not fear, do not be afraid. It's written so many times I couldn't quote them all. So when you're afraid in life, and you will be, remember what the Bible says about fear. Don't worry about the hobos."

The crew's visit had been the same routine as all their other visits, though there was a difference for me. I saw the subtle nuances of the relationships between what had become our extended family. I'd never thought about the crew's love for one another and for Mom, Dad, and me. Sam and Preacher were drawn to Mom. They would do the dishes together almost every night before sitting on the front porch laughing and talking late into the night. I figured they were drawn to Mom because they didn't have a mother and wife. Etienne stuck close to Dad and me. I imagined because his father was evil and violent; whereas, Dad was kind and gentle. I was sure Etiene's affection toward me was because together, we had all the childhood fun he'd missed out on. He never tired of shooting marbles, playing catch, or taking every opportunity to go swimming. While the twins and Tiny didn't say much, they always had a soft eye on me as if prepared to rescue me from danger. I felt like my relationships with the crew were becoming more meaningful.

On the last evening of the crew's visit, I summoned the nerve to ask Preacher what happened to his wife and Sam's mother. Uncle Clem told me most of the intimate details about the rest of the crew's families. When I asked about Preacher's, Uncle Clem, Mom, and Dad all gave me the same answer. "You'll have to ask Preacher or Sam." I took a roundabout approach. "Preacher, do you ever miss home and family? Does Sam ever talk about missing home and family?"

Preacher gave me an easy smile. "She died from the Spanish Flu in 1918. Along with a lot of other folks."

I was shocked at how easily Preacher saw through me. "I've asked Mom, Dad, and Uncle Clem several times. They always said I had to ask you or Sam. Uncle Clem told me way back in Chicago about the rest of his crew's family. Uncle Clem only said you were a Renaissance man. Why wouldn't Uncle Clem, Mom, or Dad tell me about your wife?"

Preacher put his arm around my shoulder. "It's not only about my wife. I guess they felt it would be best if Sam and I only shared what we wanted to share. Son, our situation with your uncle is complicated. Your uncle wouldn't have his crew as you know it if it weren't for me. When Clem first came to Mississippi to hire a bunch of Negroes, no one from our town would work with him unless I agreed to hire on. I wasn't going anywhere without Sam, so here we all are. I'm somewhat of a father figure to your uncle. And to the rest of the crew."

"Can I ask you another question?"

"Sure."

"How does it feel to be a Negro?"

"That's an interesting question. What if I asked you how it feels to be white? Could you answer that?"

It took a moment for me to contemplate being white. I rephrased my question, hoping for a different answer. "What is it like to be Negro? Do you understand what I'm asking?"

"I understand what you're asking, but I can't answer it in any way that you could understand, just as you can't tell me in any way I could understand what it is like to be white. It's the world we live in."

"I'm learning it's an ugly world. Does it ever make you want to cry or give up?"

"Son, don't become sad or bitter. The world's not all bad. Let me tell you something I want you to always remember. When it comes to Negroes, most white folks are thin-skinned and hard-hearted. Your Uncle Clem and your folks are thick-skinned and soft-hearted when it comes to people of different heritage."

I turned into Preacher's chest for a long hug. "I'm sorry your wife died."

"I am too, son. I am, too."

CHAPTER THIRTEEN
CURSED

While development continued on TVA dams and bridges up and down the Tennessee River, a new elementary, middle, and high school complex was constructed in 1936 on the east side of the Shoals Creek bridge. Blue Rock had the geographical advantage of being perched on a plateau above the river and the largest town west of Florence. Smaller, low-lying communities dotting the riverbank would become subaquatic ghost towns, swallowed up by the TVA's dam's rising waters.

Residents had to move to higher ground. A few moved to Blue Rock. Others moved to the small communities dotting the hills north of the river or the larger towns to the east. The new schools merged the children on the west side of Lauderdale County. President Roosevelt decreed the dirt farmers' and hill folks' uneducated progeny "must go to school for the good of the country," increasing the enrollment.

Advancing from middle school to the brand-new Robert E. Lee High School was exciting. Having new classmates from other towns and schools was an even more exciting prospect for some. Itchy and Shanks spent the entire summer anxiously awaiting bussed-in coeds. As puberty and hormones took over, my buddies had high hopes for a romantic relationship.

At the beginning of eighth grade, Itchy had a steady—a ginger who moved from Mississippi. She was a sweet girl, but after only a week, the girls in our grade convinced her she wanted nothing to do with our misfit clique. Tammy Sloan's four older brothers nipped in the bud Shanks' advances. For my part, a relationship with the opposite sex was not an option. None of the girls in Blue Rock interested me, nor did they show any interest in "the Yankee." Miss Cannon, the middle school librarian, was the only woman who stirred a fantasy in me. She had wavy blonde hair and always wore one side pinned behind her ear, exposing the side of her neck. During warm weather, she wore blouses revealing a little shoulder near her neckline. Miss Cannon was curvaceous, smelled good, and was always cheerful. She rode the school bus to Blue Rock from a town a few miles north.

The new school year got off to a divided start. A tense us-versus-them mindset between the Blue Rock natives and the students bused from neighboring towns hung in the halls. Shanks, Itchy, and I may have been the misfit clique, but now we were a subset of the Blue Rock clique. During the first few weeks of class, the bused-in boys strutted around school like peacocks rattling their fanned plumage. The new girls were generally guarded with everyone except their hometown friends. Blue Rock's student body called the invaders river rats. The outsiders were at a disadvantage. They only knew the kids from each of their small towns. The kids from Blue Rock were in the majority and attended school together for years.

The first fight of the year happened two weeks in. One of the bussed-in boys, Arthur Thompson, made fun of Scott Jenkins' raggedy clothes in front of half the school at Lunch. Scott was an angry boy from a poor family. "I'll see you after school," Scott said with a grimace.

"You don't scare me," Arthur bit back.

News of the fight quickly spread. When the bell rang at three o'clock, every student from Blue Rock rushed to the waiting buses and blocked access to Arthur's bus. Scott stood stiffly with his fists raised to his chin and almost one hundred Blue Rock kids behind him. There were only about twenty students on Arthur's bus route. They stood a safe distance from Arthur and the Blue Rock mob. They knew if it turned into a melee, there would be a beatdown of epic proportions. Before a punch was thrown, the bus driver, a burly bearded man in bib overalls, pushed through the crowd and positioned himself between Scott and Arthur. "What in tarnation is going on here?" he growled.

"They're gonna brawl," a voice called out from behind Scott.

"Arthur made fun of my clothes in front of everyone."

The bus driver looked Scott up and down, then at Arthur. "This true, Arthur?" Arthur looked at his shoes—he kicked up a little dirt. The bus driver grabbed Arthur by the ear and drug him through the laughing Blue Rock mob. Even the kids on Arthur's bus route laughed.

The first fight of the year ended before it began, but the message was sent. The bussed-in students were a minority.

The following Tuesday, I fell victim to the school consolidation. My last class of the day was at the east end of the building. Shanks' and Itchy's last class was on the west side. We always exited our respective side doors to avoid the crush of students at the main entrance. Itchy and Shanks waited while I circled around the deserted back of the school. Suddenly, my arms were pulled behind my back as if being handcuffed. My books hit the ground. A voice whispered over my shoulder. "It's me, JD from second and sixth period."

"What's your problem, JD?"

"Dirk's gonna explain it to you."

I struggled to get loose, but my captor had leverage. Dirk Johnson appeared out of nowhere. "Don't be a dick, Dirk." Before I could get another word out, Dirk landed a left fist on my right eye. Then, a right on my nose and another left on my mouth.

"Stay away from our girls," Dirk spat before landing a gut punch, knocking the wind out of me. The jerks ran to catch their bus before I had enough breath to ask them what they were talking about. I staggered to Itchy and Shanks.

"Holy crap, Asa. What happened to you?" Itchy asked.

"Not sure. Dirk and JD jumped me behind the school. Said something about staying away from their girls."

Shanks pulled a handkerchief from his back pocket and put it up to my bleeding nose. "Hold your head back for a minute to stop the bleeding." He was an expert on bloody noses. He had them frequently back in his malnourished days.

"Have you been flirting with Busty Barb and Leggy Louise? They're off limits," Itchy said.

"I've no interest in those girls or axe to grind with Dirk or JD. I don't know what their problem is."

"Well, they got a problem with you," Shanks said. "Gave you the country boy ass-whoopin' trifecta. A bloody nose, busted lip, and a shiner."

"Can y'all carry my books to Itchy's? I'll collect them later."

"What are you gonna do?" Itchy asked.

"I can't go home like this. Mom'll be on the phone calling the school and who knows who else. She'll make it worse. I'm going to the switch-yard to see my dad. He'll understand. He'll talk Mom out of making a stink."

Dad looked up from the telephone. He politely cut the call short at the sight of me in the doorway. He sighed, rounded his desk, and wrapped his arms around me. I needed the hug. While I was in his comforting clutch, he asked, "Has your mother seen you?"

"No, sir. I came straight here."

"Good. She'd be on the phone, making matters worse. Tell me what happened."

"Two of the bus rider boys jumped me behind the school. One held my arms while the other punched me out. Then they ran off to catch their bus."

"That's it? Nothing else to it?"

"Somehow, I knew what was coming, so I told Dirk not to be a dick. He took aim anyway. Made sure he got my eye, nose, and lip to make it look bad. Before he gave me a gut punch, he told me to stay away from their girls. My stomach was in my throat. I couldn't speak my piece."

Dad would have scolded me for calling someone a dick. In his fatherly wisdom, though, he knew it was not the time. He leaned his butt against the desk and folded his arms. "You were gonna get a beating whether you called him a ... um, a you-know-what or not. This was about their girls."

"Like I told Itchy and Shanks, I've got no axe with Dirk and JD and no interest in their girls."

"Asa, I can't tell you how this all came about, but I can almost guarantee those girls did or said something about you. Those boys are jealous."

"It's their problem now. I'll get my payback one at a time."

"No, you won't. It's one thing to defend yourself when attacked. Revenge is a whole other matter. Besides, you're not a fighter."

"I'm gonna look like a chump if I don't retaliate."

Dad's eyes went to the ceiling momentarily before imparting his advice. "Son, you've got to learn to pick your battles in life."

"I don't understand."

"Think of it this way. Sheriff Taylor's told me how you've handled Mayor Filbert, Vernon, and Skeeter down at Smalley's. For years, they've been trying to provoke you. Taylor says it's a thing of beauty the way your silence has gotten under their skin. Those old coots can hardly stand it. Sometimes silence can be as powerful as speaking or punching."

Dad always had a way of saying the right thing at the right time. I never knew I was getting the best of the Sit-n-Spit Club. My anger and planned vengeance quickly evaporated. "I'm going to call it a day. Let's go home and work this out with your mother."

"Oh my goodness, Asa," Mom gasped. "What happened?"

Dad took control. "He got jumped after school by a couple of bus riders. He didn't have a chance."

"For Pete's sake. Why? Who was it? I'm calling the school and those boys' parents."

"That'll only make matters worse. Just leave it alone, Dory."

"For Pete's sake. For Pete's sake, Hank, we have to do something."

Two *for Pete's sakes* in a row. Mom was really upset.

"Asa and I talked it over. He's going to turn the other cheek. Hopefully, that'll be the end of it."

"Why did they jump you?"

"Not sure."

"It had something to do with girls," Dad said.

Mom's tense posture relaxed as she sighed. "I knew this day would come."

"What? I didn't do anything. I've never even talked to Dirk's and JD's girls."

"You may have never talked to them, but I'm sure they've been talking about you." I had no experience with girls showing interest in me. The bused-in students knew nothing of me, my parents, or Uncle Clem and his Negro crew. I wasn't their pariah, yet.

"Asa, sit. I want to explain something." I sat down at the kitchen table, expecting an awkward, one-sided conversation. "The last time Clem and Preacher were in town, we were talking. Your uncle noticed how much you'd grown. Preacher pointed out how handsome you were becoming, both inside and out. He said it would be both your blessing and your curse."

I never thought of myself as handsome or ugly. I was just Asa. "This is embarrassing, Mom. What's your point?"

"My point?" Mom paused for a moment to think. "I can't believe I'm going to quote your uncle. Clem put it this way. He said, 'Your odds were good, but the goods were odd.'"

"I still don't understand. Preacher said I'm cursed?" I looked to Dad for relief.

Dad explained things. "Preacher and your uncle were saying there'll be many attractive young women fawning over you. Most will be sullied by hateful racism. They'll be ugly on the inside. That's your curse."

Mom put her hand on my shoulder. "I'll bet all those new girls have noticed you. If you get a big head about it though, I'm warning you, there'll be more beatings."

"What am I supposed to say when the kids and teachers see my face?"

"Crack a joke about it," Dad said. "Tell them they should see the other guy's face. It'll make you seem unaffected by the incident."

Mom took my hand, "Let's get you cleaned up."

Eating dinner was a chore with my busted lip. Going to sleep was even more difficult. Sleeping on one side hurt my lopsided fat lip. My swollen black eye smarted if I rolled over. I gave up and laid on my back. Added to the physical pain was the conversation about my looks and a curse. I was awake for what felt like hours.

I woke to a train whistle and tried to sit up—my pillowcase followed my face. I had rolled onto my side as I slept. My weeping bloody lip stuck to the fabric. It took several minutes of producing extra saliva and working my tongue against the inside of my lip to free myself. The bathroom mirror revealed a lumpy, rainbow-colored face. I startled Mom when I arrived for breakfast. My lopsided mouth had swollen more overnight, and my eye was completely shut. "Would you like to stay home today?" Mom offered.

"No. I'm not going to give JD and Dirk the satisfaction."

"I'm proud of your fortitude."

Itchy and Shanks did their best to keep a straight face when they saw mine. On the way to school, they promised to get to the bottom of what set Dirk and JD off. By third period, word had circulated about my beating. Stares and questions had run their course. Even the teachers learned who the perpetrators were and why they pummeled me. Miz Dockery, the principal, cornered me in the hall. I told her I talked it over with my parents and I'd rather forget about the whole matter. Her pursed lips said she was unhappy my parents had the final say.

Shanks mumbled through a mouthful of peanut butter and jelly, "Looks like Barb and Louise are sweet on you. They were passing a note back and forth all morning yesterday. I didn't see the note, but I heard they were carrying on about lovin' up on the big city Chicago boy. Wrote how cute you were and how sexy the name Asa was. Someone told them about you driving your pa's French car, and how y'all must be rich. Dirk intercepted the note during fourth period."

"You gonna pick 'em off one at a time?" Itchy asked.

"No. My dad told me not to."

Shanks had a twinkle in his eyes. "I could start a rumor Barb and Louise felt bad and were all over you, lick'n your wounds."

"That's no good. It'll sound like I told you to say that. The only thing worse than a kiss-and-tell is lying about the kissing in the first place. I'd probably get another beating to boot. The best thing y'all can do is let it go."

I wondered if Barb and Louise felt sorry for me, were mad at Dirk and JD, or got sadistic satisfaction out of making their boyfriends jealous enough to pummel me.

CHAPTER FOURTEEN
IN FROM THE COLD

The New Year of 1937 brought the second semester at Robert E. Lee High School. Snowfall dusted the nearby hills in front of an arctic blast of cold-dry air. The type of cold that makes your hair stand at attention when tugging off a sweater, followed by a shocking jolt from the next contact with whatever or whoever. On our way to school, the frozen ground crunched underfoot. During the winter months, Itchy, Shanks, and I stopped at Miz Teeny's pedestal birdbath on our way to school to see if it was cold enough overnight to freeze. Most mornings, there was no ice. Occasionally, the thin layer of morning ice disappeared by the time school let out. For the first time, the birdbath was frozen solid.

The frozen bird bath wasn't the only excitement of the new semester. Over Christmas break, old Miz Welch, the ninth- and tenth-grade English and penmanship teacher, slipped on a patch of ice and broke her hip. Miz Welch was hot and cold with me. I was a straight-A grammar and spelling student, frequently used as an example in class. However, she berated my penmanship. Old Miz Welch took her accident as a sign it was time to retire.

The bell dismissing homeroom sent native Blue Rock first-period English students charging through the halls to meet Miz Welch's replacement and claim second-semester desks. The bused-in students, not privy to the teacher's retirement, were left the seating scraps. My heart fluttered, and my temperature rose as I rushed through the classroom door. Miss Cannon, the young, single, middle school librarian and my in-fatuation, sat behind Miz Welch's desk. She had been reassigned to Lee High. I planted my butt in the front-and-center desk. "May I sit here?"

"Yes, Asa. Hopefully, everyone will behave, and seating assignments won't be necessary."

I soon learned my chicken scratch handwriting was an asset, not a liability. Penmanship was the last few minutes of class. I frequently re-ceived special attention from my becoming teacher. She would walk be-tween the desks, observing everyone's paper. When she got to my desk and leaned over my shoulder to critique my work, the sweet-subtle scent of her perfume and her breasts inches from my face always caused a stir under my desk. When the bell rang, I'd have to exit the room with *The Exciting World of Biology* covering my crotch. I did my best to mask my infatuation. If she was aware of my feelings, she never let on.

During fifth period, I received a message from the principal. A first in all my school years. "Your mother called and wants you to go straight home after school." It was mysterious. Mom or Dad would surely have ordered me home early if there were an emergency. Perhaps they had exciting news? My thoughts flashed back to the cold January evening in Chicago years earlier when Uncle Clem burst into the apartment to pitch Mom and Dad on the job opportunity in Blue Rock. Curiosity tor-mented me the rest of the school day. When the final bell rang, I bolted out the side door, around the back of the school, and whizzed past Itchy and Shanks.

"I'll tell you later," I yelled, knowing they would wonder about my rush. Halfway into the sprint, my lungs burned from huffing frigid win-ter air. I didn't let it slow me down. Mom was at the kitchen table scrib-bling on a piece of paper. "I got your message from Miz Dockery. What's going on?"

"The tracks Clem and his crew are laying at a job site are on hold un-til this cold snap ends. They'll be here around dinnertime."

"It's too cold for them to stay outside or in the pole barn."

Mom handed over her list. *"Asa To Do."* The first item, "cots from the barn—six in the living room, two in the upstairs spare bedroom." Un-cle Clem and his crew stayed with us often but never slept in the house. The list continued with various chores, including a run to Smalley's for two sacks of flour, a tub of lard, and a bag of potatoes. "Chop chop," Mom ordered.

By the time the crew trickled through the kitchen door, the sunset temperature had dropped from bitter cold to dangerously cold. Uncle Clem arrived in true form. He rubbed his hands together over the kitchen stove and declared, "Goddamn, it's cold. Colder than a witch's titty in a brass bra."

I heard Mom yell from the living room, "Clem, the boy for Pete's sake." I tucked Uncle Clem's declaration away for a laugh with Itchy and Shanks on our way to school in the morning.

Quarters were tight during the three-day work stoppage. Making matters worse, an outside concern infiltrated the thoughts of everyone sequestered in our home. President Roosevelt had been at war with the Supreme Court and Judicial branch of government. One battle was over Roosevelt's Railroad Retirement Act of 1934. The legislation required taxes for railroad workers' retirement and workplace injury annuities. The federal government would administer the taxes collected to shore up the inadequacies of private plans. Eventually, the Supreme Court struck it down as unconstitutional. Roosevelt and his people succeeded in enacting the Railroad Retirement and Carriers' Taxing Act of 1935. They had designed it, they thought, to avoid the constitutional difficulties encountered in the 1934 Act. Since its passage, the legislation and court battles had been a topic of conversation during every visit by Uncle Clem and crew. Preacher and Dad explained to the crew and me, the pros and cons of the legislation and the court battles. The legislation would affect everyone crammed in the house who worked on the railroads, including Dad and Uncle Clem. The discussions were a practical example of the three branches of government I learned about in civics class.

While an appeal was pending, railroad management and labor, at the request of President Roosevelt, formed a joint committee to negotiate their differences. Robinson was an ally of Roosevelt and supported The New Deal. He treated his people more fairly than many industrialists. Still, business was business. There was a concern Robinson might support terms less desirable for the railroad laborers. Uncle Clem had strong relationships with several of Robinson's managers in the Chicago office. He was on the phone with them frequently, getting updates on the negotiations coming to a head.

On the morning of the fourth day, there was a thaw in the weather and a break in the negotiations. Roosevelt came out on top. It meant more for the Negroes on the crew than Dad and Uncle Clem. A pension and survivors' rights were a small but welcome step toward equality and acceptance as American citizens for the Negroes. There was an exuberance in the house as the crew packed up to head back to work.

CHAPTER FIFTEEN
MIZ GAY LYNN

The frigid winter of 1937 succumbed to spring's inevitably. Daffodils sprouted at the end of February. March and April brought with them the vibrant colors of Alabama in bloom. The annual downpours raised the Tennessee Valley streams, creeks, and rivers to their high-water marks. For the dirt farmers of the region, the storms provided optimism instead of the annual despair of watching their tilled land wash away. TVA's soil-retention training for farmers over several years paid off. Fertile topsoil held its ground against the heavy rains as promised by the scientists. In anticipation of more productive farming, grain elevators and silos for crop storage sprung up along rail lines.

The last week of April, Uncle Clem and his crew were assigned a rail extension project to provide train access to a cluster of silos under construction in Florence. Everything went as planned on Monday and Tuesday. Dad drove the crew to Florence and back in the Leyland truck. I woke Wednesday morning to Uncle Clem barking into the telephone in the downstairs hallway. "I don't give a rat's ass who you call. My crew ain't working today. I suggest you keep everyone off the job site. It ain't safe. We'll be back tomorrow and we'll finish the job on schedule. Goodbye." Uncle Clem slammed the receiver on the hook.

From my bedroom window, I watched the crew, except the twins, put their cots and mosquito netting in the barn. The twins were acting strange. At the east side of the barn, they held their hands on the wood siding. They did the same against the barn's west side. After a brief discussion, the twins crossed the yard to the cluster of three ornamental magnolias on the west corner of the property. With hand movements, one twin appeared to point out to his brother how the wind was lifting the shiny dark green leaves at the top of the trees, exposing their leathery-brown underside. I thought I was witnessing a unique Native American behavior. Nature's mystery confirmed my feelings. The great horned owl that visited regularly at night, made a rare daytime appearance, alighting between the twins. The two men sat cross-legged beside the bird and began to speak to it. The bird's head bobbed and weaved, looking at whichever twin spoke. After a minute or two, the owl lifted itself with two strong wing flaps and soared east on a gust of wind.

"Asa, you're not going to school today," Dad called from his chair in the living room.

"What's going on?" I asked, bounding down the stairs.

"The twins were awake in the middle of the night," Uncle Clem reported. "Said they could smell the cold, dry breeze from the northwest mixing with the warm-moist gulf wind from the southwest. The Great Spirit spoke to them. Told them there would be tornadoes today."

"Do you really think they could know that?"

"It's their Indian half. The twins predict storms all the time. They're never wrong. Never predicted tornadoes, though. I'm not about to second guess them."

Although Dad was a skeptical man, he added his two cents with the same confidence as Uncle Clem. "I once read somewhere, probably *The Saturday Evening Post,* that indigenous peoples can predict natural occurrences. Those who live along the coast know when a tsunami is coming and rush to higher ground. I suppose it's like that for the twins."

"What does indigenous mean?"

"Hmm," Dad pondered. "I think I'd need a dictionary to give you an accurate definition."

"It means folks live where they're supposed to live," Uncle Clem said. "Like Eskimos live at the North Pole. Chinese people in China. Negroes are supposed to live in Africa, and Indians are supposed to live here."

"I suppose that's an accurate description, albeit rudimentary," Dad said.

"What does rudimentary mean?" I'd never heard the words, albeit or rudimentary. "Albeit" was obviously a conjunction.

"It's how we simple folks explain something, unlike your old man, who has to use *Saturday Evening Post* words like albeit and rudimentary."

"Where are us white people supposed to live?" I asked.

"Apparently, wherever we want," Dad said.

"Or wherever we can conquer," Uncle Clem added.

The entire conversation left my head swimming over my cheesy grits and eggs.

During the morning hours, lightning streaked the sky, thunder clapped, and heavy rain washed over Blue Rock . By the time lunch was over, crisp blue skies had calmed the Tennessee Valley. I was sure the twins were wrong about the tornadoes. However, near the end of the school day, the atmosphere changed. Low gray clouds moved in erratically from the northwest and southwest. We all stood on the front porch, fixated on the roiled western sky. Suddenly, in the distance, a thin bullwhip tornado dropped from the sky over the river. Seconds later, it was sucked back into the turbulence.

The clouds morphed into an ominous pale green. The twins ordered everyone to the basement. I clutched the porch railing with fearless curiosity. "I want to stay and watch. I want to see."

Tiny was having none of it. He lifted me off my feet and hustled me down the rickety stairs to the basement. The twins were the last to scramble to safety.

"It's gonna be big," Twin said in unison.

My ears popped. Reverse air pressure blew coal soot out of the furnace. The pile of Drumpf's empty bourbon bottles in the corner rattled. The sound of a three-engine freight train at full speed overcame the basement. Seconds later, it was over.

"The coal chute," Dad said, rushing to the east side of the basement. He lifted the small door with an eastern view.

"Let me see, let me see," I pleaded. Dad stepped aside. I saw the monster spinning toward the northeast before disappearing over the horizon.

We rushed up the stairs and out the kitchen door. "It missed us," Mom said, her voice trembling.

"Looks like it missed the whole town," Dad said.

The center of the tornado cut a swath through the woods behind the pole barn. The sour odor of green, twisted, and shattered trees filled the air. Tall trees that survived the outer edge of the tornado were stripped of their leaves and contorted unnaturally toward the northeastern path of the twister.

"Looks like you lost part of the barn's roof," Preacher said, pointing to corrugated metal strips tangled up in a barren tree.

Itchy's hollering from down the street grabbed everyone's attention. "It's the Sheriff's Office. It's the Sheriff's Office." He was out of breath by the time he reached our backyard. Itchy's parents forbade him from going on our property when the Negroes stayed with us. I knew something terrible must have happened. "The oak tree by the Sheriff's Office split and crushed the building. Miz Gay Lynn's trapped inside."

Without hesitation, everyone, including Itchy, tore out to rescue Gay Lynn. Even Mom ran. I'd never seen her run before. "I'll get Doctor Watson," Mom said, splitting off from the group.

A hopeless scene was unfolding at the sheriff's office. Split at the trunk, half of the tree stood erect. The spine of the enormous oak exposed a black cancer. The roof of the municipal building fell victim to the other half of the tree. Large wooden beams and chiseled limestone brick lay in a mangled pile. Sheriff Taylor frantically dug through the carnage with his bare hands. "Oh, Lord, please don't take my Gay Lynn. Please, Lord, please," Sheriff Taylor whimpered over and over.

Everyone joined in, pulling debris from the area where Miz Gay Lynn's desk sat. Dad and I were at the top of the pile, handing bricks, roofing material, and wood down the line. I saw Miz Gay Lynn first. When I started to call out, Dad quickly covered my mouth. Her motionless body and head were pinned between her desk and the building's main support beam. "Clem, get up here," Dad called down. Sheriff Taylor started to climb the pile of rubble. "Let us handle this, Taylor. We're gonna get her." Dad ordered. Preacher gently grabbed the sheriff by the arm.

Dad asked Uncle Clem, "Do you think we need your crew's gandy bars for leverage under the beam?"

"If she's alive, there's no time to fool with gathering up equipment. Besides, there's not enough room down there for everyone and their tools." Only a little open space surrounded Miz Gay Lynn among the rubble. Uncle Clem yelled, "Tiny, Etienne, get up here. Y'all think you can get in there and lift that beam?" Tiny and Etienne quickly climbed into the cavity. "Tiny, you get on the desk. Etienne, when Tiny lifts the beam, you push it hard to the side, out of the way."

Tiny unhooked his overalls' shoulder straps, squatted over Miz Gay Lynn and slid his forearms under the beam. He let out a loud groan as the beam slowly raised off of Sheriff Taylor's wife. My body stiffened when Tiny lost momentum. The beam lowered back down toward Miz Gay Lynn's head. With another loud grunt, he gave it one strong heave. His T-shirt tore at the seams. Blood oozed out of his ear and sprayed from his nose and mouth as he struggled.

"Now!" Uncle Clem ordered.

Etienne pushed the beam clear. Tiny rushed her limp body out of the rubble to Doc Watson, waiting in the street.

"She's got a pulse." The doctor said before forcing her eyelids open to examine her pupils. "You better take her straight to Muscle Shoals."

"I'm going with," Mom announced.

The rest of the day was tense, waiting to hear from the hospital. After a simple dinner of bread and butter, we finally heard from Mom. Blue Rock's matriarch survived. However, there was brain damage. The doctor's assessment—"she will never be the same."

From that day forward, folks in Blue Rock spoke differently about time. There was "before the tornado" and "after the tornado." Blue Rock had no physical scars except the destroyed Town Hall and Sheriff's office. However, the tornado's timing, striking at the same time as school dismissal, affected the town psychologically. While we worked to free Miz Gay Lynn, the rest of Blue Rock was in a frenzied panic over the school children's safety.

Sunday, June 27, Miz Gay Lynn was sent home from rehabilitation. She had been under the care of Miss Orla; a young Irish nurse inspired by Helen Keller's miracle worker, Annie Sullivan. Miss Orla had worked tirelessly with Gay Lynn to mend her to a minimally self-sufficient state.

A rich-savory smell wafted from the kitchen when I arrived home, famished from an exhausting day of swimming. Mom was working her Dutch oven. "As Uncle Clem would say, I'm so hungry I could eat—"

"Don't you dare say it," Mom chided before I could finish my crude remark.

"What is it? Smells delicious."

"Brunswick stew. And it's not for you."

"That ain't right, Mom. I'm starving."

"Isn't right."

"Yes, ma'am."

"Asa, do you remember our first Sunday night in Blue Rock? Miz Gay Lynn and Sheriff Taylor brought us Brunswick Stew. Gay Lynn wanted us to have a proper Sunday dinner. I thought taking her a proper Sunday dinner now that she's home from rehabilitation is fitting."

"Come on, Mom. I'm so hungry."

"Asa, mind your mores. Miz Gay Lynn is like Blue Rock's mother. It's for her. Besides, it's not much different from the stews I normally make. The lean smoked pork has gotten the best of your senses." Mom dunked her tasting spoon. "Here's a smidge. Now, make yourself a turkey sandwich to fill up on. After you eat, I want you to drive me to the Taylors'." The stew was tastier than any stew Mom had ever made for Dad, me, and the crew.

A younger version of the Sheriff on his knees was pulling weeds and vines out of a bed of daylilies. "Greetings," the man said, struggling to his feet. "Just tryin' to get some of these vines out of Mama's flower beds."

"Good afternoon. I'm Dorothy Paxton. This is my son, Asa."

"Delighted to meet y'all. I'm Stan, their eldest. I'd shake y'all's hands 'cept I'm a bit dirty, and y'all have your hands full with that, oooh-wee, pot of smokey goodness, and what I expect is a towel full of cornbread."

"No disrespect, sir, but you're not dressed for yard work," I pointed out.

"None taken. I drove straight from church in Birmingham to collect Mama from the nurse she'd been staying with. While we were helping her into the house, she surveyed her flower bed and told Daddy he should be ashamed for letting her garden go like that. It was the clearest she's spoken since the tornado." Stan chuckled, "I guess derision is Mama's best speech therapy. When she ain't mad, I can't hardly understand a word she's saying. It's like she's talking through a biscuit in her mouth. So here I am, pulling vines and weeds on a hot day in my Sunday best to make Mama happy."

"I made a large pot. I thought she might have visitors."

"That's mighty kind of you. Mama said she was tore up she couldn't fix me a proper Sunday dinner. I reckon that's what she said. Don't bother with the doorbell. I'm gonna finish up out here."

From the foyer, we heard an unfamiliar voice fussing at Sheriff Taylor about a shawl and pillow. We stepped into the living room. Half of Miz Gay Lynn's face lit up. The other half remained droopy and lifeless. I knew it was Mom she was excited to see, not me.

"Well, hey, Gay Lynn. Welcome home," Mom cheerfully greeted, in what almost sounded like a Southern accent.

Miz Gay Lynn looked at the big pot held at my waist and the cotton towel in Mom's hands. "Dory, what did you do?" Her speech was muddled but clear enough to make out the words.

"I thought you should have a proper Sunday dinner now that you're home. It's Brunswick Stew and cornbread."

Miz Gay Lynn looked away. She tried awkwardly to wipe her eyes with the handkerchief she held in her shaky right hand. She took the cloth with her steady left and dabbed her eyes and nose. The reciprocal symbolism of the proper Sunday dinner of Brunswick stew and cornbread was not lost on Miz Gay Lynn. "You Yankees done made this Southern girl cry. Y'all are too sweet."

"Aw, Gay Lynn. It's nothing you haven't done for us. We're honored. Aren't we, Asa?"

"Yes, ma'am. I never prayed harder than I did for you that day when ... well, you know."

"Thank you, Asa. Now let's get these fixins into the kitchen," she said, struggling out of her chair.

Sheriff Taylor emerged from the hallway with a pillow in one hand and a shawl in the other. "You stay in your chair, Gay Lynn. We'll take care of everything."

"Oh, hush. Nurse Orla told me struggling will make me stronger. That little nurse sure worked me hard the past few weeks." Gay Lynn led us to the kitchen, dragging her right foot. Her right arm and hand were stiffly contorted. "Put it on the stovetop."

"I'll set the table for five," Sheriff Taylor said.

"Thank you but we won't be staying." We said our goodbyes, which meant it took three attempts to make it out the door—the customary minimum in the South.

During the car ride home, Mom made an observation, "She may have lost some mobility and enunciation, but she still has her mental faculties."

The rest of the summer was uneventful in Blue Rock, with one exception. News of the damaged Town Hall quickly made it to Alabama's senators and, through them, to President Roosevelt. With no objection and without standard appropriation procedures, money was expeditiously allocated to construct a new building to house a Federal Post Office, Town Hall, and Sheriff's Office. Unlike the Post Office, the local offices had no business receiving federal funding. However, there was so much Washington pork flowing into the Southeast no one cared about the small misappropriation. The most exciting aspect of the project was funds earmarked for a New York City artist commissioned to paint a mural on an outside wall of the new post office.

The artist was a quirky woman named Solace. That was it. No first name, middle name, or last—just Solace. She was pale and thin with an angular face. She smoked an ever-present cigarette with a long meerschaum holder. The cigarette-butt end of the holder was seasoned tobacco brown. Dark red lipstick stained the other end. When she worked, she wore a loose-fitting, paint-splattered white smock. When she wasn't working, she wore all black, including a black cape. This seemed extreme in the summer heat, though I never saw her sweat. She appeared perfectly comfortable. We had the pleasure of hosting Solace for dinner twice during her two-week stay. The dinner conversation was lively with her stories of New York's art scene and the hustle and bustle of America's largest city. Mom and Dad weren't artsy, though it was apparent our guests' stories made them feel nostalgic for America's Second City.

Solace kept to the Roosevelt script. Her mural was a blend of the Tennessee River being tamed by the construction of dams, farmers behind yoked oxen pulling plows through dark-fertile soil, and a black locomotive on a trestle traversing the river. She snuck in a small, controversial image on the west end of the mural—Indians in the distance being marched toward Oklahoma on the deadly Trail of Tears.

By the time my 17th birthday rolled around near the end of August, I had learned one truism about Alabama—summers were hot. Hot at midnight, hot at noon, and hot at six in the evening. As far as I was concerned, September's cooler weather and the new school year couldn't come soon enough.

On the third Saturday of September, I was sent on a hunting and fishing expedition before Uncle Clem and crew arrived to work on a project five miles west of the switchyard. Dad offered to come with me. Over the years, I'd learned I had better luck without him. When Dad was "teaching me to hunt," I realized why it took him a year-and-a-half after purchasing the shotgun to bag his first turkey—he was loud and clumsy in the woods. He couldn't shoot worth a damn, either. Natural selection of the flock's dimwitted turkeys was the only reason he had any luck at all. He must have driven Sheriff Taylor nuts, attempting to teach him to hunt. Dad and I never once nailed a turkey hunting together.

As I headed out, I noticed Sheriff Taylor in the clearing between our house and Shoals Creek scouring for early season hickory nuts under the cluster of trees just out of the tornado's reach. Blue Rock's town folk harvesting the free nuts was expected. It wasn't like Sheriff Taylor. He was a hunter, not a gatherer. I dismissed it and went about my charge.

Uncle Clem and his crew arrived in the early afternoon on Sunday. When Mom commented that it had been a long time since we had seen them, Uncle Clem was true to form. "I know, Dory. We've been busier than a one-legged man in an ass-kicking contest."

"Clem. Please," Mom complained.

The crass statement led my thoughts directly to Shanks' one-legged grandpa. As clever as Uncle Clem's joke was, I decided not to use it around Shanks. It would be bad form.

Barely five minutes had passed since the crew arrived when Sheriff Taylor and Miz Gay Lynn came banging on our latched front screendoor. I unhooked the lock. Miz Gay Lynn brushed me aside with her contorted right hand and hurried toward the kitchen, dragging her right foot. "Where are my saviors? Where are my heroes? Where's my Tiny and Etienne?" Her speech was clear as a bell.

"She's a little wound up," Sheriff Taylor told me. He was holding a hickory pie in each hand. "She made Tiny and Etienne each a pie. I had to shell the nuts for her. She insisted on doing the rest of the baking herself. It took her all day yesterday."

"I thought it was odd seeing you foraging yesterday."

"I'd rather be huntin' or fishin' rather than ruttin' round for nuts—in August to boot. Had to buy the rest from Smalley. Gay Lynn wanted to do something special for them after she learned those two saved her life." Cooking is what she knew and did best.

"Bring those pies out back," Miz Gay Lynn ordered Sheriff Taylor. From the kitchen window, I could see Miz Gay Lynn pull each towering man down by their shirt with her good hand, whisper in their ear, and then kiss their cheek before presenting them with a pie. The exchange gave me a sense of comfort and assurance. In a world filled with racism and ugliness, I was fortunate to live in a small sanctuary of love, respect, and kindness.

After dinner and enjoying the pies Etienne and Tiny shared, everyone except Mom retired to the fire pit. Sam's soothing harmonica and the fire's wispy flames mesmerized the circle. Uncle Clem fumbled around in his rucksack. I couldn't see what he retrieved, but I could hear the unmistakable sound of a tin collar twisting off the top of a mason jar. "Who wants a snort of white lightnin'?"

"Where did you get that?" Dad asked.

"Three dirt-face brothers on a hillside in Tennessee." Uncle Clem thumbed the flat seal loose and took a sip. His jaw clenched, his neck muscles stiffened as he stomped his foot. "Goddamn. That'll take the tar off a roof," he hollered and handed the jar to Preacher. The twins looked at Uncle Clem and shook their heads in disgust. Preacher took a sip and gave the jar to Sam. Sam sipped, barely missing a note on the harmonica, and passed the shine onto Dad.

"Here's to dirt-face Tennessee boys," Dad cheered, raising the jar before pressing the glass to his lips.

Tiny and the twins passed the firewater around without partaking. The jar landed in Mack's marbled hand. He looked around the circle and said, "Now don't y'all tell Edna bout me drinkin' no shine, or she gonna snatch a knot in my ass."

Uncle Clem had told me at The Berghoff about Miz Edna—how she had her finger in his face complaining, "We don't need no white savior." He said, "Miz Edna was like an Old Testament plague sent by God—big, bad, and out of man's control."

Mack took a sip and shouted, "Whoo-hoo, dat's what I'm talkin' bout." He started to hand me the jar, then realized Dad might disapprove.

"You're old enough, son. It's up to you."

I took the container, turned it up, and filled my mouth. I had a molten volcano on my tongue. I forcefully spit the clear liquid out. The spray of moonshine hit the fire and ignited. Sparks and shooting flames sent everyone diving for cover. The laughter that ensued was embarrassing. Dad apologized. "I should have told you, son. Small sips. Small sips. Give it another go if you like."

I swished my mouth with water, took a tiny sip, and passed the jar on. After two more rounds, I'd had enough and put myself to bed.

PART THREE

CHAPTER SIXTEEN
DAMN NAZIS

Over the years, I learned the best way to ask Mom and Dad for permission to do anything was when they were together, preferably in the evening while reading in the living room. This avoided the "Go-ask-your-mum-go-ask-your-dad runaround." Or the "we'll see" non-answer I received while they were focused on a task. The dinner table was a foolish choice. Captive in front of a plate of food opened up the possibility of a more extended conversation than desired. The worst approach was to ask them anything while they listened to a show or news on the radio. "Shush" was always the answer in that scenario.

"This is not good, not good at all," Dad commented from behind the *Times Daily*.

"What's not good?" I asked.

Dad folded the newspaper and handed it over. *"HITLER INVADES AUSTRIA!"* screamed the headline above the fold. March 1938 flew in like the Nazi eagle clasping a swastika.

"Damn Nazis," Dad grumbled.

"Damn Nazis," Mom agreed. That was something new, Mom swearing.

"Hitler won't stop there," Dad added.

"What's it mean for us?"

"We can pray it means nothing for us, but I doubt it," Dad said. "They'll suck us into the fray."

"I don't understand."

"Hitler's been building up his army and menacing all of Europe. The

Nazi government is egging on the worst in human nature among its gentile citizens."

"Gentile citizens?" I still don't understand.

"Your father is saying the Christians are demonizing and terrorizing its Jewish citizens through propaganda and new laws. Add a military build-up, and it's a recipe for—" Mom bit her tongue.

"That sounds a lot like the South."

Dad agreed, "You're absolutely right, son."

Mom let out a disappointed sigh. "The rest of our country hasn't exactly treated their Negro citizens fairly either. The US has yet to atone for its original sin."

"Sooner or later, Jim Crow will get its comeuppance," Dad said. "Hopefully, without another Civil War."

After Dad's comments and the thought of war, I almost forgot what I wanted to ask. "Can I take the car to East Bluff on Saturday?"

Dad and Mom's eyes met, searching for a response. Mom eventually made a point. "Saturday is the ribbon cutting on the new bridge."

"That's why I want to go. I want to be the first car to cross the bridge from our side. They're having activities with prizes on the East Bluff side." I handed Dad the flier I'd picked up at Smalley's.

Dad read in a loud radio announcer's voice. "Grand opening of the State Line Bridge." He mumbled the list of the activities. "Sack races, three-legged race, pony rides, pie-eating contest, greased pig-catching contest." Laughing loudly, Dad repeated, "Greased pig-catching contest."

"Oh, for Pete's sake," Mom complained.

"That's the one I'm most interested in. Look under the picture of the pig. The winner gets a free sundae at Ellington Rexall Drugs' soda fountain."

"You earn enough money for a sundae without catching a greased pig," Dad said.

"Yeah, but it's better when it's free because you won it. Besides, this all sounds like a lot of fun."

"I don't know, Asa. Your dad and I went to East Bluff once. It's much bigger than Blue Rock. Lots of traffic, and it's in a whole other state. It also sounds like it'll be a madhouse with all the goings on."

Dad took the newspaper from my hand and held the headline up to

Mom. "He's not a child anymore. He'll be eighteen in a few months."

Mom and I understood Dad's prescient point—which took the air out of the room.

"May I take the car, not, can I take the car,'" Mom corrected. "You go ahead, Asa. Have fun."

CHAPTER SEVENTEEN
YOU'RE A YANKEE

Saturday morning chores were postponed thanks to my under-standing parents. My rustling around the kitchen woke Mom. "Asa, why are all those potatoes on my kitchen table?"

"I need the gunny sack ... for friction. Hand me the scissors from the junk drawer, please?"

"What are you talking about?"

"I'm making a burlap shirt to help catch the greased pig. I'm gonna make sleeve stockings for my arms from the onion sack. Once I get hold of the rascal, the rough material will make it harder for it to squirm away. It'll also protect my T-shirt. Pretty clever, right?"

"Good grief. A sackcloth shirt and sleeves to catch a greasy pig. Per-haps you should dust yourself with ashes to complete the Biblical look, less the mourning and the forbidden swine. I'm going back to bed."

I fashioned a hole in the bottom and sides of the sackcloth for my head and arms. Rubber bands secured the sleeve stockings. The dry run over my shirt was itchy in spots but tolerable for long enough to grip the slippery creature.

Shanks and Itchy's parents' position on them going to East Bluff went from a "maybe" to a hard "no" by the time Saturday rolled around. Their "because I said so" parents were the type to say "maybe" and then say "no" to almost everything for no apparent reason. I don't know why they bothered asking. Both had long since ignored the ban of the Paxton home when the Negro crew stayed with us. The boys pretty much did whatever they wanted. Perhaps leaving the state was a bridge too far for my buddies. I was on my own.

The ribbon-cutting ceremony at the midpoint of the bridge was anticlimactic. There was no Dixie-style music or a long list of speakers—only Mayor Filbert and the East Bluff mayor trying to out-bluster each other with their less-than-inspiring words. A fair amount of foot traffic headed from Blue Rock to East Bluff stood behind Mayor Filbert. Only a scant group of sure-to-be-disappointed folks headed from East Bluff to Blue Rock. Sheriff Taylor waved me through once the ribbon was cut and the pedestrian traffic cleared.

Drumpf's "suicide" train trestle paralleled the new bridge and split off toward an industrial district on the Mississippi side. The auto bridge fed straight into downtown. East Bluff was a hive of activity fueled by the TVA economy. Small specialty shops and offices lined the street leading to a sizable four-way intersection. The center of the busy intersection boasted a tall Confederate monument—an obelisk of sorts. The marker created a confusing and unnecessary traffic obstacle, a befitting memorial to the chaos of The Lost Cause. Cars lined up for fuel at a fancy Texaco station on one corner of the intersection. Woolworths' front door faced diagonally across from the gas station. Piggly Wiggly and Rexall Drugs occupied the other two desirable corners of the cross streets. A young ink-stained boy in front of the Rexall hollered, "Extra, Extra, Hitler installs Nazi government in Austria." The hawking paperboy was having great success—a newsboy cap full of coins at his feet.

White men read their newspapers on benches, in front of stores, and while leaning on parked cars. White women dressed for downtown shopping had their Negro help in tow to carry their shopping bags.

My Citroen became trapped next to the Confederate monument by a large group of cars traveling in all four directions. Some attempted to negotiate left turns in front of the memorial, others behind it. The snarl of vehicles reminded me of the traffic jam scene in Stan and Ollie's "Two Tars" silent film that made me belly laugh back when I was seven or eight. While idling helplessly, I read the bronze plaque attached to the spire's base. "Dedicated by the United Daughters of the Confederacy in Remembrance of Brigadier Gen. Gideon J. Pillow and The Men Who Fought for States Rights." I assumed he was a brilliant soldier to warrant recognition in the middle of East Bluff's busiest intersection. Once Gideon Pillow's traffic jam loosened, I continued straight and came across a police officer on foot patrol. "Excuse me, sir," I yelled from the car, holding up my flier. "Where can I find all this?"

The officer hollered back, "Keep straight. You can't miss it."

At the end of the main street, a large neighborhood park bustled with activity. I found a gap among the parked cars and trucks to squeeze my Citroen into. I lifted the top into place and waded into the all-ages crowd.

My path crossed with several classmates—all of whom ignored me.

Boiled peanuts' earthy scent mingled with the cloying aroma of caramel kettle corn. A Dixieland band, uniformed in straw boater hats, white shirts, and red suspenders, performed from a gazebo in the center of the park. Behind the musicians, a wood-slat-sided truck corralled a passel of pigs. When they became agitated with one another, their squeals added a bizarre, out-of-tune, out-of-rhythm clarinet-sounding section to the lively music. After the band completed their set, the master of ceremonies, perched on the back of a flatbed truck, made announcements through a megaphone.

"Don't you teenagers get any ideas about pony rides. Yer too big. The ponies are fer the little ones. Says so right on the sheet, or ain't they teachin' you how to read?" The emcee received a chorus of raspberries from the teenagers. "Now then ... each sack race, three-legged race and the greased pig contest will have two ages grouped together. Five- and six-year-olds together, seven- and eight-year-olds, and so on. We'll have a break at noon for lunch. The pie-eating field is set and will commence at one o'clock, followed immediately by the grand finale greased pigs. We're fixin' to start the sack races, so y'all five- and sixers gather round Miss Dottie." Finally, with gusto, the emcee encouraged everyone to "Get right with Gaawd" at that evening's tent revival.

The sack race for the five- and six-year-olds ended predictably, with only a few children crossing the finish line. In their wake, the rest of the field was on the ground, crying and struggling to get out of their sack, their parents trying to console them under a barrage of laughter from the older kids.

Before the seven- and eight-year-old heat, the master of ceremonies wisely announced that the five- and six-year-olds would not be included in the three-legged races after all. Instead, his advice to the parents was, "Y'all take the little ones for a pony ride to lift their spirits."

I found myself laughing and engaging in friendly banter with the spectators as the sack and three-legged races and other games progressed through the morning hours. Except for a few classmates in the crowd, I felt part of the community—that is until segregation and Jim Crow slapped me in the face. One by one, Negro women arrived to collect the youngest white faces in the crowd for lunch and mid-day naps. I was determined to have a good time but avoided more small talk with those around me.

At noon, the savory scent of smoke and barbeque sauce drew me to the park's far end. A portly man sold pulled-pork sandwiches and grilled ribs from a smoker grill mounted on a lowboy trailer. His round bald head beaded with sweat. He opened his mouth and repeatedly stuttered, trying to get out, "Ribs or sammich?" I suppressed my ugly instinct to laugh at the man. He eventually gave up and asked, "Hungry?"

I ordered a sandwich and an RC and retreated to the solitude of my Citroen.

An excited buzz filled the air, anticipating the pie-eating spectacle. The crowd jockeyed for position around three picnic tables lined up end-to-end, creating one long table. One female and nine male contestants were seated on one side of the table, each with three pies to consume. Opposite each participant sat a judge. The pie eaters came in all shapes, sizes, and ages. The youngest looked to be in his mid-twenties, the oldest in his late fifties or early sixties. The lone woman physically looked like she could hold her own. She was not fat, but instead, big boned. I expected her enormous chest might get in the way of a face-first dive into a pie tin. All the contestants appeared to be salt-of-the-earth farmers or laborers, sturdy and crafty. Not the type of people a finished man would want to tangle with.

The emcee turned the megaphone over to an older, rotund man in overalls, boots, and a straw hat. His mouth deftly controlled a long blade of seed grass as he barked out the rules. He repeated the warnings,

"Hands must remain behind the back," and "any judge's ruling is final."

The starting pistol cracked. The play-by-play man was off as fast as the contestants. He announced the competition in horse racing and livestock auction terms. His call of the event fueled the excitement of the spectators. He appeared to know every contestant personally and accentuated their names with nicknames. There was Barnyard Barney, Manure-mouth Manford, and Seabiscuit Sally, to name a few. I was laughing so hard I couldn't cheer on the pie-faced contestants. In the end, Wedge-Face Willy prevailed. His advantage came from a lanky build. His long arms and skinny torso made holding his hands behind his back effortless. A long-skinny neck and wedge-shaped face made his navigating the pie tins smooth and precise. Seabiscuit Sally used her huge breasts to her advantage. They helped keep the pie tin in place as she mauled it with her large mouth. She came in a respectable second. A sad-downtrodden-looking man called Lucky Luther took third place.

I was about to head to the car to retrieve my burlap garb for the grand finale pig-catching contests when I noticed a beautiful young woman gazing at me from the far end of the picnic tables. After allowing me to lock eyes with her momentarily, she demurely looked away—albeit with a flirtatious grin. She had an allure about her that went beyond her beauty. My elbows and knees went rubbery in a ticklish way. My stomach fluttered as I headed to my car. I wanted to approach her but didn't know how. They didn't teach that sort of thing in school. Anyway, it was no use self-educating on the racist coeds in Blue Rock. I needed to compose myself, but she could be gone if I hesitated. I threw on my burlap and rushed to the large oval pig pen next to the pie-eating tables. She was nowhere in sight.

As the age groups progressed, I refined my pig-catching strategy while keeping my eye out, hoping the young woman would reappear. With each increase in age group, the size of the pig increased. With each contest, the turf became muddier and more slippery. By the time the second-to-last group was summoned, I had given up on ever seeing the beautiful young woman again when I heard a sweet-soft voice behind me say, "Nice shirt." I turned around, and … there she was. She had donned a burlap sack like me, except hers was crafted with more care. The sleeves were sewn on at the shoulder and covered her arms completely. The neckline was cut in a V-shape, exposing a little cleavage and the edge of the blouse under the sack. A strip of burlap tied tight around her waist accentuated her hourglass figure. "Cat got your tongue?" she asked. The cat had gotten more than my tongue. "That swine is mine," she said as she wove her long-wavy chestnut hair into a French braid at the back of her head.

I stood silently, my mind sorting out how to respond. Awkward words eventually spilled out. "So. I guess you're … I guess you're in the seventeen- to eighteen-year-old group."

She looked at me oddly with a big smile. "Well I'll be. You're a Yankee." Her voice was as smooth and flowing as the river's deep spot past the shoals.

Before I could respond, the emcee ordered the last group into the arena. About ten boys, the beautiful young woman, and another possible girl entered the ring. Regardless of their gender, the homely teenager deserved pity. Once the pig was set loose, the competitors, except me and the object of my instant infatuation, began the chase. We stood against the pen's fencing, biding our time. She tapped her foot and held her hand at her chin. Apparently, we had the same strategy. Let the competition and the pig wear themselves out. The other contestants tripped over the wily pig and each other under the spectator's jeers. The frantic hoard passed us at least five times. They almost caught the greasy thing twice, but it slipped through their muddy hands. The pig and her pursuants eventually slowed. They lumbered our way one last time. We pounced, pinning the animal against the fence. I got a hold of it with my onion-sack-wrapped arms under the front quarter. She had the hindquarter. Between us, the pig was pressed tightly against our burlap-covered torsos. We struggled with the squirming animal and each other, our panting faces inches apart. Our eyes were locked amorously as we shuffled across the pen to dump the captive into a barrel in front of the emcee as required to win. While we wrestled the pig back and forth, trying to gain sole possession, it squealed louder and louder.

Seeing neither of us was giving up and the pig becoming overly stressed, the emcee yelled into his megaphone, "It's a tie. Now y'all let that poor thing go." We dropped the squealing swine and shook hands, laughing and breathing heavily.

"I'm Asa. Asa Paxton from Blue Rock across the new bridge."

"I'm Rosie Pickett. From around the corner."

What were the chances we would both have the idea of wearing burlap and the same strategy of letting the pig and the competition wear themselves out before attacking? I thought to myself. I sure hope this is pig-pen kismet.

"I'm sorry, y'all, but I only have one coupon left for the ice cream sundae. Should I flip a coin to see which of you gets it?"

"She can have it."

"We could share it," Rosie said, staring deep into my eyes. "I'd like that."

"You young fools are gonna paint my cheeks red," the emcee said, handing me the sundae certificate. "Now go on and git."

"Would you like to walk to Rexall Drugs?" I asked. "Or, I'm parked just up the block?"

"Ooh, you have a car? I'd love a car ride. But only after I get out of this silly sack."

Rosie lifted the tacky burlap over her head, pulling her blouse partway up, exposing her breast-filled silk-and-lace bra. The shirt fell back down before Rosie knew she'd exposed herself. I burned the image of her breasts deep in my mind.

We threw our sackcloths in a garbage can in the park. On the way to the car, I flipped open my pocket knife with one hand and sliced a pale blue hydrangea bloom from a bush in someone's front yard. "For the lovely lady."

Rosie accepted the flower, holding it with both hands under her chin. "Does this mean we're on a date?" Rosie asked with the same demure look and a flirtatious grin she flashed me when our eyes first met. Once again, my body felt like rubber.

"Hopefully, the first of many." I had no idea where this debonair persona was coming from, though it didn't seem to turn off Rosie.

She bounced excitedly when she saw the car was a cabriolet. "Can we put the top down?"

"As you wish. Unfortunately, I can't hold the door for you like a true gentleman. The only door is on the passenger side. It's a French car. You know how silly those French are."

I slid behind the wheel. Rosie followed, sitting as close to me as possible. She bridged the small gap between the front seats with my gear shift between her knees.

The soda fountain teemed with the earlier pig-catching sundae winners. An older woman in a frilly white apron with a pencil wedged above her ear greeted us from behind the counter. Her stiff, perfectly coiffed hair looked like she had a wash-and-set that morning. Suspiciously, the waitress said "Hello, Rosaleigh," while eyeballing me and the flower Rosie laid on the counter.

"How many times do I have to tell you? Call me Rosie."

"Who's this ... Rosie?"

"This is Asa. Asa, this is Miz Nadine."

I slid our free sundae certificate across the counter. "Pleased to meet you, Miz Nadine."

"Likewise, I suppose." Miz Nadine looked at the piece of paper and sighed. "I hope this is the last one. I'll be cleaning up after you greasy kids for hours once we close."

"We're hardly greasy at all," Rosie pointed out.

"We? You got in the pigsty, Rosaleigh Elizabeth Pickett? Does your mother know you took part in such a disgrace?"

"Rosie is going to order for the both of us," I interrupted. Miz Nadine readied her order pad and pencil.

"The usual, please."

"And how about Romeo?" Miz Nadine asked Rosie.

"Bring us two spoons. We're going to share."

Miz Nadine contorted her lips. "Big spender."

"If two spoons are too much trouble, you can bring only one. I'll spoon-feed Asa right here in front of everyone."

Miz Nadine walked away, shaking her head. Rosaleigh and I swiveled our barstools to face each other.

"Rosaleigh is a pretty name."

Her response was swift and stern. "I prefer Rosie."

"Yes, ma'am."

"How come you don't already have a girl?"

"Well, I uh—"

"Oh no. You're not stepping out on another girl from across the river, right?"

"No, ma'am. As I was about to say, I'm a bit of a pariah with the girls where I live. Well, actually, with most folks across the river."

"Pariah? That's a seldom used word."

"I just learned it. Describes my situation perfectly."

"So, what makes you a pariah?"

I squirmed a little but knew I had to be an open book. Because of my curse, I might be wasting time with this girl once she knew my true nature. "First of all, I'm from Chicago. 'Ain't from around here,' folks say the second I open my mouth."

Rosie responded gently. "I didn't say that. I called you a Yankee."

"Second. My uncle runs a railroad maintenance crew of Negroes and a white Cajun from Louisiana. They stay at our house when working in the area. They're like family. The Blue Rock town folk don't like seeing my uncle's crew. We must be breaking some laws putting them up, but our sheriff and his wife are friends with my parents. They're good people and make sure no one harasses us." Rosie listened intently with an accepting smile. "Finally, I have only two friends. They're a little odd. All the other kids at school call us the Misfit Clique. My crush on an English teacher is the closest I've come to a girlfriend."

"Thank god. I was hoping when you caught my eye, you were more than a handsome face. Sounds like your folks are the kind of people I'd like to get to know."

As if I had confessed my sins and was forgiven by this girl, a wave of relief washed over me. "What about you? How come you don't have a steady?"

"I've never even been on a date." Rosie's eyes widened as she gasped. "This is my first date. I've got to write about it in my diary."

"I find that hard to believe. You're so ... uh, well ... beautiful."

"That's sweet of you to say. The boys do constantly pester me. They're only interested in trapping a debutante. Frankly, the boys around here are shallow, thin-skinned, and hard-hearted. They're ugly inside and bigoted. Most everyone around here is thin-skinned and hard-hearted."

When Rosie spoke the same language Preacher once used to describe most white Southerners, she had me hook, line, and sinker. Our conversation, which seemed too deep for a first date, was interrupted by Miz Nadine delivering our sundae. "I have a mind to call your mother, young lady, and tell her what you've been up to today."

"I have a mind to call Mister Ellington and tell him you've been rude to his new customers from across the bridge."

"Romeo hasn't spent a penny yet."

To quell all the fuss, I interrupted the two women. "Oh, I'll be back, Miz Nadine. Hopefully with Rosie."

"I won't hold my breath," she quipped as she walked away.

I couldn't tell if Rosie was a performance artist or if she ate everything the way she ate an ice cream sundae. She leaned her head back, holding the maraschino cherry topper by the stem above her mouth— she slowly lowered the fruit. Her lips engulfed all but the stem. After biting off half, she gently pulled until the remainder of the sundae garnish emerged. I felt her foot wiggle between my feet at the base of my stool. Her knee forced my legs apart as she leaned into me. Her free hand slid from my knee halfway up my thigh. While squeezing my leg, I was fed the rest of the cherry. She pushed back in her seat and swooped two fingers through the whipped cream and sauce. A drip of caramel fell, landing on the exposed skin of her cleavage. It took her a long time to lick and suck her fingers clean, though not as long as I would've liked. "I made a mess," Rosie giggled as she ran a finger through her cleavage. I was so mesmerized I unconsciously leaned forward, following Rosie's finger toward her lips. Sensing her control over me, she stopped short. Her sweetened finger went into my mouth.

Next were the spoons full of ice cream, eaten in two steps. First, the scoop went into Rosie's mouth upright, and the top half of the ice cream was removed with a slow pull through her lips. Next, the spoon was turned upside down and the remaining ice cream was pulled free with her tongue. Once we finished the sundae, I thought about ordering another for a repeat performance but decided that might be too obvious.

Not wanting to end our time together, I made a suggestion. "Would you like to go for a car ride? You could show me around East Bluff. Afterward, we could cross the bridge, and I could show you around what little there is to see of Blue Rock."

"That sounds like a grand idea."

On the sidewalk in front of my car, Rosie pointed to the Confederate monument in the middle of the intersection. "That obelisk is all you need to know about East Bluff, Mississippi. A road obstruction, erected by the daughters of losers, honoring the worst general in the Confederacy."

Obelisk? She's smart. "So it's safe to say you're proud of your hometown?"

Rosie laughed. "I shouldn't joke, but sometimes it's all you can do with such absurdity."

"I got stuck in traffic next to the inscription. I can't remember the General's name now. I assumed he was a military mastermind or hero."

"It's General Gideon J. Pillow. I read somewhere, during the Civil War, he hid behind trees instead of leading his men into battle. He's not even from Mississippi."

"So what's the story with the daughters that erected it?"

"Good god. You've never heard of the United Daughters of the Confederacy?"

"No."

"Well ... they've morphed from an honorable organization into, let's just say, a bunch of mean old ladies intent on white-washing slavery, brain-washing schoolchildren, and terrorizing Negroes. The worst part for me is that my mother is the local chapter chairwoman. Let's get going. I don't want to ruin a good time."

Rosie directed me around the main streets of downtown East Bluff. She pointed out different restaurants, empty stores that didn't survive the Crash, and new stores that opened when the Federal TVA money flowed into the local economy. A new theater with a glitzy marquee had opened a year earlier. Rosie said it was the first air-conditioned building in East Bluff. She pointed out the jail, city hall, and the county courthouse complex that housed her father's office. She mentioned under her breath, her tone was both biting and dismissive, her father was the elected County Solicitor. We passed the hospital, library, and her high school at the edge of downtown. East Bluff offered so much more than Blue Rock. We continued through some neighborhoods, ending up near the industrial district.

"Stop, Asa. Don't go over the tracks."

"What's over there?"

"It's where all the Negroes live."

"So? Is it dangerous or something?"

"Dangerous? Of course not. But it's not right for a couple of well-off white kids to go joyriding in a cabriolet through their neighborhood."

"Oh, I get it. We don't have a single Negro living in Blue Rock. I don't have to think that way except when my uncle's crew stays with us."

"Turn around. I want to show you another spot before we cross the bridge."

I was guided to the end of a dirt road on the outskirts of town. "Follow me," Rosie ordered. I would have followed her through the gates of hell. We hiked down a short path to a large pond, its water eerily black from plant decay. A few yards from the water's edge, a bamboo forest with stalks at their base thicker than the barrel of a baseball bat encircled the pond. The pale-green-and-gray canes stretched hundreds of feet toward the sun, laying siege to the pond, allowing only small rays of sunshine to reach the water's blackness. The stagnant-sickly-looking pool, surprisingly, teemed with life. Bullfrogs croaked. Dragonflies buzzed from lily pad to lily pad. A row of turtles warmed themselves in the waning sunlight on a downed tree limb protruding from the water. The bamboo, stoic at its base, swayed high above in the slight breeze. The sunbeams, pond, and surrounding bamboo forest was God's artistic contrast of light and dark.

Rosie stood next to me on a short flat rock, worshiping the tops of the bamboo, her hands stretched to the sky, waving from side to side along with the swaying leafy crowns. "This place is amazing. It feels like a medieval Chinese forest," I imagined aloud.

Rosie's hands fell to her side. She paused before speaking. Her eyes moved from my eyes to my lips and back to my eyes. "For me, it feels romantic in a mysterious way."

I overcame my nerves, stepped in front of my date, and placed my hands on her waist. Her eyes closed, giving me permission. The kiss was slow and gentle at first, then became full-on and passionate. Once our lips parted, Rosie stumbled off the rock into my arms. "Wow. I can hardly stand." She lifted her forearm between us. "Look at those goosebumps. Where did you learn to kiss like that?"

"I don't know. That was my first. Maybe my parents. I've walked in on them kissing like that."

"My first, too. I brought you here, hoping you would kiss me. I've always wanted my first kiss to be somewhere special and romantic. Not awkward, like fumbling around in the front seat of a car. That kiss is for sure getting described in my diary."

The awkward nervousness I felt since I first laid eyes on Rosie melted away with our kiss.

On the bridge to Blue Rock, Rosie released her French braided locks, stood up on the floorboard, and let her hair blow wildly in the wind. She looked so happy, so free. I hoped it was all because of me.

It hadn't occurred to me until we entered Blue Rock I might be seen with a young woman in my car. Running into my parents was my biggest fear. Introducing them to a girl was something I wanted to orchestrate. I cleverly weaved through neighborhoods to avoid Shanks' house, Smalley's, and Sheriff Taylor's office. From a distance, I pointed out the switchyard on the west side of town and explained I worked there for my dad to earn spending money. We crossed Shoals Creek Bridge on the east side of town to visit the new school complex before returning to the motor bridge. "Well, Rosie, that's about it. I'll take you home now."

Rosie turned in her seat with a furrowed brow. "Wait a minute. Pull over. That can't be all there is. There must be some stores and other things to see. What about your house? Are you embarrassed or something?"

"Embarrassed isn't the right word. I think. I mean. I should prepare my parents before I bring a girl they haven't met home, or we run into them somewhere unexpectedly."

"Something wrong with them? Are they mean?"

"No. Just the opposite. They're the kindest parents in the world.

That's the point. They wouldn't want to be surprised. They would want to prepare themselves to greet you warmly, properly."

"I understand now. Must be nice. My parents are dreadful people."

"I don't believe that. They raised you right."

"Trust me. You might get a proper reception from my parents. However, it would be about as genuine as a snake oil salesman."

"Maybe you could come to dinner next weekend and meet my parents?"

Rosie batted her eyes and whined, "I don't want to wait that long to see you again."

"Me either. Tell you what. I'll ask my parents if you can come to dinner tomorrow. If they say yes, I'll pick you up. If they say no to dinner, let's meet after you get out of church. I'll walk if my parents won't let me take the car. It can't be more than a mile or so. We could go to lunch."

"Church? Are you kidding? I quit going when I was thirteen."

"I assumed most everyone down here went to some sort of church. Your parents don't make you go?"

"Not hardly. They gave up. What about you? Do you go to church?"

"We used to, in Chicago. What little I remember of our church, I liked. Now, we only say grace at dinner. I pick up the Bible on my own from time to time. New Testament, mostly. The Gospels. I don't get much out of the Old Testament, except for Psalms and Proverbs."

"Please don't think of me as a heathen," Rosie said. "I read the Bible religiously. Sometimes Jesus is the only hope I have. On the other hand, I don't believe all the mumbo-jumbo most churches use to justify misogyny, racial subjugation, and duplicitous conduct. Life's not complicated. Jesus keeps it simple in his words and actions. There's right and wrong. No Sunday message or altar call can change that."

"Duplicitous? Subjugation? Misogyny? I guess you are a solicitor's daughter."

"Don't give my father any credit. He's a big part of the problem here in the South. I've learned to think for myself."

"Okay then, Rosie Pickett, let's get you home to those dreadful parents."

She directed me to a short U-shaped street off the park where we first met. The houses were all large, painted-white brick, and well-kept.

Hers was the largest in the neighborhood, boasting a grand porch with plantation big-house columns.

"I'll walk you to the door."

"No, thank you. I don't want my parents to come out and ruin what has been a perfectly dreamy day. You can meet them tomorrow."

"I know it's the front seat of a car, but may I at least kiss you once more?"

"Babe, after that first kiss, you may kiss me anywhere, anytime."

After a tender kiss, I said my goodbye. "One o'clock tomorrow won't come soon enough."

I instinctively knew to wait for Rosie to make it safely into the house. She reached the porch stairs, stopped momentarily, then rushed back and leaned over the passenger door. "Asa. Do you believe in love at first sight?"

"I do. Just as sure as you're standing in front of me."

CHAPTER EIGHTEEN
IDES OF MARCH

B reaking my rules of where and when to ask for parental permission, I chose the dinner table to bring up inviting Rosie to Sunday dinner. I needed Mom and Dad to be a captive audience in case it took some convincing.

"Tell me about your day," Mom said.

"Did you catch the pig?" Dad chuckled.

"I did."

"Oh, for Pete's sake." Mom bit into her pork chop.

I drove the field peas around my plate with my fork. "I caught something else."

"Oh yeah, What?" Dad asked before stuffing in a mouthful of mashed potatoes.

"A girl. Or maybe she caught me."

Mom gagged on her pork chop and dropped her fork on her plate. Dad quickly swallowed his mashed potatoes and took a swig of water to ensure they made it all the way down.

Mom and Dad's wide eyes met. After a long silence, Dad's head twitched toward me while holding his eyes on Mom. She calmly asked, "What's her name?"

"Rosaleigh Pickett. She goes by Rosie."

"Rosaleigh is a pretty name."

"Mom, she goes by Rosie."

Dad resumed eating slowly, his eyes darting back and forth between

Mom and me.

"How did you meet?"

"We both caught the pig. I caught it by the north end. Rosie caught it by the south end. They declared it a tie." It was Dad's turn to gag on his pork chop.

Firmly placing her napkin next to her plate, Mom laid into me. "For Pete's sake. Rosie the hog wrangler?" She was gearing up for a rant. I beat her to the punch.

"I know what you're thinking, Mama. She's not some redneck bumpkin. I caught half the pig. Does that make me some kind of Country Boy Asa? You should be ashamed of yourself, pre-judging her and acting like I don't know how to gauge someone's character. I've had to live in this podunk town with only two real friends. I'm a Negro-loving pariah with the Blue Rock girls because of the company we keep. Finally, I met someone who doesn't care about that. I told her all about Uncle Clem and his crew. She's coming to dinner tomorrow. You'll see what kind of person she is." Mom had a look on her face I hadn't seen since that night years ago in Chicago when Uncle Clem reminded Mom and Dad they didn't have a pot to piss in.

"The boy's right," Dad said.

Dinner continued in a tense silence. After a few minutes, Mom spoke. "You've never called me Mama before." There was another long silence before Mom spoke again. "I apologize. You're right. I shouldn't have characterized her that way. I suppose I've come to expect the worst in people around here. I don't think I've ever been more proud of you than I am right now."

"So, does that mean she can come over tomorrow?"

"Sounds like you've already made the decision for us," Dad said.

"Y'all know what the crazy thing was? Rosie showed up wearing a burlap sack like me, which, I might add, worked like a charm. Once we got a hold of the pig, it couldn't wiggle out of the rough fabric. It felt like pig-pen kismet." My pig-pen kismet description lightened the mood for the rest of dinner.

I tossed and turned for hours in bed, unable to sleep. My mind kept rehashing my day with Rosie and thinking about seeing her again.

Fortunately, Mom didn't wake me until nine-thirty after my restless night. "What time are you supposed to pick Rosie up?"

"One o'clock."

"What are you two going to do until dinner time?"

"Not sure. I expect Rosie's father will interrogate me. No telling how long that'll take. I'll introduce her to Itchy and Shanks. Get that awkwardness out of the way. We'll see what happens afterward. Maybe the four of us will play cards, get a soda at Smalley's, the usual boring stuff."

"There's a list of chores I want done before you leave. I also need you to pick up some things for dinner from the Piggly Wiggly in East Bluff."

"Yes, ma'am."

I would have thought Mom was punishing me for scolding her at dinner the night before. Her long list of chores could have been whittled down to one task. Clean everything in sight. Thanks to elbow grease and Bon Ami, every surface was spotless. I was both exhausted and energized when I left to pick up my date.

Farrington Willard Pickett was still wearing his Sunday best when he welcomed me into the foyer of his home. He was a tall man, much taller than my six feet. His posture was slightly stooped, making him seem physically overbearing. "I'm Farrington Pickett," he said, offering his large hand.

I shook his hand the way Dad taught me. "Pleased to meet you. I'm Asa Paxton from across the river in Blue Rock."

"You're not originally from the South. I don't need to be the County Solicitor to decipher that." It wasn't clear if he was trying to impress or scare me with his title, though he obviously forced it into the conversation.

"No, sir. We moved from Chicago when I was younger."

"Paxton? Paxton? Where do I know that name from? I haven't crossed the new bridge to Blue Rock yet. That's not it. It'll come to me."

"I'll be down in a minute," Rosie yelled from upstairs.

"I imagine you don't know Rosaleigh very well," Farrington said. It wasn't clear if he was asking a question or making a statement.

I responded cheerily, trying not to sound lustful. "I'm hoping to get to know her better."

"You're a strapping young man. I would think there are plenty of lovely, acquiescent young women in Blue Rock."

"It's a small town, sir. There isn't an abundance of anything." I knew better than to mention why the Blue Rock girls shunned me.

Farrington put his hand on my shoulder. "What I'm trying to say, Asa … Rosaleigh isn't like most girls." *Perfect. The kind of girl I want to date.* "Think about it, son. She told me how you two met, chasing a greased pig. Her mother forbade her from embarrassing herself and the Pickett name in a pigsty. She did it anyway."

"Respectfully, sir, it wasn't a pigsty. It was temporary fencing." Farrington's hand twitched on my shoulder. "Respectfully, Solicitor Pickett."

"Well, just the same, young man. My Katherine probably won't show her face at any social clubs for a month or two. Rosaleigh is a petulant girl. She refuses to listen to me, either. If I tell her not to do something, she wants to do it more. When I ask her how she'll ever get a suitor to marry her, she says she doesn't believe in marriage. I'm only allowing this dinner charade to teach that girl a lesson. You're the first boy she's shown interest in. She needs to learn, a respectable suitor will not tolerate her nonsense. I'm sure you'll quickly tire of Rosaleigh's temperament. I expect I'll end up apologizing to your parents on behalf of the Pickett good name."

Farrington had no idea what he was talking about. He may have been a big man with a big title, but still, he was out of his league as far as I was concerned. I had the moral high ground. Rosie made it clear when she described her father as "a big part of the problem in the South."

A faint conversation emanating from upstairs steadily grew louder until I heard Rosie yell, "I don't give a damn what you think, Mother. I don't want to wear my hair that way. I didn't ask for your help or your opinion."

Farrington and I looked up the curved staircase. "See what I mean, son. Do yourself a favor and take my advice. Find yourself a girl who knows her place."

"Rosaleigh will be down in a minute," said a slight woman descending the stairs.

"Asa, this is my wife, Katherine Pickett."

"I'm pleased to meet you, Miz Pickett."

"Please, call me Katherine," she offered her hand, palm to the floor. "I regret you had to hear all that fuss. I don't know what's gotten into Rosaleigh today. She's never raised her voice before." I knew Katherine was lying, which the expression on Farrington's face confirmed. "Would you care for something to drink? Sweet tea or perhaps lemonade?" Katherine's accent was pure Ole Miss.

"No, thank you, ma'am."

"Well then, if you all will excuse me, I need to keep the help on task in the kitchen."

While Farrington was pessimistic, I sensed Katherine was hopeful, wanting to help Rosie prepare for the date.

Farrington blurted out, "Clem Paxton. Are you kin to the Clem Paxton who runs a railroad crew of niggras?"

My stomach sank and I answered with a stutter. Yes, sir. He's my uncle."

"His crew has occasionally worked on the tracks around here. I spoke to him once in an official capacity, along with our police chief. We wanted to ensure he kept his niggras in their place. Out-of-work white folks weren't happy to see a bunch of them with jobs they could use. Of course, that was then. Things are different now. We have the TVA. Plenty of work to go around, and gandy dancing is convict or niggra work." I handled Farrington's possibly racist comments like I handled the Sit-n-Spit Club at Smalley's—I ignored them.

"Your uncle works for that big-shot Robinson out of Chicago, right?"

"Yes, sir. My dad also works for him. He manages the switchyard in Blue Rock."

"I'll say this, son. Your uncle does a good job of keeping his niggras in their place, although there's one thing I don't understand. Why does he have that white Cajun on his crew?"

There was that word again, "niggras." I panicked, not knowing how to answer about Etienne when Rosie appeared at the top of the staircase with a radiant smile, saving me an explanation.

"Hello, Asa."

She differed from the practical denim and flat-shoed young woman I met the day before. Instead, she was dressed for visiting in a beautiful floral sundress and low heels. Her long hair was parted on the left and pinned behind her left ear. The rest brushed to the edge of her right eye, falling over her breast, shoulder, and back. My date looked like a starlet making her grand entrance in a Hollywood production. Rosaleigh Elizabeth Pickett was a stunning woman.

I imagined Farrington was disappointed at the sight of Rosie gracefully descending the stairs. His daughter could be the embodiment of the romantic Old South. Instead, she was a petulant rebuke of the Lost Cause and glorified plantation life the United Daughters of the Confederacy espoused. She also rejected the Jim Crow justice system her father was elected to prosecute.

"When can we expect you home?" Farrington asked Rosie.

Rosie snapped, "When I get home."

"I'll have her home around nine, Mister Pickett. If that's OK?" Farrington seemed somewhat pleased that between Rosie and me, he received at least one respectful response.

Like the day before, Rosie sat in the car as close to me as possible, straddling the gearshift. "We have to stop at Piggly Wiggly on the way home. Mom needs some things for dinner."

"First, I want to show you something around the corner." We drove to the back alley of a row of homes and horse pens converted into auto garages. "Stop here, where no one can see us." Rosie pulled the holding brake, lifted her dress halfway up her thighs, and pivoted her legs over my waist, provocatively straddling me face to face. Her hands combed through my hair to the back of my neck while her eyes bore into me. "Don't move. I want to look at you." Rosie's eyes were an exotic pale jade with shards of amber. I was mesmerized, feeling as if Rosie was mining my thoughts for an answer to a question she didn't want to ask aloud. She eventually closed her eyes and kissed me gently, then passionately, like our first kiss in the bamboo forest. Once our lips parted, Rosie had a shiver that went from her shoulders to her knees. She lifted her forearm. "Look at those goosebumps. That was no fluke yesterday. We're a natural fit," she gushed before kissing me again. She was right. Our kisses had a certain oomph that went beyond the physical connection.

The East Bluff Piggly Wiggly had the same layout as the Muscle Shoals location, with checkout lanes near the front door and dry goods organized on shelved aisles. "What's on the list?" Rosie asked.

With a straight face I replied, "Cow's liver and onions." Rosie winced. "I'm kidding."

"I would've forced it down with a smile."

"We need evaporated milk, a pound of cheddar cheese, and maca-roni noodles. Mom wants us to pick out whatever meat looks good, and she'll serve it with macaroni and cheese."

"I love, love, love mac-n-cheese," Rosie said, bending and twisting at the knees. "I know where everything is. Meat and cheese are in the back."

The butcher behind the meat counter gave us the same greeting as Miz Nadine at the soda fountain the day before. "Hello, Rosaleigh," he said while glaring at me.

"Now, Mister Cox, you know I prefer Rosie."

"Who's yer friend?"

"Nice to meet you, Mister Cox. The name's Asa Paxton. I'm from across the new bridge, in Blue Rock."

"No you ain't. You ain't from round here."

"Yes, sir. We moved from Chicago in thirty-three."

"What's good today?" Rosie asked the butcher.

"If it was me, I'd choose between the spring-lamb-shoulder roast at fifteen cents a pound, yearling-round steaks at thirty-nine cents a pound, or milk-fed-dry-picked spring chickens at fifty-nine cents each."

"Mom makes a big pot of lamb stew when my uncle is in town with his crew. It's always good, but I think Dad would prefer something dif-ferent. We rarely have steak."

"Steak sounds good to me," Rosie said.

"We'll have four of your nicest-looking round steaks, please," I or-dered. "And keep your thumb off the scale." Rosie laughed. Mister Cox didn't. "I was joking, sir. My mom would wring my neck if I got the Pax-tons off on the wrong foot with the butcher. Now that the bridge is open, I expect she'll be a regular." I hoped my backtracking worked.

128

Mister Cox returned from the cutting room with our steaks wrapped in butcher paper. "Four of the nicest steaks I have, for Rosaleigh," he said, going out of his way to hand the package to her instead of me.

"Thank you very much," I said.

"You're welcome, Rosaleigh. Tell Miz Pickett I asked about her."

"I'll be sure to."

After we retrieved the last item on our list, Rosie stopped me in the middle of the dry goods aisle. "The checkout girl and bag boy are from school. Lucy and Chip. There'll be some sort of reaction to you. Not sure what. Be prepared."

"Who's the looker, Rosie? Your first cousin, I presume," Lucy said, smacking her gum.

"You would know about cousins, wouldn't you?" Rosie shot back.

"Hi. I'm Asa from Blue Rock across the river. Pleased to meet you, Lucy."

Lucy leaned over the checkout counter, looked down at my feet, then slowly made her way up to my face. "The pleasure is all mine."

Rosie wrapped both of her arms tight around my biceps. "Stick to your cousins, Lucy." Rosie said loudly as the store manager walked by. "And don't you know it's rude to smack your gum like that?" The manager gave Lucy a disapproving nod. She removed the gum and wedged it behind her ear to resume smacking on later.

Chip avoided eye contact as he bagged our groceries. "I see there's finally someone good enough for Rosie Pickett."

"Aw, don't be like that, Chip," Rosie said.

Chip's face was an angry red. "You've never given us East Bluff guys even a chance."

"Now you're sulking. As much as you boys and my parents think one exists, no social contract says I have to give you a chance," Rosie said.

Chip pushed the bag of groceries into my chest and stormed off.

As we drove across the bridge, I had an epiphany. After all the years living in Blue Rock as the misfit, the outsider, the pariah, and the Negro lover, I was actually a fortunate soul. I could sleep with a clear conscience. I was proud of my parents. Uncle Clem and his crew welcomed me into their unusual community. Itchy and Shanks ignored the Blue Rock social norms and stuck by me over the years. And now, by a strange twist of fate, a beautiful, intelligent, and liberated young woman was clinging to my arm with her head on my shoulder. I never felt happier.

On our way home, we passed Itchy and Shanks playing catch with a football. Itchy threw a bullet while Shanks was distracted by seeing a woman in my car. He was lucky the throw was a little off target, otherwise it would have resulted in a painful incompletion. I would have stopped; however, my friends needed time to process the notion of a girl in my car, almost sitting in my lap.

I always parked on the side of the house and entered through the kitchen door. Out of respect for Rosie on her first visit, I parked on the street, and we entered through the front door. "Mom, we're home," I yelled from the foyer.

"Coming." She was drying her hands on her apron as she walked down the hall. Before Mom could get close, Rosie shuffled across the floor in her low heels and wrapped Mom up in a long hug. At first, standing stiff as a board, Mom looked over Rosie's shoulder at me in shock. She gathered herself, relaxed, and wrapped her arms around the girl.

Rosie stepped back by my side. "Mom, this is Rosie. Rosie, this is Mom."

"I'm so pleased to meet you, Miz Paxton."

"It's nice to meet you, Rosal—I mean, Rosie."

"You can call me Rosaleigh if you like."

Damn. I preferred Rosaleigh but didn't get that privilege.

"How about you call me Dory, and I'll call you Rosie?"

"Yes, ma'am. May I help you in the kitchen?"

"Thank you, but no. I'm done for now. I was about to sit down and read for a while. We'll visit over dinner. Asa, why don't you show Rosie around the house and neighborhood?"

"Where's Dad?"

"He's helping Sheriff Taylor screen in his back porch. He'll be home for dinner."

The tour of the house took less than five minutes. Outside was a different story. Rosie got a kick out of our chickens. At first, she gasped and asked if we ate them. I assured her we wouldn't eat anything we named.

"Tell me their names?"

"That one is Lily White."

"Makes sense."

"Henrietta's over in the corner. The one in back is Miss Amber Belle. That one's Black Betty, obviously."

"What in the world, Asa?"

Hearing my voice, my duck waddled out of the wooden enclosure. "He's Lucky Ducky. When he was tiny, I found him wandering alone at the river's edge. Me and the hens raised him." I bent down and poked through the hexagon wire. Lucky Ducky rushed to me and rubbed his head on my two fingers.

Rosie giggled, "You and the hens raised him. How sweet." Rosie gracefully squatted next to me and addressed the birds. "It's a pleasure meeting all of you. Keep up the good work."

We moved onto the pole barn. I explained how Uncle Clem and his crew slept in the yard or the barn, depending on the weather. She thought the setup with cots and rope with a mosquito netting canopy I described was clever. I told her how the crew had a regimented system of living together, and the routine was the same when they stayed with us. One group always used the bathroom and shower at the switchyard office. The other group used the bathroom in the house. She felt Uncle Clem showed good leadership sleeping on a cot with his crew, and only sleeping in the spare bedroom when he visited alone.

Rosie pointed to the ladder leading to the barn's loft. "What's up there?"

"You're gonna laugh if I tell you."

"No I won't."

"It's my clubhouse. Well, actually, it's me and my friends' clubhouse. You can't have a club with only one member. We spent a lot of time up there when we were younger. Not so much now."

Rosie rocked back and forth with her shoulders bent in and hands balled together at her waist. Her eyes fluttered. "I wanna see. Are girls allowed?"

"Allowed? Desperately encouraged by my buddies. Never any takers, though. I'll go up first." Rosie made it halfway up the ladder before I grabbed her hands and lifted her into my arms. "You're light as a feather."

"Are you trying to flatter me? Are you trying to seduce me in your lair?"

"Have you been reading romance novels?"

Rosie leaned into me with closed eyes. "Oh, kiss me and break the damsel curse hanging over this boyhood retreat."

"You've already broken my curse."

Rosie's eyelids sprung wide open. "What curse?"

"When I was fifteen, one of my uncle's gandy dancers said I was cursed when it came to girls."

"Well, that's not me. I'm your blessing."

Rosie looked around the loft. "Comic books, baseball cards, sports-section clippings tacked to the wall. So, this is a boy's life? When can we meet your friends?"

"Did you notice the two boys we passed playing catch?"

"They're your friends? Why didn't you stop?"

"I haven't had a chance to tell them about you. They saw you in the car. I'm pretty sure they soiled themselves."

Rosie, laughing loudly, echoed, "Soiled themselves."

"They've had enough time to get over the shock. I'm sure they're lurking nearby."

After I showed Rosie our vegetable garden, we made our way to the front yard. And there they were, across the street, sitting on Itchy's porch stairs wearing shit-eating grins.

"Hey, y'all," Rosie called out, waving both hands enthusiastically.

They jumped to their feet and ran across the street. "I'm Itchy."

"I'm Shanks," the boys said, talking over each other.

"I'm Rosie. From across the river. I met Asa at the East Bluff shindig."

Shanks' elbow jabbed Itchy's side. "I don't know why we asked for permission to go. Should've asked forgiveness after."

"We should have gone even after they told us no," Itchy said.

"Asa told me y'all were his best friends."

"Sometimes," Shanks said.

"All the time," Itchy corrected.

At that moment, I felt guilty. I didn't feel like a good friend because I was so thankful they weren't with me the day before. Who knows if things would have turned out the way they did if Rosie and I had a third and fourth wheel?

132

"Y'all want to walk over to Smalley's for a soda? I'll buy," I offered as secret atonement.

On the way, we briefed Rosie on the Sit-n-Spit Club, likely passing time at Smalley's. Shanks told her his grandpa would probably be there and how he came to be one-legged. Itchy explained the mayor's incompetence and how Skeeter's nuptials were short-lived after the pitch a traveling salesman gave Skeeter's new bride had lured her away. I described how Uncle Clem and I were the targets of race-based verbal abuse over the years, and old man Smalley abstained from said abuse because I was a paying customer.

I stopped our gang on Smalley's porch before entering. I whispered, "Please, Rosie ... please listen to me. No matter what the old men say, ignore them. I promise you, nothing gets under their skin more than ignoring their hateful words."

Rosie grabbed her hips, tilted her head, and barked loudly, "You're telling me if those nasty, mud-mouthed, old men say something mean or racist, I can't call them out as nothing but a bunch of sorry old, limp dick, mean sons of bitches?"

Shanks fell to the porch floorboards in laughter, ending up on his side in the fetal position. Itchy doubled over, holding himself up on the bench. I laughed so hard my eyes watered up. All the while, Rosie stood silent with a pleased expression. It took us boys some time to compose ourselves.

Shanks held the door while Rosie strutted confidently in. The old farts all stared at us in slack-jawed shock. We retrieved sodas from the drink box. I laid my money on the counter. It was the first time the old coots had nothing to say. They didn't talk amongst themselves. Nothing.

We sat silently on Smally's porch bench, sipping our drinks.

Itchy eventually assessed the encounter. "That was weird," he whispered.

"I know. They always try to get at me. Always."

"I have that effect on men," Rosie bragged.

"Maybe they decided to have some manners around a lady," I said.

"Not my grandpa. He makes my cousins cry regularly. Bet they heard Rosie. The old shits are right by the window. She didn't exactly whisper. Bet they didn't want another blast from Shotgun Rosie."

Rosie's soda bottle popped and fizzed loudly off of her lips. "Shotgun Rosie? If you're looking to stick me with a nickname, don't. Rosie ... is ... my ... name."

"Yes, ma'am," we boys said in unison.

After kicking a can around the neighborhood and a tour of the switchyard, we ended up teaching Rosie how to play Polish Poker at the dining room table. The combination of luck, strategy, and the frequent opportunity to screw or be screwed by the person sitting next to you made for raucous laughter.

"You lucky shit," Rosie yelled after Itchy drew a king to end the hand and knock her out of first place. Mom would have rushed from her reading to scold us if it had been one of us boys swearing. She ignored Rosie's outburst. Rosie's long-sincere hug had established a feminine kinship.

Mom sent Shanks and Itchy home in order to set the table for dinner. Rosie insisted on helping. She hugged and kissed the boys' cheeks before I walked them to the front porch.

Itchy exhaled loudly, "Dang, Asa, she's a knockout. She's fun, funny, smells nice, and good lord she's beautiful."

"I know. She's not like the girls around here."

"I'd drink a gallon of her bathwater," Shanks said.

"Please tell me she has sisters or some girlfriends?" Itchy asked. He had avoided the subject in Rosie's presence.

"I'd settle for a one-legged sister," Shanks said, which he meant wholeheartedly.

"Sorry, fellas. Her only sister is married off. As far as I can tell, Rosie is a misfit like us."

"I'll bet the guys in East Bluff are knocking down her door," Itchy said.

"That's right. I met one of them today. Chip, the Piggly Wiggly bag boy. He was none too happy to see Rosie on my arm. Made a red-faced stink about how Rosie gave none of the East Bluff boys a chance."

Climbing the porch stairs, Dad greeted us. "Good evening, gentlemen. Did the girl make it?"

"She made it all right," Shanks answered. "You better hold on to your hat, Mister Paxton."

"Asa hit a grand slam," Itchy added.

"Is that so?"

"A friendly warning, Dad. She's a hugger. She's in with Mom."

I said goodbye to the boys and walked into the living room to find Dad's back with Rosie's arms around it.

Dad and I were called to the table right on time, six o'clock. Rosie and Mom emerged from the kitchen with a plate in each hand. Once the dishes were placed, Dad pulled Mom's chair out. Dad only pulled Mom's chair when the Taylors joined us and the two times Solace, the muralist from New York City, came to dinner. I took Dad's cue and pulled Rosie's chair.

"This looks delicious. "Rosie, did you help?" Dad asked.

"No, sir. All I did was introduce Asa to our butcher for a good cut. Would you like me to say grace?"

Dad and Mom didn't let on, but I knew they were shocked. "Thank you. That would be lovely," Mom said. Rosie closed her eyes, bowed her head, and reached her left hand over the table to Mom and her right hand to Dad. Mom, Dad, and I looked at each other. We were Northern Presbyterians. We didn't hold hands during the dinner prayer. Mom took Rosie's hand and reached out for mine. Dad followed suit.

Rosie sat silent for a moment, presumably centering herself before praying. She eventually began. "Loving God, we give You thanks for nourishing our bodies. You have nourished our souls with the healing spirit of Jesus Christ. We pray for those around our country and throughout the world who are not as fortunate during these difficult times." There was a slight quiver in Rosie's voice as she said the last words. "We give thanks for Your presence and pray this circle be unbroken. Amen."

I could tell Dad was moved. "Thank you," he said softly.

"That was a lovely way to end our prayer," Mom said.

"I have a confession to make," Rosie said.

Uh-oh.

"The ending just now came to me. It's not an original thought. It's from my favorite hymn, Will This Circle be Unbroken. The Carter Family came out with a popular version a couple of years ago, however, I prefer Ada Habershon's original from 1907."

Whew. No big confession. Things were still on track.

Rosie finished her first bite of macaroni and cheese and started the dinner conversation. "Asa, did you tell your parents how we met?"

"I did."

"Dory, Hank. I can only imagine what you must have thought."

Dad and I turned deliberately to Mom, putting her on the spot. She fessed up. "I also have a confession. To be honest, Rosie, I was a little judgmental about the whole greased-pig business."

Dad bent toward Rosie and grinned. "Don't you worry. Asa straightened Dory out last night at dinner."

"I understand, Dory. My parents were horrified. Probably to a much greater degree than you."

"How so?" Mom asked.

Rosie looked at me pensively. It was the first time I sensed any hesitancy from her about anything. "It's OK. Go ahead."

"Well, Miz Paxton, Mister Paxton. Dory, Hank. I don't like to sound disrespectful. However, the plain fact of the matter is I have no respect for my parents or my older sister. My sister is married off, carrying on the Pickett way. Mother is involved in a gaggle of useless women's organizations, including the United Daughters of the Confederacy. My father has been re-elected County Solicitor three times straight. He campaigns on enforcing segregation laws. I refuse to worship at the altar of white supremacy. Socially, they put on airs. Their daughter chasing a greased pig was an embarrassment in the highest meaning of the word."

Dad leaned toward Rosie again, this time with a soft eye. "Life can be ugly and unfair. Asa said he told you about my brother and his Negro crew. I think we understand each other."

"I'm excited to meet your brother and his crew," Rosie said cheerily. I sensed she was trying to lighten the conversation without dismissing its essence.

"Speaking of meeting Uncle Clem and company, there's something I haven't told y'all."

"What's that?" Mom asked innocently.

"Rosie, when I met your father today, he said he knew but couldn't place the Paxton name. He eventually remembered a Paxton who ran a Negro gandy dancer crew working on the East Bluff tracks over the years. He asked if we were related."

"Oh no. What did you tell Father?"

"I told him the truth."

"And what did Father say?"

"He went on and on about how well Uncle Clem kept his niggras in line. Why does your father say niggra?"

"Asa!" Mom snapped.

"This is so embarrassing, but it's ok, Dory. Asa asked a good question. He deserves an answer. Some affluent Southerners use the term as a more sophisticated way of saying the word I won't dignify by uttering, but it's just as hateful. I don't understand why Father would think your uncle did a good job keeping his crew in line? It makes him sound as cruel as most white Southerners."

"Think about it this way," I said. "It's as if you and I went joyriding in the Citroen with the top down through the Negro part of East Bluff yesterday, only the opposite ... sort of. Imagine Uncle Clem and his crew rolling into East Bluff and yucking it up together as they work. Of course, white folks aren't going to take to that. It's a performance, a ruse to keep the entire crew safe."

"Oh, I get it now. Staying with y'all from time to time must be a relief from that tension."

"Well, enough about that," Mom interrupted. She knew the subject needed to be changed. "Tell us about you, Rosie. What do you like to do for fun? What are your interests?"

"Well, I enjoy most school subjects, especially science and mathematics. Challenging puzzles are always fun. I like to ride my bicycle, and I love to read. I bicycle to a few quiet spots and spend the day in another place and time with my face buried in a book. My friend Martha runs the Carnegie Library and keeps me in interesting books and musical recordings. Many of the books she recommends would surely be censored by Mother and her United Daughters of the Confederacy if they knew the subject matter. I clean Martha and her housemate Julia's home weekly for spending money. That's about all there is to know about me."

"I love to read too. What are you currently reading?" Mom asked.

"I started *Gone with the Wind* last night."

"I've heard it's popular. It's never available by the time the bookmobile makes it out here."

"It's an easy read so far, although I'm unsure how I feel about it. Martha described it as glorifying slavery and the old Antebellum South. She's taught me, like it or not, reading whatever is popular is important. What do you like to read, Dory?"

Dad interrupted. "I like to read the Bible and the newspaper. Have you kept up with what's going on in Europe?"

"Poor Hank," Mom poked, "Are you feeling left out of the conversation?" Dad went back to working on his steak. "I like just about any fiction. Mystery and detective novels are my preference. I've read almost all of the Perry Mason series."

All through dinner, Mom tried to steer the conversation toward lighthearted banter while Dad pushed the conversation toward world events and politics. One minute, Rosie and Mom would laugh about how we named our chickens based on their color and how the duck had imprinted on me. The next minute, Dad and Rosie would discuss Hitler's next move after invading Austria. Rosie wondered aloud, "Will Hitler continue east into Poland, or would he dare move west toward the heart of Europe?" She kept Mom and Dad engaged with her wit and ability to speak intelligently at every turn in the conversation. I hardly got a word in, which was fine with me. After we talked in front of our empty plates for at least an hour, Rosie insisted on helping Mom with the dishes while Dad and I retired to the living room.

"You've got a tiger by the tail, Son," Dad said from behind the broad sheets of his *Times Daily*.

"I know."

"Treat her right," was his fatherly advice.

Rosie hugged Dad goodbye. Mom escorted us to the porch. She pointed to the darkened sky. "Look at the new moon."

"The Ides of March in a couple of nights," Rosie said.

Ominously, Mom said, "Shakespeare. Beware, the Ides of March."

"Yes of course. However, I was referring to a time before Shakespeare's Caesar and Brutus. I was thinking about ancient times, Babylonian Empire. The Ides of March marked the new year. It was a time for celebration with food, drink, and revelry. Thank you for a wonderful evening, Dory. It felt like a new-year celebration with the Ides of March's blessing."

While parked in front of Rosie's house, I asked her about her favorite hymn she mentioned at dinner, *Will this Circle Be Unbroken.* I'd never heard the song.

Rosie looked down at her hands meshed together in her lap and began to softly sing. It wasn't a joyful hymn. When she finished, I was hesitant, but I said it anyway. "It's bittersweet for you, isn't it?" Rosie didn't look up. "You wish you loved your family like in the hymn."

"I learned the hymn when I was seven, maybe eight. As I grew older, the words began to take on real meaning for me. In my house, there's no circle to be broken. There won't be a heavenly reunion if Mother and Father don't change their ways."

"The hymn helped you sort out your feelings about your parents."

Rosie kept her face down. "Asa—," she started to say something, then sat silent momentarily, collecting her thoughts. "Asa. When I first saw you laughing at those crazy pie-eaters, I thought you were so handsome and full of life. When you opened up at the soda fountain and said your uncle's Negro crew was like family, I wondered, could you be for real? Our first kiss wasn't awkward. It felt completely natural. Today was so much fun, and now, what you said about my family and the hymn. No one has ever talked to me like that—about my feelings … except Addie and Martha, and they don't dig too deep. Your friends, parents, you and me together, it all seems too good to be true."

We sat quietly while I thought about the right thing to say. I thought of what Mom, Dad, or Preacher might say. "Rosie, you took a chance on me. I took a chance on you. We could have turned out to be thin-skinned, hard-hearted, and ugly. But, instead, you and I are the same on the inside. We see the world differently than Jim Crow Southerners. I don't think this is too good to be true."

"I'm excited, Asa, but I'm also scared. I just met you. This is scary and foreign to me."

"Rosie, I remember some advice from Preacher, the old-renaissance man on my uncle's crew. He said God tells us over and over in the Bible to 'fear not.' and 'do not be afraid.' I don't think God wants you, me, or us to be afraid or scared."

Rosie appeared reassured and laughed, "A Renaissance gandy dancer? I'd like to meet him."

The goodnight kiss we then shared wasn't a lustful exchange between wanton teens. Instead, it was a kiss shared by two people who cared for each other.

"Your Dad and I had a talk while you were driving Rosie home. Tell him, Hank."

A "talk" didn't sound good. Perhaps the Ides of March were not in my favor. "Rosie doesn't live too far away. However, it seems impractical for you to continue courting her without certainty of transportation."

This could go either way.

"It's a short walk to work, and I have the company pick up and Leyland if I need a vehicle."

I was starting to like what Mom and Dad's "talk" was about.

"We've decided to let you have full use of the Citroen. Almost as if it's your own car. No more asking us if you can take it."

Praise Jesus.

Mom jumped in with the conditions. "This doesn't mean you can disappear without doing your chores. No complaining if I ask you to run errands or if I need to use the car. And listen carefully. The privilege can be revoked if you act irresponsibly."

"Son, you may think your mom and I are doing this for you. Actually, we hope you'll bring Rosie around often. We were hoping for a girl but got you instead." Dad couldn't resist a playful jab.

CHAPTER NINETEEN
BONNIE AND CLYDE

Years before I experienced Eros-type feelings for Rosie, the exploits of Bonnie and Clyde were splashed across newspaper front pages and over radio airwaves. I couldn't understand what would make a young couple run amok like they had. I was so lovestruck after my impromptu date with Rosie on Saturday and her arresting aura, charming my friends and parents on Sunday, Bonnie and Clyde's passion made sense. There was no telling what I was capable of. I wondered if Rosie felt the same way and was capable of some level of recklessness. Over the weekend, Rosie hinted at throwing caution to the wind with her bombastic threat of dressing down the old men at Smalley's Sit-n-Spit Club. However, there were also moments of profound thoughtfulness. This young woman was like none I'd ever met. She had my head both spinning and in the clouds.

On Monday, Shanks and Itchy repeatedly told me to, "Snap out of it, lover-boy."

On Tuesday, my science teacher, Miz Wells, noted, "Asa. Unlike the rest of the class, you didn't complete the pop quiz. This is very disappointing B-minus work."

Miz Simms returned my Monday homework assignment in a private meeting after class on Wednesday. The project was to write an essay describing somewhere naturally beautiful. Miz Simms had several reasons to question the authenticity of my paper. My penmanship, as she put it, "has never been so graceful." She pointed out "spelling and grammatical errors, the likes of which I've never seen from Asa Paxton." Finally, she said while shaking the paper in my face, "The point of the assignment was to describe somewhere naturally beautiful. Instead, you described a beautiful young woman and a first kiss that could not have felt more natural. You barely mentioned the bamboo forest and pond. Did you pay some sappy girl to write your essay?"

I could feel my face becoming flushed. "No, ma'am."

Perplexed, Miz Simms stared at me for a moment. "Oh, good lord. A siren has caused your brain to become unbalanced. I won't accept it. Rewrite this. Leave out the girl and the kiss. Focus on the bamboo forest and the pond. Turn it back in tomorrow."

"Yes, ma'am."

Sensing my embarrassment, she gave me a spoonful of consolation. "Asa, your bamboo forest sounds like it was a beautiful and romantic spot for your first kiss."

The irritation of rewriting my essay snapped me out of my fog. According to the ancient calendar, Thursday's Ides of March would be a new day and a new year. All I had to do was concentrate. The upcoming weekend and seeing Rosie again were only a few days away. I felt alert and ready to learn.

My first-period trigonometry quiz was a piece of cake. In second-period science, I had no trouble filling in the empty boxes of the quiz on the periodic table of elements. I also knew the extra-credit bonus question—1869 was the year the periodic table of elements was created. Miz Simms read my reworked essay to the class, calling it "the best in all of my three senior English classes." She extolled my creative use of words and the picture I painted of a mysterious pond in a Chinese bamboo forest. I described the location as "a magically romantic hideaway every young damsel dreams of for her first kiss," which conjured up wistful sighs from a few of the girls in the class. When the bell rang, Miz Simms stopped me on my way out and held the essay up to my face. "Asa, you've proven you can put an elegant pen to paper. Look at this chicken scratch on your reworked essay. Creative writing and good penmanship are NOT mutually exclusive."

My "chicken scratch" was a sign I was back to normal. Or so I thought.

Itchy, Shanks, and I took our lunch sacks to the lonely Misfit corner of the cafeteria. In three-plus years we'd been attending Robert E. Lee High School, not once had the other seats at the six-seat table been occupied. Mister Monroe, the only male teacher at Lee High, was the week's lunchroom monitor. I'm sure the unruly freshman and sophomore classes of first-lunch kept him busy. The juniors and seniors of second-lunch may have been noisy in conversation and laughter, but they didn't require close supervision. Or so Mister Monroe thought. His face and focus were buried in a stack of papers he was grading. Itchy and Shanks were sitting across from me, trying out a new joke about a bartender, his patron, and a bowl of complementary peanuts when they stopped talking. Their goggled eyes looked past me with mouths agape. The lunchroom noise quieted. I looked over my shoulder to see Rosie approaching our table. Every eye in the cafeteria except Mister Monroe's was on the beautiful and mysterious co-ed.

The junior and senior boys had helplessly stupid looks on their faces, while the girls wore jealous and scornful expressions. After Rosie passed Dirk and JD's table, Leggy Louise scowled at Dirk. Busty Barb hip-checked JD right off his seat and onto the floor. The boys and I were as speechless as the rest of our classmates. Rosie pecked Shanks and Itchy on the cheek before giving me a long, tongue-filled kiss. I was shocked and confused. I also wanted to revel in the envy and scorn of my junior and senior classmates. Unfortunately, there was no time for gloating. I jerked my head around to Mister Monroe's table. He was still focused on grading papers, clueless to the quiet mayhem taking place in the cafeteria.

All three of us boys were tripping over each other's words and our own words, not knowing what to say about Rosie's unexpected and, as far as we knew, unauthorized visit.

Finally, I composed myself. "Rosie, what in the name of Sam Hill?"

"I missed you—missed y'all. So I rode my bicycle over."

"How did you get past our principal?"

"You mean Miz Dockery? I had her fooled." Rosie sat down and firmly placed her hands on the table to steady herself. In a nasally Midwestern accent, Rosie said, "I told her I was your cousin visiting from Chicago and my Aunt Dory said you forgot your lunch and asked me to take it to you."

Itchy giggled a little at first then laughed uncontrollably after making complete sense of the ruse. "You sound just like Asa's mama."

Shanks expressed his admiration. "Rosie. You are one sneaky peach with a hard pit."

"Thank you, Shanks. I'm honored to be compared to stone fruit." Rosie emptied her paper bag. "You boys want a sandwich? Addie's pimento cheese is to die for."

Shanks and Itchy looked at their dry sandwiches. "Heck, yeah," Shanks said.

"Y'all should've seen the side eye Addie gave me when I asked for four sandwiches this morning."

I couldn't think about food. I looked back at Mister Monroe. He was still oblivious, but the rest of the juniors and seniors were obviously talking about the Misfit corner of the cafeteria. "What about your school? Aren't you gonna get into trouble for cutting?" I asked.

"I told the principal I was having the worst cramps of my life and wasn't prepared for my oncoming period. He's young and awkward, and most men don't like talking about that subject. He was happy to send me home rather than have a longer conversation about my menstrual cycle."

Shanks set his sandwich down and ran his pointer finger through his crooked teeth and gums to clear out the excess pimento cheese before speaking. "Rosie, remind me to never, ever trust you. And you're right, this pimento cheese is to die for."

This may have been funny to Shanks, Itchy, and Rosie, however, I was nervous about what might happen if Miz Dockery discovered Rosie's ruse. I eventually relaxed a little and ate the sandwich. I'm glad I did. It was wonderfully fluffy with just the right amount of hot pepper.

We made it through lunch, and Rosie was on her way after giving Shanks and Itchy big hugs and me another full-mouthed passionate kiss in front of everyone—an act chaste Southern belles simply did not do; whereas, most Southern gents certainly wished they did.

In fifth period, my head was back spinning and in the clouds. A summons to Miz Dockery's office greeted me in sixth period. I had been found out. Mister Monroe was exiting the principal's office as I was heading in. His defeated expression changed to tight lips and glare as we passed. It was apparent he'd been disciplined for his lack of attention to the Misfits during second lunch. Being called to the principal's office had a sobering effect on my otherwise love-struck condition.

"Have a seat, Mister Paxton."

I sat on the edge of the chair across from Miz Dockery. She lifted her sparkly cat-eye framed glasses hanging from a chain around her neck, picked up a piece of paper, and read it silently. It was clear she had already read it at least once. After what seemed like a silent eternity, Miz Dockery lowered her glasses and held out the sheet of paper. Accepting it was my only option. I first looked to the bottom of the long letter to identify the snitch. No luck. It was anonymous, of course. I began reading from the beginning.

> Dear Miz Dockery,
> I am among the many young Lee High ladies with
> the distinct honor and advantage of attending your
> "Becoming a Christian Woman" classes at Calvary
> Baptist Church. In keeping with your teachings,
> certain events during today's lunch left me, and
> I imagine the whole Junior and Senior classes, aghast.
> Asa Paxton's female lunch guest went far beyond
> proper decorum. Her public display of affection was
> more than a gentle touch of Asa's elbow or a soft
> giggle with her hand three inches in front of her
> mouth. Simply put, there was nothing between
> her mouth and Asa Paxton's mouth. I thought you
> would want to know.

I finished reading the letter but didn't want to look up. Sensing I was done, Miz Dockery laid into me. "Well, Asa, what do you have to say for yourself and the young lady who claimed to be your cousin visiting from Chicago?"

Graduation was less than three months away. I decided to throw caution to the wind. I would not be apologetic. The self-righteous fink was Miz Dockery's Sunday-school spawn. The principal deserved to have the Bible thrown back in her face. "Miz Dockery, do you believe the human race began with Adam and Eve in the Garden of Eden?"

Miz Dockery huffed, "Whell. Of course, I do."

"Then you must admit that the woman I shared a kiss with is a distant cousin."

Miz Dockery stuttered and stammered at first before stating firmly, "Genealogy is not the point. Your act of depravity before the junior and senior class is the issue."

"Depravity, you say? I suppose you think the prostitute in Luke's gospel who kissed Jesus' feet at Simon the Pharisee's dinner party was depraved."

Miz Dockery stuttered and stammered again before composing herself. "Are you comparing yourself to Jesus?" she asked in a tone of righteous indignation, which comes part and parcel with being a middle-aged Southern Baptist Sunday-school teacher.

"No, ma'am. I'm comparing you and your disciple to the Pharisee dinner party host in Luke's gospel."

I could tell the principal's blood was boiling. "Asa, I'd call your parents or suspend you. However, I'm sure they would take your side. You tell that Jezebel she is not to step foot on school property ever again. You are dismissed."

My rebellion against Miz Dockery was nothing like the acts of shoot-'em-up Clyde Barrow, but it was definitely influenced by my very own Bonnie Parker ... Rosie Pickett. Rosie's antics that day may not have reached the level of Miz Parker, but it was clear she was capable of throwing caution to the wind.

The Robert E. Lee High School student body viewed me differently after the episode, and not in a good way. Their resentment of me only increased. As for Itchy and Shanks, they let it be known to the entire school there was a fink among the student body.

CHAPTER TWENTY
VALEDICTORIANS

Every student, every teacher, and even the principal accepted it. There would eventually be an outbreak after the senior student body returned from Christmas break for their last high school semester. An epidemic rendering every educator helpless—an illness called senioritis.

Oddly enough, senioritis and completion of the new TVA bridge were my grade-point average savior. Had Rosie come into my life a year or two earlier, my grades undoubtedly would have suffered. Also, I became so socially enlightened by Rosie, I might have recklessly rebelled against Jim Crow and the Black Codes, putting not only everyone I cared about but also my education at risk. The history books and essays Rosie's librarian friend Martha introduced me to painted a very different picture than the Blue Rock schools' history curriculum.

Over the years, Mom, Dad, even Preacher ducked, dodged, and half-answered my questions when I asked about what I thought were dubious historical claims in my textbooks. There was no secret conspiracy on my parents' part. They admitted they were trying to protect me and my grades. Dad agreed I was right to question, but he said I also needed to keep my head down and survive until I was mentally capable of what he called "moral combat."

Positioned near or at the top of the Robert E. Lee Class of 1938, I had only one thing to worry about academically. Most of the last semester was perfunctory by the teachers and students alike. The final exams, on the other hand, were no joke. They could make or break one's final grade. Rosie sequestered herself to study before her school's exam week. She believed she was at or near the top of her class. The large senior class at Rosie's school meant greater competition for the top honor than at my Robert E. Lee High. To say Rosie coveted the valedictorian honor would be an understatement of God's Tenth Commandment. My competition was Scott Jenkins. After Arthur Thompson made fun of Scott's raggedy clothes at the beginning of ninth grade, Scott went silent. Every day, he made the long solitary walk to and from his shack in the woods with a textbook open, studying, driven by poverty and anger. The only other competition was Mildred Montgomery, my sixth-grade teacher's daughter, which gave Mildred unfair academic advantages.

Mildred was a bitch. She was mean to her friends and more cruel to the least among us. She once told Shanks, "You should just crawl back into your cave and die." When she saw Itchy approaching in the hallway, she would dramatically pass his lesioned body, hugging the wall while staring him down with a look as if she were sniffing shit. I suspected Mildred penned the note to Miz Dockery, ratting me out when Rosie visited during lunch back in March. In short, at least half of the senior class had good reason to want to punch Mildred Montgomery in the throat.

As far as I was concerned, the final exams were an exercise of focus and recalling data. Rosie's absence helped my frame of mind. The grand prize, the whole ball of wax, was Miz Simms' English final. We were given a week to write a seven-hundred to one-thousand-word essay or book report of our choosing. Miz Simms was the best and most challenging teacher of my career in the Blue Rock school system. She was clever with her teaching and assignments. One hundred percent of our final exam grade was determined by spelling, grammar, punctuation, and falling within the required word count. Penmanship, praise the lord, was not factored into the score. Every student could score one hundred percent based on the technical requirements.

Miz Simms added a twist. One could sign up to present their work orally to the class for twenty extra credit points. The students who made such a presentation couldn't hurt their final grade. However, they could help it significantly. The possibility of scoring one-hundred-twenty on a final exam accounting for thirty-four percent of the overall semester grade was too good to pass up. My essay would be my swan song. I eagerly signed up for an oral presentation. So did Mildred Montgomery. Scott Jenkins' name on the sheet was a shock. He'd barely spoken in four years.

I researched my subject thoroughly and painstakingly penned my essay. I rehearsed my presentation until I could recite it by heart. On Miz Simms' scheduled exam day, my last exam, I wore my button-down shirt, black slacks, my good shoes and had Dad tie my bowtie.

My classmates trickled into Miz Simms' room and dropped their essays and book reports on her desk. Mildred, Scott, and I would turn ours in after our presentations. Once everyone was settled, our teacher addressed the class. "Mildred, Asa, Scott, please stand up. Class, these three students have shown the courage to stand before you and present their work. They deserve your utmost attention and respect. Any sign of disrespect or disruption will result in the perpetrator being required to present their work orally to the class. Understand?" There were a few mumbles. "Is that understood?" She said forcefully.

"Yes, ma'am," the class replied.

Damn. She is one tough nut. I was grateful to her for setting us on a safe stage.

"Scott, you'll go first, followed by Mildred, then Asa."

Scott, bathed and clean, took his mark next to Miz Simms desk. His permanently stained white shirt was also clean and buttoned up to the large apple he developed in his throat. Scott's denim pants were too short. His feet were swimming in what appeared to be second-hand boots. He looked over the classroom, then at Miz Simms. She gave him a soft smile and a gentle nod.

Scott introduced his reading confidently. "A Shovel Full of Dirt. A Memoir by Scott Jenkins." Scott turned his title page over, set it face down on Miz Simms' desk, and read to the class. "When I was nine, I helped Daddy bury Mama under the sour gum tree by the shed out back. I experienced a different feeling with each shovel full of dirt; anger, loneliness, fear, and emptiness. Most of all, I felt sadness."

Holy shit, I almost said out loud. Slouched in my seat, I sat up. I didn't know if my classmates recognized it, but I could tell by the look on Miz Simms' face, she knew what I knew. We were about to experience something special.

"'Scotty, you're gonna have to be strong. We're gonna have to look after each other now,' Daddy told me." Scott looked at the teacher. "I spelled it like Daddy said it, but I know how to spell all the words correctly. I hope you don't redline them."

"You're fine, Scott. Please continue."

Scott continued, weaving a memoir of a life more challenging than even Shanks'. He spoke of eating whatever he could snare, be it possum, rabbit, squirrel, or raccoon. He described winter drafts and summer swelter in his shack. The first few times Scott quoted his daddy with improper grammar and annunciation, he looked at Miz Simms. Each time, she gave him an approving nod. Eventually, he gracefully danced between proper English and grammar and the sometimes sad, sometimes funny, other times the poetic backwoods language of his father. His delivery was well-rehearsed. Each sheet of paper was handled with care, setting the pages face down on the teacher's desk in a neat stack. Using flowing prose, Scott described his difficult life through passages of witty self-deprecation my dense classmates missed, leaving only Miz Simms and me to laugh out loud. Amazingly, with all the pain and difficulty he described, there was no accompanying air of self-pity.

"My life took a turn the day back in ninth grade when it looked like I would have to fight Arthur Thompson for making fun of my tattered clothes. You, my Blue Rock classmates since elementary school, changed my life that day. If you don't recall, you all rushed to the buses the River Rats rode and stood behind me." Scott paused long enough to make eye contact with the bus-riding students in the room. "No disrespect to you bus riders."

"Arthur and I didn't brawl, but you all backed me up. I felt I was part of something bigger. I felt my destiny was to be part of something bigger than myself."

I had mixed emotions when Scott started speaking proudly about our Blue Rock classmates. I thought of most of them as monumental assholes. On the other hand, after listening to his life story, I couldn't help but admire Scott.

"In conclusion, by my choice, I don't talk or socialize much. I've been on a mission to get the best education possible. Thank you for giving me room to grow. After graduation, I'll leave Blue Rock for parts unknown to find my place in the world. Thank you."

I leaped to my feet, clapping. I was the only one—confirming my classmates were a bunch of heartless assholes. The dam didn't break for Miz Simms. She was professional and held back her tears until Scott finished. She stood up and gave him a big hug. I could read her lips. "I'm so proud of you," she whispered into Scott's ear, her eyes misty. She retrieved a tissue from her blouse sleeve, dried her eyes, and called Mildred forward. When Mildred passed Scott on her way to the front of the class, she gave him her patented upper lip quiver. Mildred took her mark and looked to Miz Simms.

"Go ahead, Mildred."

With a slight curtsey, Mildred announced, "My book report is on *Gone With the Wind* by Margaret Mitchell."

Well, this is gonna be fun. Rosie had read Gone with the Wind, in the spring and gave me her scathing book report. Adding to Rosie's scorn for the novel was an incident with the married banker where she held her passbook savings account. The banker lured her into his office and pinned her against the wall. He said Rosie's hazel eyes and buxom figure reminded him of the book's description of Scarlett O'Hara, and he wanted to show Rosie things unfit for print. It took an unexpected and well-placed knee to the banker's balls for Rosie to escape the cad.

Mildred stuck to her outline. She introduced each section of her report, which made the presentation choppy, especially the beginning, where she detailed the publishing date and page count—required details I doubt anyone could present smoothly. In the character descriptions, she likened the men to "Southern gentlemen of courage and purpose." Scarlett O'Hara was described as "a beautiful young socialite full of energy and determination—a character I can relate to." I caught Miz Simms rolling her eyes.

Rosie described O'Hara as "a spoiled little rich bitch."

"Mammy the darkie," as Mildred labeled her, "was content to be background noise, satisfied with her trappings and cackling at Miss Scarlett like a mother hen."

Mildred's description of the plot rambled. Her summary and personal feelings about the book were, "The Northern aggression was an unjust disruption of the picturesque and honorable way of life in the South." She finished and handed the teacher her papers, then addressed the class excitedly, "Now y'all, this isn't part of my book report, but I have it on good authority Hollywood is in production of a big screen version of this masterpiece."

"Well, OK then, Mildred. You may be seated," Miz Simms said.

I took the long way around to my mark to avoid giving Mildred the satisfaction of a sneer as she headed back to her desk. Miz Simms gave me the nod. "Miz Simms? If it's OK with you, I would like to have the blinds closed and the lights turned off."

"It's your presentation. Scott, please close the blinds and turn off the lights." Enough light remained to read if needed, though I had my essay memorized.

"Before I begin, I'd like to once again applaud Scott's moving memoir—a work worthy of the utmost respect. I'd also like to thank you, Mildred. The book you chose for your report could not have provided a better contrast to my essay entitled *No Way Home.* Now then, I'd like everyone to please close your eyes."

The entire class closed their eyes immediately, still sensitive to Miz Simms threat of having to present their own work.

"Imagine in front of you is a large white building on the western edge of Africa overlooking the Atlantic Ocean. The entire world you've known is behind you. Imagine you don't know where they have taken your wife and your thirteen-year-old daughter. Imagine your naked body being prodded toward a doorway by long sticks whittled at the end to a point. Imagine the flesh around your ankles and wrists worn thin and bloodied by restraints and the long journey from your village. Imagine you are taken to a hot, windowless cell and shackled to the floor for weeks with twenty other men you do not know. Imagine his anguish." I paused long enough to make the class uncomfortable. "Now, imagine he is your father."

"Imagine you don't know where they have taken your husband and teenage daughter. Imagine you are shackled to the floor of a hot, windowless cell for weeks with twenty other women you do not know. Imagine her maternal desperation." I paused again for effect. "Now, imagine she's your mother."

"Imagine you are a thirteen-year-old girl. You don't know where they have taken your mother and father. Imagine you are in a court-yard, stripped naked, along with twenty other young girls. Imagine you are forced to march in a circle while your male captors argue over who will be your rapist until the boats return." My classmates fidgeted and twisted in their chairs. I let them squirm to my silent fifteen count. "Imagine her shame and fear. Imagine she's your sister, your girlfriend, or ... imagine you are that girl. Imagine families intentionally torn apart, never to be reunited."

I glanced at Miz Simms. She looked like she'd seen a ghost. "May I continue?" I whispered.

She gave me a reluctant sigh. "It's your essay," she whispered back.

"Thank you, class. You may open your eyes."

Twenty-six sets of eyes opened. Twenty-five of them were shocked. The final set belonged to Scott Jenkins. His eyes shone with pride as he gave me an approving nod and two thumbs up. I continued. "When a boat returned, the kidnapped, soon-to-be slaves in the Americas were marched through the western door of the prison. The Door of No Re-turn. Once onboard, African men, women, and children lay on their backs, shackled to the salt-water-chafing planks in the cargo hold. The victims alternated head to foot and foot to head, consuming every inch of the floating stockade. Within minutes of departure, the waves took their toll on many of the captives. Their last meal on land spewed from their mouths uncontrollably. Communal vomit flowed back and forth and side to side in the belly of the slave ship. Imagine the stench, wors-ened with the addition of feces and urine over the months of travel. The misery of the cargo hold was only broken up by the occasional visit top-side, where deckhands made their cargo dance for exercise. If the winds were unfavorable and the voyage would inevitably outlast the provi-sions, women were shackled together and cast overboard into watery mass graves. It was a matter of economics—women were deemed less valuable than men. If the captives survived, the voyage to the Americas was just the beginning of their misery. Slave owners were free to treat enslaved humans as they saw fit. In most cases, slaves were treated only well enough to survive the grueling hours of work, contrary to the false narrative of the happy-go-lucky slave." I paused momentarily to give Mildred, and her *Gone With the Wind* book report pursed lips and an eye-roll before continuing.

"There were unthinkable acts perpetrated on our fellow human beings. They ranged from flogging, to rape, to forcing slaves fight each other for the amusement of plantation owners, to name a few atrocities."

I could sense the negative tension coming from my classmates. I could feel the nervous tension coming from Miz Simms. The tension became even more palpable when I moved into my lesson on the cause of the Civil War and the attempts of various groups to rewrite history. When I read the line, "Regardless of what is in textbooks, it is a plain fact Southern slavery caused the Civil War."

Dirk Johnson shouted, "You're a liar."

Coming up and crouching halfway out of her seat, Miz Simms threatened, "Dirk. Would you like to do a presentation?" Dirk cowed, Miz Simms sat back down, and I continued. I was prepared for Dirk or any other challenge. My essay included quotes from several official States' Declaration of Secession citing slavery as the reason for seceding from the Union.

I saved my most scathing rebuke for the UDC. "The United Daughters of the Confederacy, by inserting themselves in the textbook selection process, are sowing the fertile fields of young minds with fear, hate, and prejudice. Our white schools must throw off the shackles of ignorance and escape the plantations of Southern thought. The continued oppression of Negroes, rising from the ashes of Reconstruction, is both repugnant and morally bankrupt—a sin in the eyes of God. We must reject the mission of the United Daughters of the Confederacy. Thank you."

Most of my classmates appeared confused by my essay. No one had ever challenged their understanding of Southern societal norms. However, I could tell by the conflicting expressions on Scott and Mildred's faces they knew exactly what I was talking about. After all, they were near the top of the class and capable of critical thought. Like many Southerners, Mildred knew better but didn't care.

Miz Simms reluctantly accepted my papers. "I doubt you understand what you've done," she said in a desperate voice. "This won't stay in my classroom."

Miz Simms was both right and wrong. I knew exactly what I had done. As soon as the bell rang, Mildred enlisted JD and Dirk and made a mad dash to the office. Surprisingly, I made it through the rest of the day without being summoned by Miz Dockery. Perhaps my essay wasn't as controversial as I had hoped.

Fifth period the next day, the last day of classes before the following week's commencement, the proverbial chickens came home to roost. I was ordered to the principal's office. Apparently, Mom, Dad, and Miz Simms were summoned as well. They sat beside an older woman wearing a Sunday-go-to-meeting hat. Her white blouse completely engulfed her neck. The wide-lapel blazer and matching skirt were a drab gray, accentuating the facial expression of an angry old mule. Her only coloring was a bright Confederate ribbon bar pinned to her lapel as if she were an honored military officer. "Mom, Dad, what are you doing here?"

My parents stood up, my essay in Mom's hand. "We were just leaving," Dad said.

"I beg your pardon," Miz Dockery said in her typical indignant tone.

"Whell, I nevah," the stuffy old lady said as if she were the most important person in the room.

Mom handed me the essay. One-hundred-twenty percent marked across the title page in Miz Simms' handwriting. "Your father and I read your work. Even the penmanship was well done."

"Are you going to abandon Asa to defend his indefensible essay?" Miz Dockery asked.

Dad's eyes squinted at the principal. "Asa was man enough to write the essay. He's man enough to defend himself against what will surely be an unjust punishment." Dad wrapped his big hand around the back of my neck and pulled me toward him. "I'm proud of you, son."

"Good day," Mom said to the old mule.

At that moment, I knew I was about to engage in Dad's "moral combat."

Miz Simms sat emotionless. Mom and Dad obviously flustered Miz Dockery. Her voice was trembling as she introduced me to the mule. "Asa, this is Beatrice Comstock from Muscle Shoals. Miz Comstock is the chairwoman of the North Alabama Chapter of the United Daughters of the Confederacy."

I offered my hand. "I'm pleased to meet you." Instead of accepting my hand, she clutched the purse in her lap more tightly.

"I sincerely doubt you are in any way pleased to meet me, young man."

"I take it you read my essay."

"I did indeed. How did you come up with such nonsense?"

"Did you not read the bibliography page?"

"I did and was quite disturbed to see Muzzey's An American History on the same page as Susan Pendleton Lee's Advanced School History of the United States."

"That's the difference between you and me, ma'am. I'm not threatened by words on a page or an accurate recounting of history."

"How dare you? Neither I nor the UDC are threatened by words on a page."

"Really? You drove all the way from Muscle Shoals to confront a high school student about the words he put on a page. And you claim you're not threatened?"

Miz Comstock glared at Miz Dockery. The principal had lost control of the meeting. She didn't know what to say, so I took another swing. "You revisionists are trying to push a rope up a hill with all this Lost Cause nonsense."

"Asa, enough," Miz Dockery growled.

I had gotten under Miz Comstock's skin. Her hand shook as she pointed at me and bayed at the principal, "He does not deserve a diploma."

Miz Simms lept from her chair. "Principal Dockery can't deny Asa his diploma. He's completed all the required coursework. He may very well be the valedictorian once all the grades are tallied."

"Thanks to you and your one-hundred-twenty percent score," Miz Dockery complained.

"The score is Asa's. Not mine. His spelling, grammar, and punctuation were perfect, and he earned the extra twenty points the same as Scott Jenkins and Mildred Montgomery."

"I can assure everyone in this room, regardless of Asa's grade point average, he most definitely will not be attending commencement. Asa, you're officially banned from school property. We will mail your diploma. It's time you leave."

Beatrice Comstock looked pleased with Miz Dockery's punishment. I wanted to get in one or two more punches before exiting. "Banned from school property? I'm in good company with my distant cousin you called a Jezebel in March. Now I'll get to attend her commencement instead of your charade."

I addressed Miz Comstock once more. "Ma'am, the South would be a much better place had Grant ordered firing squads for the Confederate traitors. Sherman should have kept marching and burning, and Lincoln should have given his theater tickets to Vice President Johnson. The Confederate Lost Cause and self-loathing have made for such an ugly and pitiful state of Southern affairs."

"Get out," Miz Dockery shouted.

I avoided any acknowledgment of Miz Simms on my way out. I had already caused her grief she didn't deserve.

Itchy and Shanks gave me a report on our commencement. Scott Jenkins addressed the students, parents, and teachers as the valedictorian with a slightly altered but just as moving version of his memoir. They said Scott's father was a blubbering heap of pride.

Rosie earned the valedictorian status of her class but was not allowed to address the audience. Her principal had become wise to Rosie's independent streak and previewed her remarks. I wasn't surprised. Her speech was an eloquent feminist manifesto.

A few days after commencement, Mom handed me an envelope. "You've got mail." I tore into it and unfolded the brief note.

> *Dear Asa,*
> *You had the highest grade point average of the 1938*
> *Robert E. Lee High School graduating class. I felt you*
> *deserved to know. I'm proud of you.*
> *Sincerely,*
> *Mrs. Evelyn Simms*

I had no regrets. On the contrary, I was thrilled Scott Jenkins received the recognition. He deserved it.

CHAPTER TWENTY-ONE
SPAGHETTI DINNER

After graduation my mind was free from my studies. It was a time of both pleasant and unpleasant introspective thought. I came to appreciate how differently Rosie viewed our relationship. For most young men, courting a bonafide debutant meant surprise flower bouquets, boxes of chocolates, restaurants, and movies—on top of those expenses, a boy's personal hygiene must be elevated a few notches. Not me, except for the hygiene aspect. Rosie, my bonafide deb, never set expectations. She insisted on paying her own way. My hand-picked cornflowers were better than two dozen long-stem roses. A bottle of RC Cola was as good as Champagne. A matinee and early bird special in East Bluff was a rare treat and always Dutch. Instead of blowing money, Rosie preferred spending time with Itchy and Shanks and hanging around the Paxton home, where Mom and Dad treated her like their own child.

With all the good, by no fault of her own, there was baggage that came with dating Rosie. When Farrington Willard Pickett betrothed, then married Katherine Inez Shelby, it was a match made in Jim Crow heaven. A power couple on the right side of laws that were inherently wrong. If the Pickett's debutante wasn't ready when I arrived for a date, our cordial small talk made me feel dirty, as if I were betraying my gandy dancer brethren. Add feeling like a pariah in my hometown and a stranger in East Bluff, I was of two minds filled with doubts. Doubts about what, I did not know.

The Sunday after graduation, Rosie and Mom make a spaghetti dinner for six, complete with warm garlic bread and salad. Mom and Dad wanted to celebrate us Misfit graduates. Until then, Itchy and Shanks were always welcome to join us for breakfast or lunch. However, a dinner invitation was never extended to the boys. That was reserved for Rosie. Mom and Dad were captivated by her intelligent and affable conversation.

As had become custom, Rosie said the dinner prayer. Tension hung over the table when Dad grabbed Shanks' hand to his left, and Mom took Itchy's at the other end of the table. Once the circle was complete, Rosie's thoughtful prayer assuaged the boys' discomfort. She concluded, as always, with, "We pray this circle be unbroken."

Shanks surveyed the bowl of pasta passed his way. "Huh. The noodles aren't stuck together like Mama's."

"Dory taught me that trick," Rosie said. "First, you stir the noodles regularly, especially when they first go into the boiling water. After you strain them, pour one ladle of sauce over the pasta and mix it in. The sauce keeps the noodles from sticking together."

The bowl of meat sauce was passed to Shanks. "Huh. There's no layer of grease on top of the sauce."

"That's because you brown the meat and strain off all the greasy fat before you add the tomato sauce," Rosie said.

"I can't wait to tell Mama."

"Don't you dare, Shane," Mom snapped. "Your mother would not like hearing you came to dinner and talked about her sticky noodles and greasy sauce."

"Yes, ma'am."

Dinner started off awkwardly. After a few minutes, Shanks told Mom and Dad a joke to break the ice. They laughed, and the comedy routine was on. The boys went back and forth, playing off each other's jokes, omitting or modifying the dirty ones. Mom and Dad were in stitches. Although Rosie and I had heard them all before, watching Mom and Dad laugh breathed new life into the act.

Dinner ended with the presentation of a chocolate cake Mom secretly bought at Buttermilk Bakery in East Bluff and hid in her bedroom. "Congratulations Graduates" scrolled across the middle in white icing with our names around the cake's outer edge.

After dinner, I took Rosie home earlier than usual. Parked in front of her house, I avoided eye contact. "Rosie, can I tell you something?"

"Of course. You can tell me anything."

"Sometimes I have strange feelings. I feel doubtful. I'm not sure why."

"I've sensed it. Are you having doubts about me? About us?"

"I don't think so. I'm always happiest when I'm with you. When we're apart, I only want to get back to you. Rosie, I don't feel like I belong here—here in this place. The South. I'm sick of all the hate."

"You just graduated from high school. Maybe your doubts are about the next stage of your life."

"Maybe."

"May I make a suggestion?"

"Go on."

"Let's just appreciate today's graduation celebration. We'll see what tomorrow brings."

"As you wish."

Rosie giggled, "Request permission to come aboard, captain."

"Welcome aboard."

Straddling me face to face, Rosie kissed me goodnight. Somehow, her kiss was different. There was something sexier and sultrier about it. Her lips and tongue felt softer and fuller than usual. Her breath was warmer and smelled sweeter than ever. Once our lips parted, she whispered, "Sleep well, my handsome captain. You need your rest."

I returned home to an envelope resting on my pillow. On the front, my name was written in cursive and underlined with an infinity symbol with two lines dashed in its midsection—a bow of sorts. Red candle wax sealed the backside. There was no stamp or return address. It had to be a graduation card, but I had already received a card from my grandparents stuffed with two silver dollar certificates. Uncle Clem wasn't the card-sending type and definitely wouldn't have used a wax seal. I couldn't think of anyone else. I removed the thick-fibrous note paper. *My handsome prince, please pick me up at one o'clock tomorrow for the afternoon. I want to take you somewhere special.* It was signed, *Forever Your Girl.* Rosie had snuck up to my bedroom during the day and left the envelope on my pillow.

CHAPTER TWENTY-TWO
WATERFALL

Rosie was standing on her porch when I arrived at one o'clock, frocked in a sleeveless linen square neck dress, loose from the hips down. Tight laces crisscrossed her midriff to the top of her cleavage and finished with a bowknot holding everything firmly in place. Her summer outfit was completed with a floppy-round hat, an oversized straw bag, and strappy leather flats. The large bag was unusual. A small-fashionable purse or clutch was her style. The tote landed on the back seat. An aluminum foil package and two RC Colas were visible at the top. "What's in the foil?"

"Addie's leftover fried chicken. She makes it for lunch every Saturday, along with collards and rice with white gravy. We might get hungry."

Rosie directed me onto the road out of East Bluff toward Corinth. After a mile or so of sparsely populated countryside, we turned onto a windy dirt road shaded by a thick canopy of hardwoods, ending abruptly on a cliff overlooking a peaceful lake. "Rosie, this place is amazing."

"Just you wait. Follow me."

We descended an overgrown trail along the lake's edge. At the bottom, a concrete dam restrained water below our feet on one side. On our other side, the steep dam wall bottomed out at a murky pool of stagnant, frothy water, a likely home to largemouth bass, water moccasins, and bullfrogs. "We're not there yet. Keep walking."

Across the dam, we picked up a narrow rolling path through stout mature trees and wiry sweetbay magnolias boasting their late-blooming flowers. After a hundred yards or so, the trees thinned, giving way to sunshine and the distant sound of rushing water. Rosie skipped ahead, rustling her hands through honeysuckle blossoms, releasing the flowers' sweet scent. Her perfumed fingers stroked her hair and caressed her face and neck.

At the end of our journey, I was treated to a place where both God and man had left their fingerprints. A twenty-five to thirty-foot crescent-moon-shaped dam filled the valley with water from what was once a swift creek, creating another finger of the double-dammed lake. Excess water from the reservoir spilled over the rim and splashed onto the curved structure's concrete anchor, forming a pool the size and shape of a baseball park's infield. Round fortifications at each end of the dam reached well above the lake. A natural flume of stone, worn smooth over the millennia, encircled the pond. Opposite the dam wall, the flume narrowed and sloped into a tree-lined stream babbling into the wooded distance.

A gentle cough grabbed my attention. Rosie's eyes locked into mine with a resolute gaze. Her fingers tugged at the bow knotted above her breast. She slowly loosened the laces. The dress fell to the ground, revealing her undergarmentless figure. Rosaleigh Elizabeth Pickett's naked body was more beautiful and awe-inspiring than the surroundings. Like an ethereal being, she gracefully backed into the sparkling pool. With water up to her neck, Rosie called to me. "Come join me. The water couldn't be more perfect. Not too warm, not too cold."

"Your note said nothing about swimming."

"Don't be shy. The water feels so much better when there's no swimsuit binding everything up." Rosie floated backward a few more feet. "It's too deep here for me to touch. Quickly, come hold me up."

Rosie didn't need me to hold her up. She had been swimming with me and the boys. She was a strong swimmer. I was reluctant to join her. I wanted to, badly, but I was becoming tumescent after seeing Rosie naked. Stripping down would make it evident. I turned my back to her, undressed quickly, and dove in, hoping cold water would tamp things down. Rosie was right. The water temperature was perfect, and swimming naked felt much better than bound up in swim trunks or a pair of cutoffs. The effect only increased my arousal. Where Rosie was treading

162

water, I could touch bottom, my head and shoulders above the surface. She wrapped her arms around my neck and pressed her body into mine.

"You're right," I said. "The temperature is perfect. I suppose it's the sun-warmed water at the top of the lake spilling over the dam. See how it's a thinner sheet in the middle. The center of the dam is higher than the sides." My nervous small talk felt awkward.

"I like to ride my bicycle here after a hard rain." Rosie inched her wet lips into mine, barely touching. "It's too dangerous to swim, but a spectacular show."

Next, she gently kissed my neck and worked her way up to my ear. "So much water gushes over the dam." She nibbled my earlobe as she spoke. "The sound is deafening. The deluge feels passionate and out of control."

She moved back to my face and gently bit my lower lip, then sucked it before releasing. Her eyes bore deep into mine. "That little stream opposite the dam becomes a torrent of raging rapids. It's the lake's only way of releasing its pent-up pleasure ... I mean pressure."

Rosie pushed away, swam to the thin sheet of water spilling over the dam's center, and pulled herself onto the footing. Her head disappeared into the air pocket between the waterfall and the dam wall. Water splashed over her shoulders, breasts, and thighs. Her face eventually re-emerged with a coquettish grin. Her right hand waved to me while her left hand patted the footing next to her. I couldn't refuse my seductive water nymph. Seated next to Rosie, she looked at my lap with a loving smile. I could feel warm blood rushing to my face. The rest of my blood had already filled the most instinctive part of my body. Rosie slid her hand into the crease at my hip, leaned into my ear, and whispered, "Don't be embarrassed. May I have that?" I nodded nervously, yielding to her advances.

Rosie straddled me, spat into her cupped palms, then tucked her hands under my chin. "Your turn."

I produced as much saliva as possible and added my share. She prepared herself with our spit before gently guiding our bodies together. Rosie's warm-soft torso moved rhythmically over mine while passionately kissing my neck, ears, face, and lips. Lake water splashed over my shoulders and back, exploding into sparkling droplets. The bright sunshine refracted the mist on the pool's surface, creating a rainbow of color. A gentle breeze laced with the sweet scent of honeysuckle added to the erotic sensations. It wasn't long before I lost control.

"Don't move," Rosie ordered. I couldn't move if I wanted to. My heart continued to pound, pushing blood through my veins while, at the same time, I felt weak and drained. Rosie repositioned slightly. She slid two fingers into her mouth, twisted out more saliva, then began to massage the sensitive flesh below her navel. Instinct overtook my inexperience. My lips went to her nipples. I clutched her locks with enough force to elicit an approving nod. Rosie found her rhythm. I felt myself returning to full strength inside of her. My mind became singularly focused—control myself so my girlfriend might reach the same climax I had experienced. After several minutes of grinding her body into mine, breathing heavily, her free arm wrapped around my neck. Her thighs tensed, and her knees tightened around my hips as the rest of her body shuddered before falling limp in my arms. I would soon learn; Rosie's climactic trembling was more than a physical release. She was closing one door while opening another.

Once her labored breathing ceased, Rosie fell backward into the water, allowing the current to carry her back to the middle of the pool. "Asa, please," she called out. "Come, hold me up again." Something was on her mind. Something was not right. I could see trouble in her eyes. I swam to her and lifted her into my arms. Rosie's hands cradled my face. "I want to tell you something ... something I'm not obligated to share."

"I don't understand what you're saying." Had she been hiding something from me since we first met?

Rosie bit the edge of her lip, then spoke. "You remember the first time we kissed? I told you it was my first."

"Go on." I was expecting her to tell me she had lied.

"It really was my first kiss." She swallowed hard. "You would probably think what we just did was also my first time." Rosie's jaw began to tremble. "It wasn't. I'm not a virgin."

Shocked, words were difficult to find. "I'm confused, Rosie. I'm not sure what I'm supposed to think or say. I don't understand."

She gasped for air and looked away. "Goddammit. I practiced telling you over and over so I wouldn't cry." Her shaky voice and erratic breathing were like a frightened child. "When I was twelve, almost thirteen, my father's older brother, Uncle Oakley, started raping me. It was so scary. I'm scared now, telling you."

"Started raping you? Oh god."

Attempting to speak, Rosie retched before choking out, "I was afraid you would feel that way. I understand if you don't want me any—."

I interrupted her with my lips in a long, tender kiss. Rosie squeezed her arms around my neck so tightly it hurt. She whispered through her tears, "I was hoping you would see it that way. You're the best friend I've always wanted, always needed."

"You said, 'started raping you.' I'm so sorry. How long did it go on?"

"Are you sure you want details?"

"I'm your best friend, aren't I?"

"You can tell me to stop if it's too much."

"I'm okay."

"My father was up for re-election at the same time my uncle ran out of money after the stock market crash. He came and stayed with us. My parents thought it was a good situation. Uncle Oakley would look after me while Mother and Father campaigned together, nights and weekends." Rosie stopped to take several deep breaths. "It went on for months after my thirteenth birthday. Most times, he was sober. Other times, he was drunk. I'll never get over the nasty smell of cigarette smoke or chewing tobacco and alcohol on his breath. His salty sweat dripped all over me." Rosie shivered. "After each time, drunk or sober, he would threaten me. If I told anyone, he would take me into the woods, kill me in the most awful way, then kill himself. Imagine a heavy hand over your mouth so you can't call out, can't scream. It hurt. It always hurt when he did it."

Her words landed in the pit of my stomach. Rosie sensed I was shaken. Her instinct to comfort me took over. She brushed my hair to the side and kissed me tenderly. "Asa, I want you to know this. If you couldn't tell, making love to you felt really good for my body. It also felt right. Right for my heart. I'm going to want to do it more. A lot more."

"I'm okay. You can go on."

"When I finally got up the nerve to tell Mother, she made it sound like it was my fault. She said I should act and dress more like my sister.

Told me it wasn't ladylike to talk about such things. I went to Father, hoping he would help. He said his brother would never do such a thing. They were so wrapped up in their ambitions they didn't want to face the truth. And just like always, they dismissed me."

I couldn't believe what I was hearing. Rosie had hidden her pain so well. "Now I understand why you're always curt with your parents."

"When I turned up pregnant, they couldn't ignore me anymore. Father finally ran Uncle Oakley off. My parents sent me to what they called a spa. 'To take care of things' is how they put it. The goddamned doctor tore me up inside. Afterward, I was so sick. I missed half the school year with delirium. Mother told the school I had pneumonia. I'm lucky to be alive. Mother warned me if word ever got out, I'd never have a bona fide suitor."

Rosie looked exhausted after her testimony. "I don't know what to say or do. I feel like the only thing I can do is be a good listener when you need to talk."

"You're the only person I've told. I doubt I'll ever tell anyone else. This place is my escape. I've never seen anyone here. When my mind goes to the dark place, I come here to scream at the top of my lungs or cry until I'm too weak to shed any more tears. The water spilling over the dam and the stream fading into the woods carries my pain away. At least for a time. Please don't bring Itchy and Shanks here to swim, and please, please don't tell anyone what happened to me."

"I won't. I promise. Baby, I want you to listen to me. This is important. No matter what your mother says, don't ever think it was your fault. And you don't need any other suitors. You've got me."

"Thank you. Now, let's go eat and talk about something else. There's nothing better for a picnic than Addie's leftover fried chicken." We sat on a blanket wrapped in towels and dug into Addie's cooking.

"When Addie was hired three years ago, I instantly connected with her. Before she came along, Mother couldn't keep good help. She was too difficult. Mother wasn't too difficult for Addie, though. She is a master manipulator when it comes to Mother's peccadilloes and contrary personality." Rosie paused for a bite of chicken. She kissed her greasy fingertips as she chewed.

"My god, you're an amazing woman," spilled out of me from a place

I didn't know existed. I felt embarrassed at first. Her shoulders relaxed. With a full mouth and fingers on her lips, she inhaled deeply and exhaled emphatically through her nose. Her delicate smile and sparkle in her eyes said she was relieved and moved by the turn in our relationship. She released me from her loving gaze, pressed the soda bottle to her lips for a sip, then continued her story. "I keep my bedroom and bathroom spotless. There's never anything for Addie to clean. When working upstairs, she pretends to clean my bedroom. Instead, she closes the door and reads a few pages of whatever I've checked out of the library. If any strike her fancy, I'd find them on my pillows." Rosie winked, "The book magically finds its way to her bag before the end of the day. It's become game-like. I told Martha about Addie. She recommends books she thinks Addie might like. Who knows if other Negroes have secret library cards with Martha."

Rosie went on to describe Addie's wit. "She's got a tongue so sharp when she uses it on Mother, an Ole Miss graduate, Mother's too dumb to know she'd been cut. Of course, Addie knows better than to try those shenanigans on legally trained Father."

After lunch and a caffeine-sugar boost from the RC Cola, one thing led to another. We made love on the picnic blanket. Afterward, we were back to frolicking in the pool. The afternoon carried on. The sun ducked behind the distant cliffs. Rosie swam to me one last time, wrapped her legs around my waist, and crossed her wrists behind my neck. With our faces inches apart, she said it. "Asa Alan Paxton, I love you."

I carried her to the blanket, and we made love a third time. Exhausted, we rested in each other's arms. The grind of cicada song lulled Rosie to sleep before I drifted off. I woke to sniffles and tears on my chest. "Why are you crying? Did I do something wrong?"

"No. Not at all. You've done everything right. They're happy tears. I thought I would never want to be with a man after what my uncle and doctor did to me. There were only three people in this world I trusted— Addie, Martha from the library, and her housemate, Julia. That all changed the day I met you. I felt safe with you. I laid in bed that first night we met, hoping this day would come."

"I can't think of anything more painful than what you went through. How have you been able to cope?" My question hung in the air. Her eyes said she had an answer but couldn't decide if she should share it. I let it go.

Rosie moved on from my question. "I feel like I've been baptized and born again after making love to you under the waterfall." She took me by surprise, bursting into laughter. "I can only imagine what self-righteous Christians would say about me being baptized and born again while fornicating."

Once I settled into bed, I should have drifted off to sleep in a euphoric state. Instead, a good night's sleep was impossible after hearing Rosie's painful testimony. Her young age and the brutality with which she lost her virginity were haunting. She had been terrorized by a sexual predator in the next room—no thanks to the parents God entrusted to keep her safe. And yet, she beautifully choreographed my first sexual experience. I had been, by one measure, ushered into manhood by Rosie's capable hands and body. Hours of angry thoughts twisted knots in my head, first causing a numbness, followed by a dull ache, and finally, a tense pinch at the nape of my neck.

Relief came from an old friend outside my window. As if the natural world sensed my torment, a male great horned owl alighted on the peak of the pole barn roof. His majestic form perched in the glow of a gently ascending full moon. Every fall and winter, he came and faced the woods behind our property and called his mate with his signature hoot. She kept hidden in the thicket and replied with screeches, inviting him to commence their annual mating. I'd never seen or heard the owls during the summer months. When the female joined the male on the roof, my mind was shaken free of negativity. The wise birds perched and stared at me for the longest time. They eventually took flight and went out of their way to fly straight toward my window. At the last second, they turned and headed back into the dense woods. I took their visit as a sign I should appreciate the here and now. To settle my uneasy feelings, I decided to use the sage words Rosie spoke the day before when I had described my unsettled feelings. "We'll see what tomorrow brings."

CHAPTER TWENTY-THREE
INTEROSCULATION

After graduation, our family developed a new routine. Before work, I picked Rosie up and brought her to the house. Mom and Rosie spent mornings doing whatever women did while Dad and I went to work. TVA projects had made the switchyard busier than ever. Dad convinced Robinson he needed a part-time gofer on the payroll. Of course, I got the job along with more responsibility. I'll never forget the feeling of my first paycheck—Northern Trust, proudly embossed across the top, and, Pay to the Order of—Asa A. Paxton handwritten and signed by Robinson's payroll clerk. I slept with it under my pillow the first night. The next day, Rosie and I headed to the Bank of East Bluff to open an account. Her father kept his money there, so she trusted the bank with the cash she earned cleaning Martha and Julia's house. "Baby, are you coming in?" I asked.

Rosie grimaced. "The manager will have to open your account. I don't want to see him."

"Oh, sweetheart. I'm sorry. I didn't think about that."

"It's okay. I asked to come with you to see the check and your face. You're beaming. I'm so proud of you. Maybe one day I'll have a real job and receive a proper paycheck rather than cookie jar money."

Inside the bank, the security guard directed me to the manager's open-door office. A suited man with slicked-back hair and a waxed mustache sat behind a heavy oak desk. "I'd like to open a passbook account," I said from the doorway.

"Well, come on in and have a seat." The manager was a little too smiley for my liking. "I'm Thomas Chelmsford. Branch manager."

"I know who you are. I'd rather stand."

"Excuse me, son?"

"You heard me. Rosaleigh Pickett told me all about you. You're lucky she didn't tell the Solicitor about your advances."

Chelmsford fumbled with some papers. Scribbled on two of them. His hand trembled as he gave them to me. "Here. Sign these and take them to the teller. The office door slammed behind me.

Like previous summers, I worked from eight in the morning until noon. After a shower and lunch, Rosie and I spent the rest of the day living our best life, alone, in blissful love or looking for trouble with Itchy and Shanks. Like clockwork, dinner was on the table at six. Rosie always said the prayer. After Rosie's insightful prayer, an insightful conversation ensued. The empty dinner plates frequently sat in front of us for an hour or so. Every evening after dinner, we all digested in the living room, playing chess, reading, or listening to the radio.

On one rare occasion when Rosie didn't stay for dinner, Mom asked a question. The inflection in her voice and Dad's attentive demeanor told me they had rehearsed the query. "Asa, don't you think it's odd Rosie spends so much time here? I wonder what her parents think?"

"You've gotten to know Rosie well enough. She's more like us than her own family. They sit around the dinner table and discuss things like the Daughters of the Confederacy's latest schoolbook approvals or Farrington's prosecution of an uppity niggra. Rosie says she hates being around all that talk."

"Asa. Don't use that term, even if you're only criticizing Mister Pickett's language."

"Yes, ma'am."

"Hank," Mom prodded.

"Son. We love having Rosie around. She's always welcome. Although, we worry about causing strife in her home." If Mom and Dad knew what Rosie's uncle did to her and how Farrington and

170

Katherine handled it, they wouldn't have worried about causing strife. They would have tried to adopt Rosie or send her north to live with Grandma and Grandpa.

The best part of the summer of 1938 was Rosie's and my explorations of each other's bodies. She had been liberated from her uncle's abuse. I was her willing accomplice. We made love in the pole barn, dam, and bamboo forest where we first kissed. The Citroen was our mobile venue. The T3-2 Trefle model's single-centered rear seat provided what Rosie cleverly described as "perfect interosculation."

By mid-summer, I had earned Dad's confidence to leave me in charge of the switchyard for two weeks while he and Mom went to Chicago for the first time since our move to Alabama. Cash was set aside to pay Itchy if I needed an extra hand. Uncle Clem wasn't far away in case of an emergency. Rosie and I made the most of the privacy. We made love in the shower, on the stairs, in my room, in the guest room, and on the couch. The only corner of the house we didn't defile was Mom and Dad's room. The switchyard office was not immune to our passion.

"Hobo lovers," Rosie called us after making love in an empty boxcar. The idling vibrations in the cab of the switchyard's diesel locomotive made short work of Rosie's amorous cravings. We flat wore each other out.

Once, while making love, Uncle Clem's words from way back in January 1933 surfaced from the deepest depths of my psyche. "I walked in on Drumpf banging his secretary Vulva." After all those years, it made sense. I couldn't help but laugh, interrupting Rosie's gyrating on top of me.

"What is it? What the hell are you laughing about? And why now?"

I tried, unsuccessfully, to explain what Uncle Clem said years earlier and how until just then, I didn't understand what he meant by banging. "It's not very funny to me. I was almost there. Now the mood is broken. Ugh. Thanks for nothing, Clem Paxton."

Uncle Clem may have ruined the moment, however, it caused me to evaluate my view of our sexual relationship. Uncle Clem's term "banging" evoked a steel spike hammered into a rail plate and wooden railroad tie on a bed of crushed granite—cold, stiff, and lifeless. Our sexual relationship was more complicated. Sometimes, it was tender lovemaking and emotional with joyful tears. Other times, playful. We could be opportunistic. It was always passionate in one way or another. I resolved to never cause Rosie to feel like she was being "banged." She deserved better after what her uncle did to her.

In between making love, we played house. Rosie had a candlelit dinner ready when I arrived home from a full day's work. After dinner, she introduced me to romantic French music like Erik Satie's innovative "Gnossiennes" and she taught me to dance. We read poetry and passages from books borrowed from the library. If Rosie had her way, she would have slept over every night during the two weeks Mom and Dad were gone. That was a line I wasn't ready to cross with Solicitor Farrington Pickett. I always had Rosie home by nine o'clock and insisted on keeping the streak alive.

CHAPTER TWENTY-FOUR
HAPPY BIRTHDAY

D ad's track maintenance work order he put in for the end of August happened to coincide with my eighteenth birthday. Rosie was over the moon with the excitement of meeting Uncle Clem, our adopted gandy dancer family, and the birthday party she and Mom planned for the Sunday afternoon the crew was scheduled to arrive. The backyard was prepped as usual for the crew's sleeping quarters with the festive addition of ribbons, balloons, and the phonograph mounted on the kitchen windowsill.

Dad began slow-cooking four whole chickens and two pork butts early in the morning on the grill he and I had made out of an empty steel barrel from the switchyard. We cut the drum in half and added hinges, a handle, and a wood-chip box.

Mom had prepared a big batch of mac-n-cheese the night before. She spent the mid-afternoon with Perry Mason's *The Case of the Shoplifter's Shoe,* held open under her elbow while shelling fresh peas. Rosie was charged with assembling a large platter of sliced cucumbers and garden tomatoes. She worked at the dining room table while playing Hearts with me, Itchy, and Shanks. She was a master multitasker and even took every heart and the queen of spades one hand, extending her lead significantly. The girl could count some cards.

Around four o'clock, Uncle Clem stormed through the kitchen door with half of his crew in tow and declared loudly, "Dory, I'm so hungry I could eat the ass out of a skunk." Causing Rosie to burst into laughter.

"Why Clem? Why?" Sam wailed.

"Clem, the girl. The girl, for Pete's sake," Mom shouted.

"What girl?" Clem asked.

Rosie leaped from her chair and ran into the kitchen, wrapping her arms around Uncle Clem and burying her head in his chest.

"Who are you, pretty gal?"

Rosie stumbled backward. "I'm Asa's girlfriend. Speaking of a skunk's ass, you smell like one." Everyone had a good laugh at Uncle Clem's expense. Even Mom giggled a little.

"What do you expect? We've been working in the August heat for a week without a shower."

"I see you're a hugger. I'm too sweaty for a hug," Sam said.

Uncle Clem asked, "You got a girl, Asa?"

"Yes, sir. Her name is Rosie."

"Well damn, boy. Ain't you about as smooth as a gravy sandwich?"

"I'm standing right here, boys," Rosie complained. "Don't act like I'm not."

Uncle Clem smiled from ear to ear. "Pretty gal, I like you already."

I immediately started making introductions to keep Uncle Clem from further ruining Rosie's first impression.

"I've heard so much about y'all. But where's the rest?" Rosie asked. "Where's Tiny and the twins?"

"They're getting cleaned up at the switchyard office," said Uncle Clem.

"Dory, may I use the downstairs tub?" Sam asked.

"Of course. Make yourself at home," Mom told Sam.

One by one, the crew emerged, clean, refreshed, and ready to visit with my girlfriend. I kept my distance to avoid being a distraction. Although I couldn't hear their conversations, it was evident by the facial expressions of the crew, they were delighted by Rosie, and vice versa. "*Hesci*," Rosie yelled across the backyard when the twins approached after bathing at the switchyard.

"*Hesci*," the twins yelled back as they upped their pace to greet her. They wore uncharacteristic smiles. I could see from a distance Rosie was attempting to speak Muskogee. The twins obviously understood her well enough to correct her several times. Eventually, Rosie gave up with a pirouette and a stomp of her foot. The three of them had a good laugh and started what appeared to be a pleasant conversation in English. It was so unusual to see the twins casually converse with someone.

I could only imagine what Rosie said to Mack. Standing inches before him, she pressed the three vitiligo dots on his face with her finger before gently tracing the lines separating light skin from dark across his nose and cheeks. When she finished, Mack kissed her gently on the cheek. A deadly sin in Alabama.

Rosie had a way about her. She made no attempt at pretense or Southern social graces and niceties if she felt strongly about a matter. She could be as firm and straightforward as she was with Miz Nadine at the Rexall Drugs soda fountain and Lucy and Chip at the Piggly Wiggly. Rosie could also make anyone drop their guard and fall in love with her almost instantly, with her unabashed sincerity. I suppose that's how it went with Mack.

When the crew was in town, dinner was typically spread out in small groups around the property. Rosie was having none of it. She insisted we all eat together. The backyard was one large circle of humanity. Rosie asked for Dad's approval to say an invocation and for Preacher to say the prayer. Of course, Dad agreed. Rosie might as well have been his own daughter the way she had him wrapped around her little finger.

As I expected, there was a brief hesitation when Rosie asked everyone to join hands. Those of us who had experienced dining with Rosie, led by example. Preacher prayed first, giving thanks for the bounty, the gathering, and the gift of my life. His prayer ended "in the name of Jesus." Rosie followed Preacher with her invocation. It was unlike any other time she prayed before dinner. Rosie called upon the Great Spirit of the original people to join our gathering in celebration of my life. She ended speaking in the Muskogee language. I didn't know what the words meant or where she learned them, but when I opened my eyes and looked up, both twins were wiping tears away. Rosie later told me it was an excerpt from an ancient Indian proverb about the circle of life. Rosie's effort to recognize the twins' humanity likely caused the tears rather than the actual words in the invocation.

My birthday party was a tremendous success. Dad's chickens and pork butts were smokey and drenched in a tangy barbecue sauce Uncle Clem bought at a joint called The Pokey Pit in a small prison town near

Tuscaloosa. He also brought two jugs of buttery smooth whiskey called Uncle Perlie's Mash-Up, purchased in a Negro enclave outside of Lynchburg, Tennessee. One jug was a birthday gift for me. That Uncle Perlie fella sure had mastered the art of distilling corn mash. Shanks and Itchy came with a big appetite. Sheriff Taylor and Miz Gay Lynn brought two homemade lemon-blueberry cakes with the number eighteen dotted out on top in whole blueberries.

Between Uncle Clem running his loud mouth, Itchy and Shanks holding comedy court, and Rosie spinning flapper music she checked out of the library, dinner felt more like a festival than a birthday party. Creamy-sweet lemon blueberry cake chased with buttery whiskey was the perfect end to a perfect birthday party. I wanted the good time to last forever.

CHAPTER TWENTY-FIVE
$\mathcal{H}$ELPLESS, $\mathcal{H}$OPELESS

Rosie climbed into the Citroen. There was no kiss. She leaned against the closed door instead of her usual spot; as close to me as possible. She had called me twenty minutes earlier in a panic, asking me to come and get her. She needed to talk but couldn't on the telephone. Her voice trembled, "They lynched a Negro man near Tupelo. I overheard Mother and Father talking about it with the Jacksons. They're in the parlor playing dominoes and carrying on."

Rosie's words shook me. It was the closest I'd come to the terrorism of the Deep South. "What do you mean they lynched a Negro? Who are the Jacksons?"

"Mister Jackson is the Lee County Solicitor. He said a mob got a tip about a white woman and a Negro man. They found her in the Negro's bed at his farm on the outskirts of town last Sunday morning." Rosie paused for a deep breath. "They hung him from a tree in his front yard. Cut his genitals off and stuffed them in his mouth."

"Good lord."

"They shaved the woman's head in front of First Baptist Church a few minutes before the eleven o'clock service." Rosie took another deep breath. "The woman ran off on the next freight train headed toward New Orleans. Mister Jackson and Father had a good laugh over the details. Mister Jackson said the mob cost him a miscegenation show trial."

"They joked about it in front of their wives? It sounds so sadistic."

"Of course they joked about it. Mother and Miz Jackson feigned disgust over talk of genitals but agreed the woman got what she deserved."

"We have to get you out of that house. It's not good for you there."

Rosie whimpered, "I feel trapped, Asa. Trapped in my own home."

"We could get married?"

"Don't be ridiculous," Rosie snapped. "Then we'll both feel trapped."

"Maybe you should go to Ole Miss and live at the sorority your sister was in. It would make your parents happy. We could see each other on weekends."

Rosie once told me about her dream of attending Wellesley College in Massachusetts. Her friend Martha and housemate Julia met at Wellesley. They told Rosie all about the prestigious Women's College. They inspired her with stories of rigorous studies and the annual Wellesley Women's March—the student body dressed in all white commemorating women's suffrage. Farrington and Katherine scoffed at Rosie's ambition. The only school they would pay for was Ole Miss. Her mother insisted she receive a bid from Chi Omega and an engagement before she graduated. Rosie's grandmother was the Chi Omega chapter president back in the day. Katherine felt cheated out of her legacy after they closed down the sorority in 1912. Katherine was instrumental in re-establishing the sorority in 1926 and couldn't have been more proud when Rosie's older sister Vernell received her Chi Omega bid.

"Asa, really? Can you imagine me in a sorority?"

I couldn't. All I knew about sorority life was what Rosie told me about Chi Omega, her grandmother's legacy, and her mother's disappointment when the sorority shut down. "It seems better than the hell you're living in right now."

"I'd rather have my head shaved in front of First Baptist Church and shipped off to New Orleans." That was the end of the conversation—the closest we had come to an argument. I drove to a dead-end road overlooking the river. We sat in a helpless, hopeless stupor for at least an hour, Rosie's head on my chest with my arm around her shoulder.

CHAPTER TWENTY-SIX
JUG FISHING

By September 1938, the complexion of the Tennessee River and Blue Rock had transformed dramatically. Tennessee River's new dam near the tri-state border of Alabama, Mississippi, and Tennessee increased the river's depth to ten fathoms in spots. The Lynchin' Tree swing, one of our favorite swimming holes, was swallowed up by the river. An exhilarating fifteen-foot dive from Shoals Creek Bridge was reduced to a dull flop into the water. Shoals Creek's egrets and herons that once plodded along the rocks and water lilies in search of a meal would have to migrate farther upstream for shallow hunting grounds.

With the dam's completion came apprehension about the economic future of the Tennessee Valley. Dirt farmers, having accepted the TVA scientists' best practices, would continue to thrive. Men with electrical or mechanical engineering skills had job security. There was always work for a crafty grease monkey. The general laborers who bent and tied rebar, nailed wooden molds together, and poured concrete were rapidly losing their jobs.

Fortunately for Itchy, his parents made the most of the good times. They mimicked the Paxton model of making do with less and investing for the future. A chicken coop for hens and eggs ensured a healthy breakfast each morning. Their vegetable garden turned over with each season for maximum production of spring, summer, and winter vegetables. Unfortunately, Itchy had a severe outbreak of what Doc Martin called eczema. No amount of expensive balm could help him. Poor kid went untreated.

Shanks was less fortunate. His father and one-legged grandfather spent every penny they could sneak away from Shanks' mother on shine and the prostitutes who worked the TVA job sites. Between me, Itchy, and Rosie, we made sure Shanks was fed.

The second Saturday of September, I was charged with catching as many catfish as possible to feed Uncle Clem and his crew scheduled to arrive the following day. During Mom and Dad's summer visit to Chicago, they explored the new Chinatown district and brought back a tub of Asian sauce. Sweet, salty, and tangy, the Far East fare was delicious paired with meat or vegetables and served over rice. The distinct muddy flavor of catfish didn't have a chance against The Kingdom of Cheng Han sauce. Mom was excited to serve something not typically found in the South or anywhere other than big-city Chinatowns.

Rosie and I invited Itchy and Shanks to spend the afternoon swimming before fishing for channel catfish. Jug fishing with rancid raw chicken and turkey pluck was the most efficient way to load up on catfish. I knew just the honey hole. Before the dam was built, Jemison Creek was shallow, rocky, and fed into the Tennessee River between the base of two steep hillsides. Once the dam was completed, river water backed into the creek, creating a deep and ideal channel cat habitat. The water at the narrow confluence swirled, keeping the buoyed fishing jugs from floating into the river.

"I've got Addie's pimento cheese sandwiches for a picnic," Rosie said, shaking a paper sack in front of Itchy and Shanks.

"Hot damn," Shanks said. I doubted he'd eaten breakfast or lunch.

"I'm going to get changed." Rosie disappeared into our downstairs bathroom.

"Y'all help me collect Drumpf's bourbon jugs from the basement." With six hands, it took one trip from the basement to the Citroen. Itchy ended up buried under the jugs in the back seat. I sent Shanks to the pole barn to retrieve fishing line, cotton rope for stringing up the catch, needle-nose pliers, and leather gloves for protection from a cat's nasty dorsal and pectoral fin sting. I retrieved the two mason jars of bait from the icebox.

"Bring back whatever you don't use," Mom said. "Make sure you seal the jar tightly and rinse it in the river. I don't want to smell a hint of that nastiness when you get home."

"Yes, ma'am."

"And Asa ... good luck."

Other than when Rosie and I skinny-dipped in private, Rosie always wore one of her fashionable yet modest bathing suits and a loose coverup to the swimming holes. Not that day. She emerged from the bathroom barefoot and braless, in denim-cutoff shorts and a thin, tight-fitting sleeveless T-shirt. Her hair was pulled back in a ponytail, which had the effect of accentuating everything from the neck down. Mom was no prude, but she winced at the voluptuous sight. She buried her face in her novel, ignoring Rosie's naive exhibition. Mom would have said something about her attire, not to judge but to protect Rosie's reputation. However, Mom knew Rosie didn't care what people thought or said about her. A characteristic my parents admired.

"Have fun," Mom said without looking up. Itchy and Shanks looked like the cat that ate the canary as Rosie approached the car.

We stopped at Smalley's for chocolate bars and RC Colas for the picnic. Rosie bought a bag of peanuts to tide Shanks over. I'd never seen him shell peanuts so fast. Poor fella.

We arrived by the trailhead at the end of the secluded road. Rosie and I gave each other the familiar glance. We were hotter than the mid-day sun. "Y'all take what you can carry on down to the water," I instructed. "We'll carry the rest down in a little while."

Clueless, Shanks asked, "Y'all ain't comin' right now?"

Rosie handed Shanks the sack of sandwiches and the goodies from Smalley's. "You boys, go ahead and start eating."

Itchy shot me a look of anger, disgust, and disappointment wrapped up in one nasty glare. "Come on, Shanks," Itchy ordered.

By the time Rosie and I were through scratching each other's itch, our T-shirts were soaked through with lover's sweat. Rosie's ponytail had come loose. Her hair was teased into a hopeless mess from my hands and the humidity. At the swimming hole, Itchy and Shanks were seated facing each other, talking on a large flat rock at the water's edge. They immediately broke off their conversation. Itchy turned his back to us. Shanks rolled sideways into the deep water.

"Did y'all eat?" Rosie asked.

Itchy ignored her. Shanks submerged his head. I was peeved they disrespected my girlfriend. "What's gotten into y'all?"

Itchy pointed to our provisions a few feet away. "Naw, we ain't ate yet."

"What's wrong with you, Itchy?" I asked.

Itchy stood up and turned to face Rosie and me. Shanks broke through the water by the bank below Itchy's feet. "What's wrong with me? What's wrong with you two?"

I was momentarily taken aback by his tone. "Oh, I see what's going on here. For crying out loud, you're jealous. Rosie, can you believe this?"

Rosie's face revealed her shame. She quickly internalized how Itchy and Shanks felt after we ran them off in order to get each other off. Rosie's lips trembled as she wiped away the tears forming in her eyes."I'm sorry, Richard. I'm sorry, Shane."

"What the hell, Rosie." I wasn't asking a question.

"We ain't jealous," Itchy shouted. "It ain't right for you to invite us to go swimming and fishing, then when we get here, you run us off like you're at the dinner table, and we're no better than a couple of dogs."

"I can't believe this. If the shoe was on the other foot, would I be bellyaching? I'd be happy for you."

"Asa, the shoe ain't ever gonna be on the other foot," Itchy shot back. "That's the point. I ... we're happy for y'all. It's nice to see y'all kiss each other hey and bye and when y'all hold hands. We're even happy knowing y'all get to do, you know what when we ain't around, but not like this. Not when we had plans together."

"This is ridiculous."

Rosie squeezed my hand and whispered, "Asa, stop."

Itchy wasn't finished. "Asa, you think you're like Shanks and me—a misfit. You ain't. All the kids in Blue Rock don't hate Shanks and me. They pity us. They don't want any part of us. As for you and Rosie, they envy y'all. The beautiful couple. The smart couple. The Negro-lovers with no big trouble. Look at me with my leper skin. Look at Shanks with his ... um .... just look at him. The shoe ain't ever going to be on the other foot."

Tears were streaming down Rosie's face. Shanks didn't say a word. He didn't need to.

"Y'all are just feeling sorry for yourselves."

Rosie snatched her hand away from mine. "Asa! Stop! Just stop, god-damn it! Take a hike and think about how you are treating your friends. Think about what kind of man you want to be. I don't want to be around you right now. I'm sorry y'all. Sorry for my part," Rosie sobbed, burying her face in Itchy's chest.

I grudgingly took the walk Rosie ordered. Back at the car, I laid across the front seats and stared at the sky. It took a few minutes for me to accept Rosie and my behavior was a dark cloud on what should have been a sunny day. After a few more minutes, I admitted I only made matters worse. It took longer to gain the courage to rejoin the group after my heartless response to Itchy's and Shanks' feelings. Rosie, not wanting to be around me, was the deep cut I needed to get my head straight. After a half-hour or so of rehearsing what I would say, how I would apologize, I headed back expecting a frosty reception. I found Shanks floating effortlessly on his back in the water. Rosie was kneeling at the water's edge next to a small mound of mud she had mixed up. Itchy laid shirtless on his back next to Rosie's knees. She gently dabbed mud on his lesions. When Rosie saw me, she leaped to her feet, ran over, and wrapped her arms around me. Having been forgiven so quickly, my shocked heart pounded. Itchy got to his feet and wrapped his muddy body around Rosie and me. I forgot everything I was going to say in my apology. "I'm so ashamed. I'm so sorry."

Shanks yelled from the water. "I ain't coming up there. You can't make me. You're forgiven." The way Shanks said it made us laugh, breaking the tension and the group hug.

"Asa, you should eat," Rosie said. "Addie's pimento cheese is good for a wounded heart. Helped me, Itchy, and Shanks feel better." Rosie was right. Addie's sandwich was like a salve on my self-inflicted wound. A dip in the water after eating helped wash away my guilt.

Rosie continued to work on Itchy's skin. Shanks toyed with me in the water, dunking and splashing my face. Fighting back was futile against the boy with feet and hands like flippers.

Once Rosie covered all of Itchy's lesions, she called Shanks to the water's edge. "I want to tell you two something. What Itchy said earlier is true. Asa and I are fortunate, but it doesn't mean we are any better than you boys. In fact, you two are better people than all the low-down folks making up this hateful place. Y'all may feel like the shoe will never be on the other foot. I don't believe it. Not for one minute. Y'all are too sweet, too honorable. God won't forsake you." The boys hung on Rosie's every word.

"I once felt like you. Like I was wandering in the desert, destined to be alone. When I least expected it, God presented Asa in the most un-expected way—wrangling a greased pig. Not only did God give me Asa, God also gave me you two. Be patient. Good things come to those who are patient." Once Rosie finished her pep talk, she kissed Itchy on the forehead, leaned over the water's edge, kissed Shanks, and dove in and swam to me.

The afternoon carried on. The September sun hung low over the west-end curve of the Tennessee River, casting long autumn shadows. Cicadas began to sing louder. Crappie and bream began to jump. The cats would be ready to eat. "We gonna do this, Asa?" Shanks called out. "These fish ain't gonna catch themselves."

"Let's do it."

Rosie watched intently as the boys and I worked purposefully, tying hooks to fishing lines and feeding them through the finger holes of the corked bourbon jugs. "How can I help?" Rosie asked.

The boys both looked at me with devilish eyes. "The bait," they said.

"Can you pop the top off of those two mason jars?" I asked.

Rosie retrieved a jar of aged-brown chicken and turkey organs, twisted off the outer ring, and popped the flat metal seal off the glass with her thumbs. Her head snapped back. Her cheeks drew in. She tried to speak. "Oh, ewe, I ca—I can't. Dear god," she choked out before drop-ping the jar in the dirt and running to the nearest bush. Throwing up pimento cheese is almost as arduous as throwing up peanut butter—a slow process.

Once Rosie finished upchucking, she couldn't help but laugh at herself. The back of her hand wiped her mouth. A string of pimen-to-cheese-colored saliva dangled from her chin. Rosie winked at Itchy and Shanks before looking straight at me and teased in a British accent, "How's about a kiss, love?" Rosie had us boys in tears.

The empty bourbon jugs went into the water. In no time, the cats started hitting fast and furiously. We could hardly keep up. Itchy and Shanks chased the buoyed lines and delivered them to me on the shore. As quickly as I unhooked one fish and re-baited, the boys returned with another catch. All the action delighted Rosie, however, she kept her distance from the bait. Once it was all over, we had enough fish to feed an army. At the end of the afternoon, we all were physically and emotionally exhausted. I wish I had known it would be the last time the four of us would be together in our favorite place—a swimming hole. I might not have treated my friends so poorly.

CHAPTER TWENTY-SEVEN
IGBOLAND

Rosie's Mary Janes stepped onto my work boots. With a sparkle in her eyes and her pinky fingernail dug into her teeth, she made a request. "Asa, promise you'll say yes."

"What is it?"

"Addie wants to meet you. We've been invited to Igboland's annual harvest feast this Saturday."

"Addie? Your maid?"

"I don't like to think of her as only our maid. She's my friend, too."

"OK. I'll bite. What's Igboland?"

"It's her neighborhood. It's what she, maybe everyone living there calls the neighborhood. The name comes from the area of Africa where their people came—where they were taken from. I've never been that far over the tracks. The closest I've come is when I clean Martha and Julia's house."

"What? Martha lives on the other side of the tracks?"

"Just over the tracks. They live at the end of a side road overlooking the river. They don't say they live in Igboland. They call their property Hermitage."

"Hermitage?"

"It's French. Never mind all that. What about Saturday?"

"Tell Addie we'd be honored."

Rosie squealed, crossed her wrists behind my neck, and planted a wet one. "Don't dress up. I don't know what people will be wearing. We don't want to show anyone up."

"I understand."

The first Saturday of October was one of those glorious autumn days in the South. September had beaten back summer's oppressive heat and humidity, ushering in crisp, cool nights and softly warm October days— perfect weather for the Igboland harvest celebration. Chores took up my Saturday morning. Rosie's morning was taken up with cleaning Martha and Julia's house. The women of Igboland's mornings were taken up by East Bluff's unofficial standard of working, "only" a half-day at the homes of white folks. Much of the celebration details were left to the Igboland men.

"We need to make a couple of stops along the way," Rosie said when I picked her up.

"Yes, ma'am. Where to first?"

"Rexall Drug."

Rosie was in the store less than five minutes and returned with a sack of candy and chocolates. "Next stop, Willy's Smitty Shoppe. Circle around Pillow's monument and follow Jefferson Davis out of downtown. Willy's is the big red barn on the right."

After once again getting jammed up at the United Daughters of the Confederacy's monumental traffic obstacle, I followed Rosie's directions to the blacksmith's shop. Below the pitched roofline, a forged sign read, Willy's Smitty Shoppe. The open barn doors at each end provided a throughput of fresh air. A lanky figure feverishly worked in front of a fire pit and anvil while pumping a contraption on the ground with his foot. A cable attached to the floor pedal led to a spindle hanging from a support beam above the blacksmith's head. The line was connected to a bellows providing life-giving oxygen to the fire with every pump of the smitty's foot. He retrieved his project from the red-hot coals with long, steel tongs and held it on top of the anvil. Sparks flew as he hammered relentlessly on the glowing iron before burying the project back into the pit.

I found the entire operation fascinating enough. Too fascinating to let

Rosie go it alone. Willy caught us out of the corner of his eye. No easy feat, given all of his leather garb. He looked like an evil character right out of a comic book. Dark-tinted goggles looked sinister. A towel under a leather fedora kept his hair in place and safe from flying embers. A leather wedge strapped over his face and neck resembled pictures of people masking up during the Spanish Flu of 1919. His shoulders to his knees were covered in a leather apron. Gloves creased at the elbow reached halfway up his biceps. "That poor cow," I whispered to Rosie.

Rosie giggled while giving my pinky a stern tug. "Shush."

"Well, hey, Rosie. Who's yer friend?"

"I'm Asa Paxton from 'cross the river.'" From time to time, Southern diction and enunciation snuck up on me. Willy removed his glasses and the leather from his face. I couldn't contain my excitement. "You're Wedge-Face Willy from the pie-eating contest. The winner."

Willy's huge mouth almost reached his ears as he shook my hand enthusiastically with his warm glove. "Four outta last five years. I was robbed one year by Lucky Luther."

I liked him immediately.

"I got yer piece in here." Willy opened the gate to one of the pens in the barn. "I shaped it close as I could to the parchment cutout you gave me." It struck me when he called whatever Rosie ordered 'a piece.' The only time I'd ever heard the word piece used like that was when Solace, the muralist from New York, visited Blue Rock. Solace talked about works of art and pieces she had on display in New York. Rosie commissioned an iron dinner bell in the shape of the African continent.

"It don't rang like regular dinner triangles. Hope that's OK," Willy said.

"Asa, hold it up please." I held the bell by the long, thick leather shoelace threaded through a loop Willy forged at the top of the bell. It was a large piece of ironwork, almost half my six feet. Rosie clanged the iron striker around the wide section at the continent's top. The ringing was deep before rising to a higher pitch as the vibration reached the more narrow Sub-Saharan Africa. Rosie silenced the bell with her hand. She clanked the southern end of the continent, which rang in a high pitch, followed by the lower hum of the Ivory Coast, the Sahara Desert, and, eventually, the Mediterranean coast. Rosie sighed dramatically, "Willy, I never imagined it would sound like this. It's beautiful." Willy had on his

188

face the proud look of one who had been rightfully acclaimed as an artist. Rosie dug into her purse. "How much do I owe you?"

"No charge. You tell them it's a gift from you, me, and this feller. What's yer name again?"

"Asa."

"Tell them it's from you, me, and Asa."

Rosie gave Willy a tender kiss on the cheek and wrapped him up in a big hug. Because that's what Rosie did to everyone she had affection for. I said my goodbye, proud to have met the man.

Once in the Citroen, Rosie held her hand over the ignition switch. "It doesn't matter with Willy—white, black, Indian or Asian. He doesn't have an ugly bone in his body."

We crossed the tracks, passed the road to Martha and Julia's house, and arrived at the Negro section of East Bluff called Igboland only by its inhabitants. To countenance such an outward and proud recognition of heritage would have been deemed unacceptable by the racists in charge of East Bluff. "I don't think white folks around here will like the dinner bell," I told Rosie.

"They'll keep it under wraps when necessary."

Upon our arrival, a swarm of children surrounded the Citroen. They expected our arrival and knew something different was afoot with us two white folks. Rosie held up her bag of chocolates and hard candies and gave me a wink. "Leave the bell in the car for now."

Rosie began handing out the treats. She insisted the littlest ones be served first. After we discharged the young ones with hard candies, she gave the teenagers the decadent chocolates, knowing they would appreciate them more than the younger children. For a moment, I imagined Rosie was being manipulative with her treats like ill-intended colonial explorers or missionaries so often glorified in magazines and library books. I reminded myself how all the important people in my life instantly fell in love with Rosie. I was wrong to question her motives.

After the hoard of children dispersed with treats, we were greeted by Addie and an old man aided by a cane. Addie looked me over. "Ooh-wee. Rosie wasn't lyin'," she gushed. "Said you were a handsome thang."

I offered my hand. "I'm pleased to meet you, Miz Addie." She presented her hand. I turned her palm to the ground and kissed its backside. Goose bumps and hair on her forearm rose above my lips.

"I never expected to be touched by a white man like that." Addie turned to Rosie. "Let me have it." Rosie kissed her on each cheek. An apparent loving tradition between the two women.

The old man switched his cane from right to left and offered his free hand, uninhibited by social norms. "I am Addie's father, Adjo Oduro—my African name," he announced proudly. "I was named Cesar by the master when I was born." With a high-pitched laugh, he asked me, "Do I look like a Cesar to you?"

"No, sir. Adjo Oduro is a fitting name for a man with such a firm grip."

Adjo released my hand and addressed Rosie with a big smile. "You must be Rosaleigh Elizabeth Pickett. Oh how Addie talks you up."

"I'm pleased to meet you, Mister Oduro." Rosie gently kissed his cheek.

"Call me Adjo."

"Yes, sir."

He laughed again and turned his back to us. "I never been kissed or called Adjo or sir by white folk," he said as he shuffled toward the first house in front of the community of modest homes.

"Come," Adjo directed. "We must wash your feet." A high-pitched, joyful chortle followed almost every sentence Adjo spoke. I looked at Rosie. She lifted her shoulders and, with wide eyes, shook her head slightly.

As if he knew what we were thinking with his back to us, Adjo explained the foot-washing ritual. "You are probably thinking about Jesus washing the disciples' feet or another foot-washing story in the Bible. Over the centuries, in my African tribe, we welcomed the guest and the traveler into our village and homes and washed their tired feet." On Addie and Adjo's railingless front porch sat two chairs, two wash basins with matching water pitchers, and a small corked vessel. A neatly folded towel laid across the top of each pitcher. "Sit, and hold each other's hand," Adjo ordered.

We climbed the porch stairs and took our seats. Our Christ-like servants faced us from the ground. Addie removed Rosie's sandals. Adjo removed my shoes and socks. They first massaged our feet for several minutes. The massage relaxed my feet and my apprehension over the ritual. After the washing, they anointed our feet with an aromatic and refreshing astringent before our footwear went back on.

"Asa, we should walk while Father gets to know Rosie." Addie guided me around the left side of the house. Adjo and Rosie moseyed to the right of the house and out of sight.

"Let me tell you about Igboland. My father was born a slave on this land in 1850. My deceased mother was born here one year later."

"That would make him eighty-eight now. Right?"

"Correct. As soon as the War Between the States ended, and Father was declared a free man, he went to his former master and negotiated a business arrangement for himself and the rest of the master's slaves."

"A bold move for a fifteen-year-old."

"You know it was. Father learned to be strong from African Igboland traditions and stories passed down over generations by our people."

"Like foot washing?"

"That's right. Father believed he was born to be a tribal leader on this land. The deal he struck included a property deed. Because the slaves had worked the land for generations, they knew the fertile patches to farm and where to build a community. Master didn't know he was giving up his best land. It comes to about thirty-eight acres."

"Why did he give up any of his land?"

"Father and his former master heard about General Sherman's Forty Acres and a Mule Field Order for freed slaves. Master figured, with a labor contract in hand marked by all of his former slaves, he might keep most of his land, the Big House, and his money when Sherman's Field Order came to the rest of the Confederate states. Father could read and write. He didn't fall for any contract trickery."

By this point in Addie's story, we had reached a tree-lined grassy square in the center of the community. Picnic tables were shaded under mature oaks. The sound of metal clamoring on metal grabbed my attention. At the east edge of the common, a sturdy man wielding a shovel banged on a barrel lying sideways. Both ends of the can were removed. A metal grate divided the top from the bottom of the large tube. Branches and split logs burned on top of the grate. With each strike of the shovel, hot coals dropped through the mesh to the lower half of the barrel. A few feet away, another man tended two large pieces of corrugated metal lying on the ground. Wisps of savory smoke seeped out from under the metal lids.

"Can we go have a look?" I asked Addie.

"Of course."

"This here's Asa Paxton we talked about the other day. Asa, this is Isaac and Benjamin."

"What've y'all got going on over here?"

"Hold up a minute, and we'll show you," Isaac said. He banged his shovel on the side of the barrel again, shaking more hot coals onto the pile. He scooped out a shovel full of embers. Benjamin lifted one of the corrugated metal sheets, exposing a headless, gutted, and butterflied whole pig lying stomach down on top of a grate. Isaac added his fresh coals to the smoldering pile. Rendered fat dripped and sizzled.

"Good night that looks and smells delicious."

Benjamin lifted the other corrugated piece of metal, exposing a roasting lamb.

"We've been tendin' 'em since five this morn," he said.

I noticed a large pot boiling over a limestone-brick fire ring. "What's in the pot?"

Benjamin grabbed a long meat hook and fished the pig's head from the broth.

"Nothin' goes to waste," he said matter-of-factly, dropping the head back into the boil.

"Be ready on time, right?" Addie asked.

"Yas'm," Benjamin replied.

"Nice meeting you both."

"You come visit anytime, mister Asa."

"Thank you, Isaac."

Several houses we passed had men cooking on outdoor stoves and fire rings. Unfamiliar sweet-and-savory aromas of the pot-luck dishes mingled along our way.

"Now, where was I?"

"You said the former slaves were under contract."

"That's right. For every dollar of cotton picked by the freed slaves and sold by their former owner, Father got twenty cents. Of that twenty cents, Father paid the picker fifteen cents. President Lincoln was shot three months and one day after Sherman's Forty Acres and a Mule Field Order. Lincoln was dead, and so was the promise of a fair start for former slaves. Praise Jesus, by then, Father and the other freed slaves had Igboland up and running. They had their former master's cotton and Igboland's cotton in the ground. They also planted a large crop of corn, okra, sweet potatoes, and such. Before the first harvest, a Yankee soldier from Massachusetts approached Father about buying a small section of land overlooking the river. He hated the Massachusetts cold and snow. That Yankee loved his land and the river," Addie said, with what sounded like admiration. "Father took the money from the property sale and bought goats, hogs, sheep, and chickens for breeding and harvesting. No one went hungry in Igboland. Just like African Igboland."

"Is that when y'all started your harvest festival?"

"Not exactly. There was a small celebration of what they made of themselves the first years. It grew from then, and so did the Igboland population. You know what the funny thing is, Asa? When hard times came in '29, we Negroes in Igboland never had it as bad as a lot of white folk. We knew how to survive, but we had to do it quiet-like."

"That's quite a success story for such a young man."

"Well, there were bumps along the way. Bumps started in 1878. That's a story for another time."

"You can't tell me now? You've captured my interest."

"Alright. I'll give you a little more. Things began to break up for us Negro folk in 1878. I was just a little girl. Father knew things would be different when President Grant gave up on us Negroes in the South. Mother grew up learning to cook with Gran in the master's kitchen. In 1879 Father sent Mother and me to Memphis to work in a fancy hotel. That's where I learned all about keeping house and cooking. I'm the last of a long line of women cooks. Father thought we might go back to being slaves. He told us to save a portion of our hotel earnings and run to Chicago if things got bad. They got bad, alright. Never went back to being slaves, but you know how it is here in the South. When Mother got sick, I brought her home. I've been here ever since—cooking and housekeeping for white folk."

"I don't like what I see in the South, but it's all I know. I don't remember much about living in Chicago. Mom and Dad tell me things are not much better for Negroes in the North."

"Rosie told me all about you and your people. Y'all ain't like most white folk. That's why we trust you to come visit. I wanted to see for myself."

At that point, I knew the invitation was a test.

By the time Addie was finished telling her father's story, we had reached a rocky hillside at the edge of the community and a fork in a creek. "From right here where the creek splits, to the top of this hill, and back to the train tracks is our property line."

Fenced in on the hill, goats bounced from stone to stone, nibbling on shrubs and weeds. Built into the base of the hillside, a limestone wall the size of an icebox with a pipe in the center fed sparkling water into a grate-covered stone basin. At the bottom, a small drain hole released excess water into the creek.

"Asa, have you a drink from God's own water pipe."

I filled my cupped hands and drank the cold, crystal-clear spring water. "Dang, Miz Addie, that's good."

"It's heaven-sent and never runs dry." Addie sat down at the basin's edge and patted the chiseled limestones beside her. "Have a seat. The best lesson Mother and Father taught me was to do everything with purpose. Father taught me to read and write to continue improving myself. Mother taught me to be the best cook I could be so white folk would have a use for me. The kitchen is where we women descended from Africa feel safe—feel in control.

"Rosie said your cooking is the best in all of East Bluff. I've had some of your leftover fried chicken, and your pimento cheese is to die for."

Addie pursed her lips. "I know about you and my fried chicken. Anyhow, if you look over Igboland, you can see how Father designed everything with purpose. Our hog and sheep pens, chicken coops, and mule sheds run along the base of this hillside to help protect them from the storms that come from the southwest. The slaughter and smokehouses are all the way on the other side of the town, so the livestock don't hear or smell what will one day be their fate."

"That's a humane way of thinking."

"Animals know when things ain't right. Makes for better meat too if they're kept calm."

"You haven't said anything about cows."

194

"I told you. Everything we do has a purpose. Cows take up too much land. It makes more sense to milk our goats or buy cow's milk."

"That's the opposite of what I would have thought."

Addie pointed down the creek bank. "We've harvested our summer vegetables, but you can see by the gleaning, our crops line the creek for easy watering. Father planted the hedgerow of red tips along the train tracks to keep Igboland hidden away. The red tips he planted atop the hill by the river hold the ground in place."

"You sound like my Mom and Dad. When we first moved to Alabama, we lived lean. Every penny spent or saved had a purpose. They called everything an investment. They planted a big garden, bought hens for eggs, good fishing poles, and a shotgun for turkey hunting."

"Your people were raised to do for themselves. Round here, up until fifty years ago, slaves did all the work. Plantation owners paid poor white folk to keep the slaves in line. White folk here are full of hate because of how the war turned out."

"I didn't realize how complicated things were until they built the bridge from Blue Rock, and I met Rosie. Her librarian friend Martha lent me a school book they use up North. It tells a different story than the school books we used down here. In Blue Rock, there isn't a single Negro except when my Uncle Clem and his crew come around."

"Rosie told me all about your uncle and his crew, how interesting they are, and how your uncle is a real salty cracker."

Until then, I suspected our private stroll wasn't about getting to know me. Addie had yet to ask me a single question. What she said next confirmed my feelings. "Let's talk about Miss Rosaleigh Elizabeth Pickett."

Uh-oh. First, middle, and last name. I didn't like where this was headed.

"Let me give you a piece of advice. Don't ever bring help into your home like rich white folk do. Unless you want them knowing all your business."

"I don't understand. I thought you wanted to talk about Rosie."

"We'll get to Rosie. But, first, I know just about everything there is to know about the Pickett home, if you can call it a home. There ain't no love in that house."

"I've sensed it, too."

"Miz Katherine Inez Pickett is as cold as a block of ice. She only cares about three things—being married to a big-shot lawman, her social clubs, and get'n Rosaleigh Elizabeth Pickett married off to a respectable family."

"Well, my family's not high-falutin and rich, if that's what you mean by respectable."

"Did I say you were respectable in Miz Pickett's eyes? You ain't. She thinks you're a last resort since Rosie run off every respectable boy in the county."

"Last resort? I'm feeling a little disrespected."

"Addie ain't gonna lie to you."

"You could at least use a sweeter, softer touch."

Addie lowered her chin and glared at me over imaginary spectacles at the end of her nose. "Boy, I'm just gettin' started with you."

"Great. You're just getting started with me."

"Now, as for Mister Farrington Willard Pickett. That man only cares about winning at everything, money, and keeping Miz Pickett out of his hair. In that order. He'd be just as happy to marry Rosaleigh off to you as any of those other boys that came callin'."

"How do you know all this?"

"I know all this because I heard them say it. Like I told you, don't be bringing help into your house unless you want them all up in your business."

"Well, they can kiss my ass. Rosie and I don't need them."

"That's the spirit. Now, I got some things to say to you, and you ain't gonna like 'em. Let me think on how to soften it up. Sweeten it up for you."

"Maybe you shouldn't say them."

"No. I've got to speak my mind. When I came to the Pickett's three years ago, I could see a pain in Rosie's eyes. Over the last three years, I've come across her sleeping. You know, taking naps, sleeping extra on weekends. Many times, she'd be struggling in her sleep. Calling out. Saying things like don't and stop."

I knew where Rosie's nightmares came from and her secret. I lowered my head and focused on the dirt at my feet.

"I know what happened to that innocent girl. I just don't know who done it to her. If I ever find out, they may as well go on and hang me

196

from a tree." Addie proclaimed in a shaky voice, "I love that girl. I'm gonna protect her with my life if I have to." I kept my head down. "Look at me, Asa. Look at me." Addie's fuse had been steadily growing quicker and shorter. I looked up, but would not say a word. I promised Rosie. Addie locked in on my eyes. "You know, don't you, boy." I kept silent. "You know. I can see it in your eyes. Now it all fits together." My eyes went back down to the ground.

"When Rosie met you, she changed. Cupid done went and shot an arrow into her heart. The pain she's been carrying in her eyes went away. But when she slept, her demon kept creeping back because the hurt was deep inside. I don't know who done it to Rosie or when. But I know exactly when the demon in her sleep was cast out. It was right after she graduated. She ain't called out in her sleep once, and I ain't never seen her more comfortable being a woman since that day she ran off with you and my leftover fried chicken."

Addie was bringing up things I wanted to avoid talking about. This was no friendly get-to-know-you stroll through the neighborhood.

"Young man ... I wash Rosie's clothes, including her lady undergarments. I know when she has her time of the month ... and it best keep coming. You been planting your seed in her ... regularly. Her undergarments are like the sugar glaze on my lemon pound cake after she's been with you." I gave Addie a testy look. "Was that a soft and sweet enough touch?"

"Rosie didn't need to run any gentlemen callers off. She just needed to introduce them to you."

Rosie called from down the way, "Hey, y'all."

Addie wrapped things up before Rosie and Adjo reached us. "You unburdened Rosie. You cast out her demon. I guess you make her feel like a deserving woman. I ain't gonna judge what you and Rosie do when no one's looking, see'ns how you make her happy and all, but don't you never, ever do her wrong."

"Yes, ma'am."

Rosie bounced up to me and Addie. "Did y'all have a nice visit?"

My response,"Baby, I am never, ever getting a housekeeper."

Rosie gave me a confused look, then turned to Addie. Addie's scolding demeanor and facial expression morphed into a sweet, innocent smile.

Adjo said in his high-pitched laugh and labored breathing, "I can't walk much faster than a turtle."

Rosie couldn't contain her excitement. "Adjo told me all about the ways of his African ancestors. He told me they lived in village groups— like our towns and farmed the land. The villages had elders, not kings, who made decisions that benefited everyone in African Igboland. Disputes were settled by mediation. They had their own calendar with a four-day week and a seven-week month. Oh, and they even had a banking system. They had a democracy and a more perfect union long before our Preamble and Constitution were written."

Adjo raised his old hand. "Rosie, I like your comparison of democracy and the talk of a more perfect union, but Igboland did have a few villages with kings. Only a few."

Rosie looked at the pipe poking out of the hillside. "Is that spring water? I'm thirsty."

"You have got to try it," I told Rosie.

She filled her cupped hands and took a long, slow drink. Then another. "Wow, that's good. Adjo, this must be your fountain of youth."

Adjo laughed. "We should be getting back. Soon it will be time to eat."

Along the way, we came across a small fenced-in cemetery. Adjo held open the squeaky-rusted gate. "Let us have a quick visit." We wove through several graves with simple headstones until we came to three gravestones side by side. The first stone had Ophelia Oduro 1901 carved into it. "Here lies my beloved Ophelia," Adjo said. His signature laugh did not follow. Beside Ophelia's headstone, Sampson Freeman 1910, marked another grave.

Rosie whispered, "Sampson was Addie's husband."

Next to Sampson, Our Baby Girl Rose Freeman 1910 was carved into a headstone. Rose Freeman's grave was covered with end-of-season tea-rose petals. Thorny vines crowned the headstone. Addie knelt on the ground, brushed the rose petals into a pile, scooped them up, and tucked them into her sweater pocket. She carefully pulled the thorny vine aside and kissed the marker.

Rosie gently asked, "Who is Baby Girl Rose?"

"She's my baby."

"Oh, Addie. You never told me."

"It's hard enough to tell folk about Sampson and the accident. It's too hard to talk about when it's your baby girl. Rose was with Sampson that day."

Addie was struggling to keep it together. Rosie held Addie's hand and wrapped her free arm around Addie's neck, pulling her friend's face tight against her chest. I choked down the lump in my throat. The similarity between Rose and Rosie's names was either a blessing or a source of heartache for Addie. A question I wouldn't dare ask. One thing was clear. Addie had given me a stern talking to because Rosie was the closest thing she had to her deceased child. Addie choked out, "There's been times I almost called you Rose by accident."

"It's OK if you call me Rose by accident or on purpose if you ever need or want to."

Addie took a deep breath. "We should go."

At first, our walk was a somber hike back to the center of Igboland. Strolling ahead of me, Addie held Rosie's hand and rested her head near the top of Rosie's arm. Adjo shuffled along behind me. I contemplated all the emotions Rosie and Addie must have felt. They both lost a child though under very different circumstances. At that moment, being a man felt much easier than being a woman.

As we passed houses along the way, we were joined by families headed toward the neighborhood square. Several had food to offer the celebration. One woman balanced a large square wooden board on her head, stacked at least a foot high with thin, unleavened flatbread rounds. A husband and wife held the side handles of a large round serving platter with what appeared to be steaming chunks of sweet potato. By the time we reached the square, as many as forty people had joined our parade. It had become a joyful ruckus of parents talking with each other and children laughing and running together. Another fifty or so neighbors had already descended on the common.

"Asa. Quick. Run and get the dinner bell," Rosie said.

"Don't start, please?" I asked Adjo. "We have something in the car for Igboland. I'll be right back." Adjo laughed. I returned with the large piece of ironwork, struggling to keep it hidden behind my back. Adjo, Rosie, and I stood in front of the large gathering.

The patriarch addressed his community. "It's been ninety-one weeks, a full year by our calendar since we last celebrated. God has bestowed upon us a bountiful harvest and a year of harmony in our land. Let us give thanks for the harvest and for our guests, Rosaleigh and Asa."

"Rosie yelled to the crowd, "Asa and I are honored to join you. We brought a gift from Asa, me, and Willy. Y'all know Willy, the blacksmith, right? Show them, Asa."

I swung the bell from my backside and held it up to Adjo and the crowd.

"It's a dinner bell," Rosie shouted.

There were oohs and aahs from the folks near the front of the crowd. A woman yelled toward the back of the crowd, "A dinner bell shaped like Afrika."

The way she pronounced Afrika was different than I'd ever heard. The "R" rolled off of her tongue, and the "I" sounded more like a long "E." The entire crowd joined in on the excitement of the gift. Benjamin and Isaac pushed their way to the front, took the bell, and hung it from the lowest branch of a juvenile oak tree. Isaac presented the striker to Adjo in a reverent posture. He clanged the heavy striker around the top of the bell with the strength of a man half his age. The crowd cheered at first. Adjo stopped clanging the bell, and the tone changed to a higher pitch in the southern part of the continent. The audience went silent, mesmerized.

Once the ringing faded, Adjo announced, "Let us eat."

Benjamin put his hand on my shoulder. "You all go sit. We will serve you." He returned with a large platter filled with seasoned shredded pork and lamb. Aromatic brown rice had unidentifiable ingredients mixed in. A large helping of collard greens was served in the center. Bright orange chunks of sweet potatoes had a recognizable scent I couldn't pinpoint. Isaac and a young girl arrived with four small soup bowls with crushed peanuts floating on top. A different girl handled a pitcher of spring water and four mismatched, repurposed jars from the Piggly Wiggly shelves for us to drink from. Benjamin rushed off and returned with a handful of flatbread. The pit master looked at me with a grin. "Remember the boiling pot?" He swirled his hand over the feast in front of me. "Remember, nothing goes to waste? It's in there, somewhere."

"We'll eat Afrikan style," Adjo said, tearing apart a piece of flatbread. He folded the bread over some shredded lamb and dipped it into what appeared to be yogurt before putting it in his mouth. I looked around and saw some folks using utensils while others ate Afrikan style. Some families feasted in a circle on the ground, others at picnic tables.

Addie picked up the small rustic bowl and sipped the soup. She lets the peanuts slip into her mouth like Shanks, with his RC Cola and peanuts. I followed Addie's example and took a sip of the broth. The bold flavor and hot spices exploded in my mouth. "That's spicy," I coughed out. Adjo and Rosie laughed at me.

"Eat the sweet potato," Addie instructed. "It will cut the heat."

I quickly tore some bread and folded up a chunk of sweet potato. Addie was right. The fire was slowly extinguished. They had cooked the sweet potato in coconut milk—the aroma I hadn't been able to identify. Everything except the collard greens had unfamiliar flavors and textures. Sharing one big platter and eating with bread and my hands felt like an Afrikan utopia. I was in a dreamy state until Adjo brought me back to reality.

"If this were Afrika, there would be joyful dancing and singing with drums, hollowed gourds and rain sticks. Our people left all that behind when we were brought here. It wouldn't have been allowed even if we could remember the song and dance."

There I was, a guest of honor in a neighborhood oppressed by my race. I was angry. After the Civil War, the States made little progress toward a more perfect union. Worst of all, I was helpless. "I don't know what to say, Adjo. What can I say?"

"Our people need more freedom to make new music and dances. I am told there is new Negro Delta music, but they must take it to Chicago or New York. Our time will come," Adjo said confidently.

Rosie and I left with full stomachs and on a high note. The entire community lined up at the Citroen to say their goodbyes with handshakes, kisses, and hugs. I doubt most of them ever had a caring physical exchange with white folks. I felt honored to have been welcomed into their community.

PART FOUR

CHAPTER TWENTY-EIGHT
STOVE UP

O n the fourth Sunday in October, Uncle Clem and his crew arrived on an early evening freight train from Jackson, Mississippi. They cleaned up, ate dinner, and settled in for the night. I had Rosie home before nine o'clock. An East Bluff police car and paddy wagon were parked out front. I didn't give it much thought. It wasn't my first time seeing a patrol car parked in front of the Pickett home. After all, Farrington Pickett was the County Solicitor. As had become custom, Rosie stood on the first step to the porch, eye level with me for our last kiss of the day.

I was saying my goodnight to Mom and Dad in the living room when the crash of the front door flung into the foyer wall shook the house. Rosie was gasping for air. She had ridden her bicycle from East Bluff in the dark. "They're coming for Tiny and Sam. They're coming. We have to do something."

"Who's coming?" Dad asked.

"Father and the police. I heard them. I can't breathe. I can't—" In her panic, Rosie was hyperventilating.

Dad wrapped her up in his arms. "I've got you, sweetheart. I've got you. Take a slow, easy breath." Mom peeled Rosie's hands from Dad's back and meshed their fingers together. After a few staggered breaths

202

and one deep breath, Rosie was calmed enough to talk. "There now. Tell us what happened."

"They were talking about a woman who said she was raped on the freight train from Jackson earlier today. She got off the train in East Bluff and went to the police. Police Chief Stuckey and another officer came to get Father. They're coming over the bridge to find Tiny and Sam."

Mom asked, "Are you sure you heard everything correctly? There must be a mistake."

"I know what I heard," Rosie chided. "Stuckey told Father the woman identified the entire crew, including the Twins, Etienne, and Mack, with his marbled coloring. Said it was the big one and the little one who raped her."

"They know you're here?" I asked.

"I don't think so. I walked right between them talking in the foyer. I said good night and started up the stairs. Once I realized what they were talking about, I took the server's staircase back down and out the kitchen door."

"Asa, go get your uncle and Preacher. Don't tell them anything," Dad ordered.

The crew abandoned their cots and followed me from the backyard into the house. At the same time, Sheriff Taylor and Miz Gay Lynn arrived. "I got a call from Virgil Stuckey, East Bluff's police chief," Sheriff Taylor told everyone. "Said he needed to talk to Clem and crew. Wouldn't tell me what about. I reckoned it wasn't good. He wants me to show him where to find y'all. I figure y'all wanna meet at the switchyard office instead of your house."

"We're not going anywhere," Dad said. "Rosie, tell everyone what you told us."

Rosie repeated what she heard.

"What? That's a damn lie," Sam shouted.

"Rape?" Tiny quivered.

Sheriff Taylor's hand wiped his forehead and slid down over his face. "Oh, good lord. I was afraid it was some nonsense. They're gonna wanna lock them up in East Bluff."

"Hell's bells," Gay Lynn mumbled.

"That don't make no sense," Mack said. The twins nodded in agreement.

"Tiny was in a boxcar with me the whole trip," said Etienne.

"How long have we got?" Uncle Clem asked Sheriff Taylor.

"I told them it would take me an hour to get Gay Lynn situated before I could meet them at my office and lead them to the switchyard. We've got about forty minutes to come up with a plan."

"We'll just tell them about Sam," Mom said. "That'll be the end of it."

"It ain't so simple, Dory," Sheriff Taylor said. "They could get five years for mixing."

"That's right," Preacher said.

"Hold on," I interrupted. "I'm confused. What are y'all talking about?" A strained silence overtook the room. The Twins turned their backs on everyone. Mack and Etienne looked down at their feet. Tiny looked up at the ceiling. Preacher took a deep breath and rubbed his stubbled cheeks and chin.

"It's time you tell the boy," Sheriff Tylor told Uncle Clem.

Sam stepped across the room next to my uncle. I could feel the temperature on my face rise. "Tell me what, goddamn it?"

"Asa, Sam's my wife."

I had no words at first.

"Ha," Rosie blurted out. "I knew something wasn't right the moment I met you, Sam. The way you jumped all over Clem, your boss, when he said he could eat the ass out of a skunk and the way you avoided me. You've got a lot going on under those baggy clothes."

"Samyra's my baby girl," Preacher said.

"Dang it y'all. All these years? I feel so stupid."

"We were legally married in Chicago back in twenty-three. It had to be kept a secret here in the South where mixing is illegal. No one wanted to burden you with that knowledge."

"The cat's out of the bag now," Sheriff Taylor said. "We ain't got time to dwell on it. We've got to plan."

Samyra went to Tiny, took him by the hands, and looked up at his scared, innocent face. "Tiny, Twin and Mack are going to take you back outside while we talk. Don't you worry 'bout a thing."

"What are we looking at?" Dad asked Taylor.

"Biggest concern is a Klan mob getting word. I don't think it's a problem yet. The Solicitor ain't gonna want any part of a lynch mob. He's gonna want a show trial."

"Klan mob" struck a nerve with Dad. He went to the shotgun on the mantle over the fireplace and dropped a shell in the barrel.

Gay Lynn garbled out, "If things get ugly, Hank, you're gonna need more than one barrel."

"Here directly, the problem is Rosie," Sheriff Taylor said. "If Pickett and Stuckey find Rosie here, it'll poison the well."

"I can't go back home. What if I pass them on the way? They'll know I've been here."

"We'll put your bicycle in the barn, and you'll have to stay out of sight. Hopefully, your father thinks you're in bed," Dad said.

"What's the best plan?" Uncle Clem asked Sheriff Taylor,

"They're gonna want to take the two of them back to the East Bluff jail to be arraigned in the morning. We can't keep them safe if we let that happen. Word of the rape will get out and rouse folks."

"There was no rape," Samyra complained.

"Yes, ma'am," Taylor conceded. "I'm gonna tell Stuckey they can't take them because I don't trust the East Bluff folk. We'll lock them up here in Blue Rock. I'll deliver them to the East Bluff courthouse in the morning. They got no jurisdiction to take Sam and Tiny from Alabama to Mississippi without y'all waiving extradition rights. Stuckey and Pickett know the law."

"I don't like it," Uncle Clem said. "Maybe the three of us should head up to Chicago."

Sheriff Taylor wasn't hearing of it. "Runnin' is the same as pleading guilty."

"Taylor's right." Preacher agreed. "He's right about the whole thing. This needs to play out in court rather than in the streets with a mob. They were married in Illinois. There's a states' rights argument to be made."

Rosie raised her voice almost to a scream. "Look y'all. Father doesn't care. He'll charge Clem and Samyra with miscegenation and Tiny with rape. He doesn't care about facts, states' rights, or whether he wins or loses in court. And I doubt he'll lose. The fight itself will be a political win for him."

Sheriff Taylor replied calmly. "We need to get through the arraignment.

Take things one step at a time." Rosie crossed her arms and turned her back to everyone.

"Is this the best you've got?" Dad asked Taylor.

"Fraid so. It would be best to have a lawyer representing y'all tomorrow. They got to be Mississippi Bar lawyers to practice. No time to round one up. Hopefully, y'all will get a bail you can afford."

Uncle Clem headed toward the telephone nook. "I'm calling Robinson about putting up bail."

Sheriff Taylor first addressed Rosie and me. "Asa, put Rosie's bicycle in the barn. Rosie, you need to stay out of sight. Asa, you need to be seen, not heard, except to say hello to Pickett." Sheriff Taylor then addressed everyone. "Now y'all listen here. We want Hank and Dory to answer the door and talk to us on the porch when we get back with Stuckey and Pickett. Clem and Etienne, y'all back them up. Asa, let them see you. If spoken to, be respectful until your folks send you to your room. Preacher, park yourself out of sight but close enough to hear everything said. You can explain it to the rest of the crew later. The rest of y'all hole up in the kitchen or out back and don't make a sound. Things could get ugly. We don't want any Negroes involved. No one let on y'all know why we've come calling." The sheriff seemed to have the situation, at least for a time, under control.

Sheriff Taylor and Gay Lynn returned, followed by Chief Stuckey and Farrington in a patrol car and a paddy wagon driven by what must have been East Bluff's burliest police officer. Mom answered the door with Dad by her side. "Well, hey, Gay Lynn, Sheriff Taylor. What brings you all out late on a Sunday night?" Uncle Clem, Etienne, and I sat in the living room within eyesight and earshot of the front door.

"This here's Police Chief Stuckey and County Solicitor Pickett from East Bluff," Sheriff Taylor said.

"What a pleasant surprise. It's so nice to meet you, Mister Pickett. It has been a joy getting to know your daughter. Is everything OK with Rosie? Asa took her home a little while ago." Mom was lying like it came to her naturally.

Pickett looked past Mom and Dad at me. "Hey, Mister Pickett. Everything OK with Rosie?" I said as I walked toward the door.

"Rosaleigh is fine, Asa. She's gone to bed."

Dad said in a polite but assertive tone, "What brings you all out at bedtime on a Sunday night?" Dad inched his way in front of Mom and out the door, forcing Pickett and Stuckey to the edge of the porch. Chief Stuckey leaned over the porch railing and spat a long stream of tobacco-laden saliva from the plug bulging in his cheek. The shoulder and upper end of his uniform sleeve were tobacco-stained from projectiles that hadn't cleared his body.

Stuckey stepped in front of the Taylors and Pickett. "We've come to collect two of Clem Paxton's niggers for raping a white girl on the Jackson freight today."

"Hold on, Stuckey," Sheriff Taylor interrupted. "You didn't say nothin' about rape when you called. You said you wanted to talk to them, not collect them."

"What's going on here?" Uncle Clem asked, rushing to the door with Etienne.

"Asa, you need to go to your room," Mom ordered.

Rosie was perched by the open window in my bedroom overlooking the porch roof and yard with the bedroom lights off. She whispered, "I can hear every word. Stuckey said he was there to arrest the biggest and the smallest, you know what, on Clem's crew."

We heard Uncle Clem shout, "The hell you're taking them. My crew didn't rape anyone."

"Fine, you can keep 'em," Stuckey shouted back. "I guarantee you'll have a lynch mob here before midnight. They'll have every one of them niggers swinging from a tree."

The sound of boots scuffing the porch flooring and a couple guttural grunts preceded the sound of wood cracking. Stuckey's threat set Etienne off. He punched Stuckey so hard that he crashed through the porch railing, landing in the front yard. Etienne jumped off the porch and onto Stuckey. We could then see the two men from our vantage point. Etienne landed several more blows before the police officer, Dad, and Pickett scrambled off the porch and wrangled him off the police chief.

Stuckey struggled to his feet, gagging and coughing. "I swallered my plug. I swallered my plug. Taylor, you best arrest this crazy Cajun."

"Ah, pipe down, Virgil," Rosie's father scolded before turning his animus on Uncle Clem. "We didn't come here for him. We came for the Negroes, and we intend to take them."

Gay Lynn limped off the porch and into the front yard. Standing toe to toe with Pickett, Gay Lynn growled, "Over my dead body, and I mean it." Her normally handicapped speech was as forceful and clear as a bell. She was angry. While Gay Lynn was shaking her gnarled right hand in Pickett's face, she fished a pistol from her apron pocket with her left hand, cocked it, and jammed it into Pickett's ribs. "I ain't too stove up to pull this trigger. Them folks saved my life once. I owe 'em. Like I said, over my dead body."

Everyone froze. Sheriff Taylor was still out of sight on the front porch, but I could hear him speak uncharacteristically gruffly. "I tell y'all how this is gonna go. They'll be in my lock-up until morning. I'll deliver them to your courthouse by nine a.m. for arraignment. As far as a lynch mob getting any ideas, I got a loaded Thompson and every right. I'll mow 'em down like it's Saint Valentine's Day. That's a promise. Now, you boys tuck your tails between your legs and head back over the bridge." Gay Lynn stepped back but kept her pistol aimed at Pickett.

"Nine a.m.," Pickett shouted, pointing his finger over Gay Lynn's head toward the front porch. "Nine a.m." Farrington then confirmed my fears. "Paxton, I've got no ill will toward your boy, but he best stop calling on my Rosaleigh." Dad didn't respond.

"Never," Rosie whispered.

"Holy crap," I whispered back. "Sheriff Taylor said nothing in the plans about Miz Gay Lynn and a pistol."

The East Bluff posse sped off into the darkness.

Mom tapped gently on my bedroom door. "Rosie, may I come in?"

"Yes, ma'am."

"I'm sorry," Mom said, wrapping her arms around Rosie while kissing her forehead.

"They're all such horrible people. They're scary. They're embarrassing and make me so angry."

"We'll get through this," Mom assured Rosie. She went to my closet, pulled out my collared dress shirt, and handed it to Rosie. "You can sleep in this." Mom kissed her on the head again, then me, and headed for the door.

"Mom, uh, um ... wait," I stuttered. I didn't know what to say about the sleeping arrangements.

Mom flashed us a wry grin. "Asa. Rosie. You two think Hank and I don't know? Now get some sleep." Mom and Dad must have agreed, Rosie and I had just seen enough to deserve more respect than petty pretenses about our carnal knowledge and separate beds.

CHAPTER TWENTY-NINE
Pontius Pilot

Rosie and I sat alone at the breakfast table with only a few benign words spoken. We poked at the bowl of cheese grits and runny eggs. Rosie's distant eyes blinked and darted from side to side. I tried but failed to purge my fear that Solicitor Pickett would discover Rosie spent the night at the Paxton home—another justification to end our relationship. My concern was selfish and insignificant compared to what Uncle Clem, Samyra, and Tiny were facing. Our stomachs could have used dry toast instead of what would generally be a comforting and solid start to what was sure to be a difficult day.

"Rosie, why don't you take a bath? It'll perk you up." Mom suggested. "I have a dress you can borrow if you like."

"Yes, ma'am."

While Rosie was in the tub, Mom and Dad joined me at the kitchen table. Dad spoke first. "We want you sitting with us behind Tiny and Samyra at the arraignment. The Taylors agreed to sit with us, and Etienne will be there also. We need as many supportive white faces behind the defendant's table as possible. Robinson is prepared to pay any bail amount. Hopefully, Samyra and Clem's marriage can remain a secret for now. The rest of the crew will have to stand in the back if they're allowed in. I'll carry everyone over in the Leyland. You drive the Citroen."

"Yes, sir."

Mom took my hand, "Rosie will want to be there. Her presence will do more harm than good. She can stay here. You can take her home, to the library, anywhere except the courthouse. And make sure you're in your seat no later than eight-thirty."

"Yes, ma'am. I'll talk to her."

I heard tub water draining from the upstairs bathroom and my bedroom door close. I went to talk to Rosie about staying away from the courthouse, but her demeanor had changed since breakfast. "Let's go. We don't have much time," Rosie said, rushing down the stairs and out the front door in her clothes from the previous day.

"Go where? What's the rush?"

"We're going to see Father at the courthouse." Rosie held the singular car door open for me.

"Hold on. Mom and Dad think you should be anywhere but the courthouse. I agree."

"Fine. I'll ride my bicycle."

"Baby, don't be like that."

"You Yankees living on this side of the bridge with no Negroes don't understand how things work. You've got to fight as dirty as they do when it comes to their hate and ugliness. We fought a war over this, and it still wasn't enough. Am I riding my bicycle, or are you driving me?"

"What are you going to say to your father?" Rosie cocked her head and scowled at me. I could see the resolution in her eyes. "Fine. I'll drive you."

We didn't say a word during the quick trip to downtown East Bluff. It was evident upon arriving at the courthouse that word had gotten out about the alleged rape. Shops were closed. TVA laborers took the day off. The local paper's one-man publisher, editor, and photographer was in position. Police officers kept the curb and stairway in front of the courthouse cordoned off for a perp walk. After crawling the streets in search of a parking space, we finally found one three blocks away. I was late. Rosie marched double time to a side door at the courthouse.

"Hello there, Rosaleigh," said the policeman guarding the courthouse side entrance. "Who's your friend?"

"I'm here to see my father."

"I've got strict orders to secure this entry."

"Those orders don't apply to me. I wouldn't want to be you if Father finds out you wouldn't let me see him."

"Yes, ma'am," the officer cowed and held the door open.

We passed a closed door with a large brass "Judge's Chambers" sign. The Solicitor's office next door had a smaller sign. Across the hall, the courtroom rumbled with excited townsfolk. Rosie held her father's office door handle. Her eyes closed, her chest expanded, and her shoulders raised. I felt like I might hurl. Rosie exhaled and barged in. "What in the world?" Farrington said from behind his desk. "And what are you doing here, Asa?"

Rosie looked at Chief Stuckey sitting on the other side of the room. "Get out, Stuckey. I need to talk to Father in private." Stuckey's jaw slacked. He looked at Farrington, who had an equally shocked expression.

"What's this all about? At breakfast, Addie said, when she arrived this morning, you were leaving on your bicycle with a basket full of books—figured you were off to read in the park." Addie had instinctively covered for Rosie.

"Tell Stuckey to get out," Rosie ordered her father.

"Virgil, take Asa with you."

"No, Father. Asa stays." Farrington dismissed Virgil with a head nod. My heart raced because of Rosie's risky actions and what I had gotten myself into.

Farrington said dismissively, "Well, Rosaleigh? I'm waiting?"

"You're going to drop the charges on those two Negroes. You know as well as I do they didn't rape that woman. She just wanted a hospital bed and three square meals for a few days. She probably needs a break from selling herself to survive."

"Have you lost your mind, Rosaleigh? Stuckey had to rush the arrest and booking paperwork this morning. Their arraignment is the only thing on the docket. Those Nigras are the reason the courtroom is packed with voters."

"Father, I'm not stupid. All you have to do is tell the judge you're dropping the charges."

"Do you think you're going to be those Nigra's savior?"

"God dammit, Father. You would think that way, wouldn't you? I don't—"

"Don't you take the Lord's name in vain, young lady," Farrington scolded.

212

"I don't care who is being oppressed. Those men don't need a savior. They already have one in Jesus. Regardless of skin color, what they need is an ally. I intend to be just that. Drop! The! Charges!"

"I most certainly will not drop the charges."

"Yes, you will. And here's why. If you don't, I will ruin you and Mother's lives."

"The heck you will. I don't know what nonsense the Paxtons have been feeding you, but I've heard enough out of you."

Rosie leaned across Farrington's desk. "Now you listen, and you listen closely. If you don't drop the charges, I'll tell everyone in East Bluff what you and Mother allowed your brother to do to me. How you and Mother knew it was happening but were too busy campaigning to make it stop. It'll be so graphic no one will ever be able to look you or Mother in the eye. I'll describe Uncle Oakley's sweat and tobacco spit covering my body as he raped me over and over. I'll describe his panting like a dog as he pounded his body into mine until he soaked my insides."

Farrington's look of indignation turned into shock and horror. "Asa, it's time you leave."

Rosie's courage inspired me. I dug deep. "Oh, I know all about it, Farrington. You can't intimidate me. And don't blame the Paxtons for Rosie's enlightenment. She had your sinful Jim Crow and Black Codes figured out long before I came along."

"Don't look at Asa, Father. Look at me. I won't only tell you and Mother's society friends about the months y'all made excuses while I was being raped. I'll tell them about the abortion you arranged and the pain and the infection the so-called doctor caused me. You won't be a pillar of the community anymore. When your society friends see you and Mother, they'll see incestuous white trash. And then, when I'm finished humiliating you and Mother, I'll leave East Bluff, and you will never see me again. Ever."

Farrington stood up and walked across the office to his framed law degree hanging on the wall. "You think you're being a hero, Rosaleigh. I think you're being a fool," he said, tapping his finger on the diploma frame.

"Father, sometimes a fool can be a hero. And sometimes, a hero is only a hero to fools. You have to choose. Will you be a hero to all those hateful fools in the courtroom? Or will you, for once in my life, be my hero?"

There was a long silence while Farrington lost himself in his ornate Ole Miss certification. I was already deep in the mess. I decided anything I said couldn't do more harm. "Farrington, this isn't a political calculation. You don't need to worry about me. Your secret is safe as long as Rosie wants it that way. Everything said in this room stays in this room. Listen to me, Farrington. Every son and daughter wants to be proud of their parents."

There was a soft tap at the door. "Solicitor Pickett. It's time," the bailiff said from the hallway.

Through clenched teeth, while staring her father down, Rosie said again, "Drop the charges." Walking toward the door, she stopped at a painting on the wall. "One more thing, Father. Take your pale, straight-haired, blue-eyed Jesus down. Christ was probably dark-skinned like those two innocent Negroes, who you, just like Pontious Pilate, are willing to crucify for political gain."

We entered the courtroom from a private doorway reserved for the judge, solicitor, and bailiff. All eyes were on Rosie, me, and Farrington.

Tiny looked at Farrington for only a second before fixating on the tabletop. Samyra's contemptuous eyes followed Farrington all the way to the solicitor's table. Sensing Samyra's defiance, Sheriff Taylor nudged his wife. Gay Lynn leaned over the railing and said something to Samyra. Samyra released Farrington from her glare and looked down. Rosie marched past the accused and their supporters without as much as a glance. She wedged herself into a seat on the first bench behind her father. I took the saved seat between Mom and Dad. I'm sure my parents were both confused and furious with me. Furious because I was late. Furious because I'd driven Rosie to the courthouse. Confused by our entrance with Farrington. Dad started to speak under his breath. "Asa—"

"Don't ask," I interrupted.

"All rise," the bailiff ordered.

The judge, a tall-slender white-haired man, took his seat. He appeared to be at least seventy years old. Old enough to have witnessed the post-Reconstruction chaos creating the Black Codes and Jim Crow. "You may be seated," the judge told the crowded courtroom. "I see we only have one item on the docket. Not even a few weekend drunk and disorderly arrests. Yet we have a full courtroom for a simple arraignment. Bailiff, you're up."

The bailiff read a series of numbers from a piece of paper and the rape charges.

Farrington stood up and asked the judge, "May I address the court?"

"What's on your mind, Solicitor Pickett?"

Farrington turned and took a slow look at Rosie, then Tiny and Samyra. After surveying the gallery, his eyes landed back on Rosie.

"Get on with it, Pickett," the judge grumbled.

"Your Honor, I believe it is my responsibility to explain to the fine citizens of our great county my investigation of the rape accusation before this court. After speaking with the doctors who examined the alleged victim, I believe the accuser is more a victim of our economic times than of rape. The doctors confirmed evidence of intercourse but none of violence or force. After speaking to the victim, I can assure you she comes from the finest Southern stock but has suffered, as so many of our Southern brothers and sisters have suffered. I find comfort in knowing the young woman has rested her weary head and relieved her hunger pangs in East Bluff's hospital."

I could hardly believe it. Farrington was pulling on Lost Cause heartstrings. He then pivoted. "Also, I have firsthand knowledge of the accused's overseer. He would not allow such behavior from his Negroes. It is also important the citizens of our great county know the accused's financier in Chicago is responsible for many of our TVA construction jobs. I will not bite the hand that feeds our people. To wit, I am dropping all charges against the defendants." The solicitor looked over the gallery and made one more pronouncement. "I assure anyone bent on harming the accused will be prosecuted to the fullest extent of the law."

The befuddled judge's left eye twitched. "Are you sure about this Solicitor Pickett?"

"Yes, your Honor."

"Well then, case dismissed. Court adjourned," the judge ruled with a strike of his gavel. Tiny let out a big sigh. From behind Samyra, I could see her jaws pulsating.

"All rise," the bailiff ordered. The judge retired to his chambers.

Except for a few mumbles and sighs, the courtroom was unexpectedly hushed. I knew the blood-thirsty gallery had not seen this show before. Dropped charges was not how the performance was supposed to play out. There were several acts still to be performed over the coming days. The selection of an all-male white jury. A brief trial and closing arguments. A jury deliberation long enough to have lunch brought in at the court's expense. Afterward, the anticlimactic fifth act. A predetermined guilty verdict, followed by the final act. The resolution. The sentence. A lynching like the good old days, or at the very least, a stiff jail sentence for the Negroes who had defiled The Lost Causes' most prized possession.

Farrington lumbered off to his office in a hangdog posture, avoiding eye contact with everyone in the courtroom. It was no time for a celebration. Sheriff Taylor advised us to stay put until the courtroom cleared and for Tiny and Samyra to return to Blue Rock in the back of his patrol car for security reasons. I expected Rosie to join us on the winning side. She knew better than to confirm her role in the proceedings. The disappointed crowd exiting the courtroom was indeed suspicious of what they considered a miscarriage of justice. Once the room emptied, Sheriff Taylor and Gay Lynn led the way. Chief Stuckey slouched in a chair next to the central doorway where he held guard during the arraignment. With his battered face from the night before, Stuckey looked like a whooped dog who had submissively rolled over and pissed on himself. Sheriff Taylor stopped, without a word, put his hand on Stuckey's shoulder, squeezed, and then patted his back before exiting.

Rosie was nowhere in sight on the courthouse square. I found her leaning against my car door. I was ecstatic. "We won. You won."

"Nobody won, Asa. Just like today, there will be another case and another still. There will be more false accusations. There will be more lynchings and lawless white men and police killing Negro men and women for a long time to come."

My heart sank upon hearing Rosie's assessment. "Sadly, I suppose you're right."

"We got lucky today. I had something to bargain with." Rosie put her hand on my cheek. "I don't mean to scold. One good thing came out of today."

"What good thing?"

"Our first time, you know, at the dam. You helped me heal in a special way, but I still had a festering wound. I closed the open wound I had with my father today. I'll always have a scar, but I can move on in some respects."

"I understand."

"Now take me home, please. I'm sure they're waiting for us." I knew she meant the Paxton home.

My parents, Uncle Clem, Preacher, and Samyra, sat at the dining room table, waiting. They had added three folding chairs to the regular seating for four. Two chairs sat empty, alone, on one side of the table. "Where's everyone else?" I asked.

"They went straight to their cots out back. They're emotionally exhausted," Mom said.

"Have a seat," Dad ordered. He was the chairman of the inquiry. "Son. Tell us what happened back there."

Rosie put her hand on my thigh under the table and gave me a trusting smile. If she had thought I would reveal her wounds, scars, and secrets, she would have given Dad a non-answer before I could speak. "There's nothing to talk about."

Mom stiffened in her chair. "For Pete's sake. What do you mean there's nothing to talk about." She wasn't asking a question.

"There's nothing to talk about," I repeated.

Uncle Clem spoke up. "Rosie, this concerns Samyra and me. What happened back there?"

"We'll say one thing, Clem. Afterward, there's nothing else to discuss. Asa and I assure you, my father knows nothing about Samyra's gender or about you two being married."

After a brief silence, Preacher imparted his wisdom. "I'm satisfied. I suppose if anyone at this table isn't satisfied, they can go discuss it with Solicitor Pickett."

That was that. End of story. Rosie never took credit, and no one ever again asked what occurred behind closed doors at the courthouse. Everyone knew Rosie had somehow carried the day.

CHAPTER THIRTY
THE ASK

Rosie didn't go home the night the charges against Tiny and Samyra were dropped. Instead, like the night before, she slept in my bed. Farrington didn't call or come to collect his daughter. He knew controlling Rosie was a lost cause. The Paxton Yankees had won the skirmish, the battle, and the war for her heart. Life would never be the same for the Paxtons or the Picketts. It couldn't be the same after the revelation of Uncle Clem's marriage to Samyra and Rosie standing up to her father. The mixed-race couple slept in the spare bedroom across the hall from my room. Arrangements that could have sent Uncle Clem and his bride to jail or worse if discovered by local racists. Rosie bedding down with me could be punishable by fornication laws, but Sheriff Taylor policed with a soft touch, and we were out of Chief Stuckey and Farrington's jurisdiction.

"Clem, Asa, breakfast," Mom yelled from the bottom of the stairs.

I had been awake, admiring the angelic woman sleeping inches away. Rosie's eyes flickered open. A big smile engulfed her face. "I never want to leave here," she said before burying her lips between my neck and shoulder.

"We have to. Mom doesn't like her food getting cold."

"No, silly. I'm saying I never want to leave this house, this home, this life. What would Dory and Hank think if I said it to them?"

"Whoa, Rosie. I don't know what to say. They've told me you're always welcome here, but—"

218

"I know, Asa. It's honestly how I feel, though. I love you and your family. I want to live here. Will you ask Hank and Dory? Please, Asa? Please?"

"Alright then. We've talked about getting you out of the Pickett house before. We can bring it up after breakfast. I gotta tell you though, I'm nervous about their reaction."

We bumped into Samyra and Uncle Clem in the tight hallway at the top of the stairs. Uncle Clem was wearing only trousers with his belt unbuckled. Rosie was sufficiently covered in my dress shirt. My eyes were fixated on Samyra. She filled out a pair of Uncle Clem's boxers. His sleeveless T-shirt clung to her curves. All those years, there was never a hint of a female under baggy work clothes and right under my nose. I was shocked, chagrined, and angry when I first learned the Sam I had known was a woman. Seeing the real Samyra that morning hit me differently. Her skin was as smooth and silky as an expensive chocolate. Years of physical labor sculptured her arms and legs. Her face was round with soft-puffy cheeks, almond-shaped eyes, and full lips. She was beautiful.

Uncle Clem broke the awkward silence. "Ladies, after you."

Mom and Dad were already eating at the dining room table. There were four more place settings with two folding chairs. Uncle Clem and I instinctively left the comfortable seats for Samyra and Rosie. A platter of pancakes, a plate of sausage patties, and a half-empty milk bottle sat in the middle of the table. A syrup dispenser bobbed in a bowl of warm water. The pancakes were passed in one direction, the sausage in the opposite.

"Coffee?" Mom offered, filling white diner mugs from the percolator. "How did everyone sleep?"

Samyra answered sarcastically, "Better than the night before last."

"Clem?" Mom asked.

"The bed's a little soft."

Samyra gave Uncle Clem a look and gently grabbed Mom's wrist. "The bed is perfect, Dory. Thank you for asking."

"Rosie. How about you?" Mom asked.

Rosie chose her words carefully. "Better than in a bed in East Bluff."

The whole scene was surreal, as if I was in a dream, where you know the setting and actors, but they're out of place, doing things that don't make sense.

Breakfast continued with the sounds of cutlery on plates, spoons stirring coffee, and the soft sound of chewing, which, even with the best effort, is loud when coming from a large group of full mouths. Dad and Uncle Clem sat beside each other in conversation about their boss. Rosie, Mom, and Samyra were in a lively discussion about ladies' undergarments. I learned there is no such thing as a perfectly fitting bra. They were laughing about how men have no idea what it's like to be a woman. Samyra joked under her breath, "Clem oughta have to wear clothespins on his nipples at the same time of the month when mine are painfully sensitive." Mom's laughter exploded through her nose. Rosie dropped her fork and covered her mouth. The girls carried on, becoming more and more animated and agreeing with each other. I was already dizzy, anticipating a conversation about Rosie moving in. I wanted to take my plate somewhere, anywhere, and find someone, anyone else to eat breakfast with, but I was afraid to stand up—fainting was a distinct possibility.

Suddenly, I was snapped out of my fog as if someone had waved smelling salts under my nose. Rosie suggested excitedly, "I know a great ladies' shop in East Bluff. We could all go shopp—oh no ... no ... n ... no," Rosie stammered. She had slipped. "I'm so sorry, Samyra."

The table went silent, with everyone fixated on Rosie. Samyra stood up, walked around Mom, and took Rosie's hands in hers. "God bless you, child. You forgot the color of my skin." She lovingly kissed the back of Rosie's hands, stepped behind Uncle Clem's chair, wrapped her arms around his neck, and kissed his ear. "I'm going to get dressed for work. I love you."

Uncle Clem reciprocated sweetly, "I love you, too."

Eating resumed except for Rosie. Dad and Uncle Clem went back to their conversation about Robinson. Not knowing what to say, I stuffed my mouth. Crushed, Rosie stared silently at Samyra's empty chair. Mom tried to console her. "It's OK, honey. You didn't make the rules."

Uncle Clem finished eating and excused himself to, as he put it, "drain his main vein," leaving the four of us alone at the table.

"Mom. Dad. Can we talk to you about something?" I had never been so nervous about a conversation with my parents. I felt like my nerves were a sign I was not yet mature enough for what I was about to ask them.

Mom topped off her coffee. "Sure, honey. What's going on?"

"We all know life's been crazy the last two days. Thank goodness things worked out the way they did. However, now there's a pall over Rosie and me at the Pickett home."

Dad's eyebrows tightened. "We hadn't thought about things for you two going forward."

"Right. Going forward. Going forward is what we wanted to talk about. I ... I I mean, we. We were thinking. How would you feel about Rosie moving ... you? You know. Living here?"

Dad's eyebrows loosened. He sat back in his chair. He looked dazed like he'd been sucker punched. Mom wrapped her hands around her coffee mug and took a slow sip. The silence was excruciating.

"I hate to say this," Rosie said, filling the void while fiddling with her napkin. "I love you two more than my own parents. I feel more at home here than in that big, fancy house. I love your son with all my heart, and I know I'm ... we're ready for this."

Mom looked at Dad. His disoriented expression hadn't changed.

"She's practically lived here since we met." I pointed out. "Except for, you know, sleeping. It wouldn't be much different."

Rosie chimed in, "I would pull my own weight. Every week I clean Martha and Julia's house for spending money. I could get another job to pitch in with expenses. Hank, Dory, I want to be part of this family. Please. This is where I belong."

"First of all, this isn't about money," Mom said. "It's about your relationship with your parents. I know how I would feel if Asa told me and Hank he didn't want to be part of our family anymore."

Dad sat up in his chair. "Maybe a little distance between Rosie and her parents would be good. It wouldn't be that strange. You and I weren't much older than Asa and Rosie when we got married and lived with Mom and Dad until we got on our feet."

There it was again. Rosie had Dad wrapped around her little finger. Rosie's eyes grew, and her lips tightened.

"I do like having another woman in the house," Mom admitted.

"Sooo?" I prodded.

"Fine. But you've got to work on your relationship with your parents," Mom told Rosie.

"That goes for you too, Asa," Dad said, pointing at me. "You need to stay on the high road with her parents." Dad didn't point at me often. When he did, I knew he was serious.

"I will. I promise," I assured Dad.

Mom and Dad weren't aware they were expecting us to go along to get along with parents guilty of neglect. A bitter pill Rosie and I would have to swallow. The matter was settled. Rosie became family in every way except name.

Rosie developed a routine after moving in her belongings. Every Saturday, she cleaned Martha and Julia's house. Afterward, she went to the Pickett home for fried chicken, collards and rice with white gravy at the kitchen table with Addie. After lunch, at least an hour was spent visiting with her mother. "It's not like sitting around with Dory," Rosie told me. "There's a stiffness, a phoniness that comes part and parcel with being proper for most Southern women."

Sunday dinner was dedicated to Rosie and me at the Pickett house. The table conversations were awkward initially. Dad's insistence I work on my relationship with Farrington and Katherine was good advice. In the beginning, I could feel Rosie's parents' anger. Rosie chose an unconventional and embarrassing lifestyle, but they were also happy to be rid of the liberated daughter who, while under their roof, broke the Lost Cause and Jim Crow norms. Over time, the Sunday dinners thawed.

CHAPTER THIRTY-ONE
CHRISTMAS

Less than two months had passed since the desperate woman made her rape accusation. Uncle Clem and crew rolled through East Bluff and Blue Rock on their way to job sites several times without incident. Rosie, the addition to the Paxton home, blended in seamlessly. She and Mom handled most of the domestic chores. Dad and I kept the home fires burning. Domestic chores, though, are where gender roles ceased. Rosie frequently initiated conversations at the dinner table or afterward in the living room about scientific hypotheses, religion, or the nature of humanity. Mom, Dad, and Rosie were skilled conversationalists and dug deep into the subjects. Each brought a different angle to the discussions. If a consensus could not be reached, Rosie, in her stubbornness, would return to a subject after visiting Martha at the Carnegie library for documentation to justify her position, which Mom and Dad respected. I learned much from the three of them. Even though I graduated top of my class, Rosie, a young woman ahead of her time, place, and age, frequently left me in awe. I realized I would have to hold on to Rosie for dear life. She was no shrinking violet and would not sit back and let the world pass her by.

Mom dropped an envelope in front of me at the kitchen table. "You've got mail." The envelope was expensive, heavy stationery addressed to

Mr. Asa Alan Paxton and Ms. Rosaleigh Elizabeth Pickett. A gold wax stamp embossed with the initials *KIP* sealed the correspondence.

"Mom. It's addressed to Rosie, too. Are we supposed to open it together?"

Mom laughed and didn't answer the question. "Welcome to an adult relationship."

I found Rosie reading in the soft chair we positioned by our bedroom window after she moved in. "Here. You open it."

"Oh, good grief," Rosie sighed, "Not the annual Christmas party. It's a dreadful affair with all the Who's-who."

Rosie retrieved her fancy letter opener from her writing table in the spare bedroom and returned to her seat. She slid the blade under the triangular fold of the envelope and separated it with a soft puff of breath—one of the minor differences between Rosie and the Paxton family. A Paxton would've ripped open the envelope with reckless abandon.

"Hmm. This is interesting," Rosie said. "It's not the annual Christmas party ... praise Jesus. We've been invited to a family dinner or luncheon on Christmas Eve or Christmas Day. Mother wrote she wants to work around the Paxton family's traditions. I can't believe it. Mother expects the world to revolve around her. She wants us to RSVP."

"It would have to be Christmas Day. We always have a special dinner on Christmas Eve. Rosie, what exactly does RSVP mean? I've heard the term before and understand its general purpose, but I don't know the exact details of those four letters."

"Répondez s'il vous plaît," rolled off Rosie's tongue. "Please reply is the translation."

"Wait. I didn't get that. Say it again."

Rosie said slowly, *"Répondez s'il vous plaît."*

I know a good opportunity when presented. "Respond, see you play?" I asked, leaning in.

"No, no, no. *Répondez s'il vous plaît.* Watch my lips. *Répondez s'il vous plaît.*"

"OK, OK. I think I can get it. I need you to say it one more time. Only this time, in my ear, softly, slowly, sexy like."

Rosie hit me over the head with her mother's invitation. "You are incorrigible, Asa Alan Paxton." She stood up, pushed me into the chair, and obliged my ear with her steamy breath, *"Répondez s'il vous plaît."* She then kissed my ear and neck, knelt down, unbuckled my pants, and obliged me with her French kisses.

Rosie sent the response, accepting the Christmas Day luncheon invitation.

We all worked diligently to ensure everything in our home was just right by Christmas Eve. Dad and I hiked deep into the woods in search of the perfect Christmas tree. Mom adorned the house with thorny boughs of red winterberries. The dozen candles Rosie bought softly illuminated every corner of the living and dining rooms and dinner table. Dad harvested a pile of small green cedar branches to add crackle and a balmy aroma to the gentle fire.

Dinner's main course came from a handwritten recipe book Addie authored for Rosie and presented over their lunch date the Saturday before Christmas. It was a dramatic and colorful stew of lamb, diced yams, and purple-hull peas baked in a hollowed-out edible gourd.

After dinner, we relaxed in the living room over eggnog spiked with the last of my Uncle Perlie's Tennessee whiskey. Rosie laid her head in Mom's lap, reading Beatrix Potter's *The Tailor of Gloucester* aloud while Mom gently ran her fingers through Rosie's hair. Rosie drifted off halfway through the story. She often fell asleep on the couch in Mom's, Dad's, or my arms. Carrying her limp body up to our bed was an honor.

I could sense a soft tapping in my dream. The sound turned into a full-on knock, pulling me from my slumber. "Wake up, you two. It's Christmas," Dad said from the other side of our bedroom door.

"We'll be down in a minute," I said.

"Don't lolly. Santa came."

Mom and Dad were teetering on the edge of the couch wearing Christmas morning smiles. The two packages Rosie and I placed under the tree several days earlier were joined by two additional presents. Since Dad's gift put a dent in our funds, Rosie and I agreed to spare each other the pressure of a gift exchange.

"Y'all go first," Rosie said, handing Mom and Dad each their present. "They're from the both of us."

Dad tore away the gift wrapping of what was obviously a large book and read aloud, "The Holy Bible. A Complete Study Guide."

Rosie said, "Martha, at the library, suggested this version would be good for a Northern Presbyterian. It has historical context at the bottom of each page."

Dad examined the cover, spine, and back of the enormous book. "Text is meaningless without context," he said.

"We had to special order it at the bookstore," Rosie said. "The bookseller told us, 'We don't sell this sort of thing around here.' I took that to mean folks around here prefer to make up their own biblical context," Rosie opined with a grin. Mom, Dad, and I had a good chuckle over Rosie's observation of the Southern state of Christianity.

Dad was positively glowing as he thumbed through the pages. "It's perfect."

"Your turn, Dory."

Mom peeled the paper away from the thick-soft-oval package. Her eyes grew large while at the same time blinked several times. "Look, Hank, it's a needlepoint of Buckingham Fountain. It even has the seahorses ... and, oh my, the water spouting up. The thread is so shiny and silvery. It sparkles like real water. What made you think? How did you?" Dad handed Mom his handkerchief.

"Yes, ma'am. Remember? You told me all about the fountain while we were doing dishes the first night y'all had me over for dinner. I started working on it a few days later. We had Addie make it into a firm throw pillow."

"It's so detailed and taut. This must have been difficult."

"Yes, ma'am. I'm not trying to complain or brag. It was challenging. I copied a picture from a library book about Chicago landmarks. To see your expression, it was worth every needle pull."

"I've never received such a thoughtful gift. Thank you. I love it." Mom hugged the pillow before hugging us both.

"Asa, your turn," Dad said. "It's the one wrapped in newspaper."

"What is it? A fish?"

"Oh, Asa. Don't be funny," Mom chirped. "We didn't have any wrapping paper. Smalley's was sold out." Mom and Dad gifted me a pair of leather driving gloves and a wool driving cap. "Rosie helped pick them out. Now you'll look proper with the top down in the Citroen."

"Your turn, Rosie," Dad said excitedly.

"Hold on." Rosie retrieved a package hidden behind the tree. "This is for you, Asa. I couldn't resist."

"I thought we agreed—"

"Hush. Just open it." Rosie purchased a muffler matching the riding hat perfectly. "Now you'll look like my handsome Frenchman cruising down the *Champs-Élysées.*"

"Rosie. Don't start speaking French." Rosie snickered at our inside joke about my Franco-linguistic fetish.

"Your turn. Your turn, Rosie," Dad said nervously while cleaning out his ear with a key on his keychain.

Rosie picked up the remaining small package wrapped in lined legal paper. "Oooh. It's heavy." She slid her fingers under the taped paper seam, revealing a thick rectangular cardboard box. Rosie looked at Mom and Dad. "Only expensive things come in a sturdy box like this. I hope you didn't do too much." She separated the top of the box from the bottom. Her face lit up. "Look, Asa." Rosie removed a small camera, pulled off the lens cap, and raised the viewfinder to her eye. "It's too much, y'all."

"We thought you would like it," Mom said.

"It's a thirty-five-millimeter. Nice and compact," Dad bragged. He leaped to his feet and separated a skeleton key from the rest of the keys on his chain. "Follow me, Rosie." Dad doubled up the stairs to the spare bedroom with Rosie, Mom, and me lagging behind. He fiddled with the skeleton key to the normally unlocked room. "For crying out loud. I hate skeleton keys."

"For Pete's sake, Hank. Let me."

Dad found the sweet spot. "Got ya." He pushed open the door and flipped the light switch. A red glow illuminated the room. "It's the rest of your Christmas present, Rosie."

Rosie stepped into the red glow. "When did you do all this?"

"Last night. While you were sleeping."

"He was so excited to play Santa for you. He planned everything out," Mom said.

The bed, dresser, and writing table had been rearranged, making room for a workbench of two wooden boards supported by two empty lubricant barrels from the switchyard. The windows were darkened by layers of old newspaper. Above the workbench hung a cotton rope with clothespins for drying processed photos. Dad pointed under the workbench. "Everything you need to develop your photos is in those bins."

Rosie sprung off the floor, wrapped her arms around Dad's neck, and kissed his cheek. "I'm so excited. It's chemistry. It's science. It's art. This is going to be so much fun. Thank you, Hank. Thank you, Dory."

CHAPTER THIRTY-TWO
BEAUREGARD PARCELL

The biscuits and gravy had barely settled when we arrived at the Pickett house a few minutes after noon. I never understood why the big Thanksgiving, Christmas, and Easter meals are always served shortly after noon. Rosie rang the doorbell rather than letting herself in. It was her way of making the point she no longer considered the Pickett house her home. To our surprise, it was Addie who opened the door. Rosie was incensed. "Addie, what on earth are you doing here on Christmas Day? That's just wrong."

"Don't you worry, child. I dictated the terms. Addie's gonna get her porch screened in," she said with a belly laugh and a little two-step. "Besides, when I heard you and Asa was comin', I couldn't help myself. I wasn't gonna subject you to Miz Pickett's cooking on Christmas Day. That would be, just wrong." Rosie wrapped her arms around Addie and kissed her on the cheek. "Now, the other side," Addie ordered. Rosie did as she was told. Addie gently rubbed Rosie's lipstick in, bronzing her brown cheeks. "Am I glowin' now?" Addie asked.

"Your cheeks are always glowing. You don't need my lipstick."

"Just like the good old days. I do miss you, child," Addie lamented.

"At least we have our Saturday lunch routine."

"That's right." Addie kissed me on the cheek. "Merry Christmas, Asa."

"Merry Christmas, Addie."

"Asa, when you gonna make an honest woman outta Miss Rosaleigh?"

"I already asked her once."

"You suggested it in a moment of despair. You didn't ask," Rosie clarified. "Even if Asa got down on one knee with a diamond ring, I wouldn't say yes. I'm an independent woman."

"You somethin' child. Anyway, before we step inside." Addie twitch her head toward the porch ceiling.

Rosie and I tilted upward. Rosie's head paused, then fell completely back. Her eyes closed as she sighed. She looked back down at Addie and shook her head. "When did she do that?"

"Last week. Sal was spit'n mad paint'n it. Oh well. Y'all come on inside."

Addie pointed to the closed parlor pocket doors, "Your peoples are in there. Now, I best get back in the kitchen."

Once Addie was out of earshot, I asked what the issue was with the ceiling. "Sal is short for Salifu. His Gullah basket name. His mother was a Carolina low-country slave girl. She was sold off after he was born." Rosie lowered her voice. "He's lighter skinned. I bet his father was the master. His wife probably made him sell her and Salifu out of state when she saw the baby. Haint blue is a Gullah Geechee color meant to stave off evil spirits. Mother's co-opted Salifu's heritage."

"I'll never understand the South."

Merry Christmas was coming from every corner of the parlor. "Merry Christmas, everyone," I announced to keep things simple. Rosie and her sister Vernel gave each other a disingenuous hug. They had not seen each other in two years, and it was painfully obvious they didn't miss one another. Vernel was eight years Rosie's senior with a toddler son and a six-year-old daughter whom she had popped out on schedule— precisely forty weeks after her wedding day. Vernel spent Christmas with her in-laws in Nashville the previous year to keep things fair between the two families. Rosie once told me she and her sister were too different to have a close relationship. The difference was immediately obvious to me. Rosie was naturally beautiful, moved gracefully, and was confident. The heavy makeup was no help to Vernel. When she stood up from the settee to hug her sister, her ankle twisted in her high heels, her knee buckled, her hips gyrated, and her arms flailed about before she regained her balance. After greeting me, Vernel tried to introduce me to her daughter Punkin—short for Penelope. Punkin fish-hooked each side of her mouth with her pointer fingers, stuck her tongue out at me, and ran off before Vernel could scold her. Vernel's toddler son, Jackson, waddled up and kicked me in the shin.

"Jack!" Grandfather Farrington bellowed, causing Jack to fall on his behind, screaming, his arms and hands extended, shaking uncontrollably.

Rosie whispered, "Let's nickname him Heart Attack Jack."

Vernel was a flustered mess seeing to Heart Attack Jack, so Rosie stepped in and introduced me to her brother-in-law, Beauregard Parcell. "Nice to meet you, Beauregard." While I was shaking his hand, my mind wandered. The name Vernel Parcell had a funny ring to it, and other than Rosie, the only thing I had in common with everyone in the room was the letter P at the beginning of everyone's last name.

"Call me Beau," he said in a forced voice as if he had dropped it an octave to sound more impressive.

"Nice to meet you, Beau."

Beauregard was a typical Ole Miss frat boy. Privileged and overconfident. I knew him better than he knew himself. To use Uncle Clem's phraseology, if Beauregard were actually confident, he would have cut someone other than Vernel out of the herd.

Addie appeared with a serving tray, balancing three cold drinks. "Your usual, Rosie." She handed Rosie a glass of half lemonade and half sweet tea. "Sweet tea or lemonade for you, Asa?"

"I could really use a snort of Uncle Perlie's Mash-Up whiskey," I whispered.

"Oooh, I know that's right. This place is a mess," Addie whispered back.

"I'll have the lemonade, thank you."

"Five minutes, Miz Pickett," Addie told Katherine.

The dining room table looked like it was set for royalty. The silver was polished to a spotless shine. A low-cut centerpiece bouquet provided an unobstructed line of sight between the guests. Seating arrangements were predetermined and marked with each guest's name written in ornate calligraphy on white cardstock mounted in silver holders. I was thankful my name was Asa. Looking at the cards, I couldn't distinguish between Rosaleigh, Farrington, Katherine, and Beauregard. The cards all looked like a jumble of herky-jerky thin and fat lines depending on how the ink pen rotated in the calligrapher's hand. Farrington was, of course, seated at the head of the table. Beauregard was on his right with Punkin seated between him and Vernel on a stack of Montgomery Ward catalogs. Heart Attack Jack sat behind a tray in a highchair at the corner of the table between Vernel and Katherine, who was seated opposite Farrington. I sat to the left of Farrington, directly across from Beauregard, with Rosie to my left.

Addie pushed through the butler pantry door with her butt, each hand holding serving dishes. She placed a large platter of perfectly pink, sliced beef tenderloin in front of Farrington. A green bean casserole was placed at Katherine's end of the table. Addie noticed Jack becoming restless in his chair. She scooped a handful of oyster crackers from her apron pocket and spread them onto the boy's tray, immediately grabbing his attention. She returned from the pantry less than a minute later with a large basket of steaming, golden-brown yeast rolls glistening from melted butter brushed over them. She placed a large, shallow baking dish in front of Rosie and me. "This is in the recipe book I gave you. Creamy baked middlins with golden raisins, spiced pecans, and the top drizzled with maple syrup." The dish looked and smelled like soulful culinary genius—both elegant and inexpensive.

Katherine asked suspiciously, "You gave Rosaleigh a recipe book?"

Rosie answered for Addie. "Yes, Mother. It was a lovely gesture. She hand-wrote them in a journal."

Thankfully, Farrington interrupted Katherine's moment of insecurity by clearing his throat. "Let us pray," Farrington said with his eyes closed.

The prayer could have been the opening statement to a jury. Farrington laid out the facts, choosing his words carefully. He began with "Virgin Mary" rather than stating "Mary was a virgin." "Joseph was obedient to God," rather than "planning to divorce Mary." Farrington mentioned the star in the east and the wise men with their gifts—the manger, swaddling clothes, and, of course, the baby Jesus. He made the event sound so quaint. All I could think of was my education from Dad, Rosie, and Mom one night at dinner about the likely, actual life and times of Jesus, including whether there actually was a virgin birth. And Golgotha, rather than Calvary, was the name of the garbage dump where Jesus was crucified. The one firm belief we all had was the gospels provided the best guide for righteous living.

Dinner immediately became chaotic when Vernel clumsily dropped the heavy serving fork on the platter of steak, startling Heart Attack Jack. He exploded into screams with his hands shaking in front of him. Vernel tried frantically to calm him. Her panic upset him more. Punkin clapped her hands and laughed hysterically. Useless, Katherine sat beside the boy disappointedly while Farrington put his big hand on his forehead like he was shading his eyes from the sun. Vernel's hero, Beauregard, didn't miss a beat. He cut a huge piece of meat from his plate and stuffed it in his mouth. The meat was perfectly tender, although, when you stuff as much meat into the mouth as he did, it's gonna take a while to get it down. Staring blankly across the table and straight through me, ignoring Jack's meltdown, he chewed and chewed.

"Damn it, Vernel," Rosie chided after what seemed like an eternity of Jack screaming. She grabbed a yeast roll, leaned as far over the table as possible, and tossed it onto Vernel's plate. "Here. Give Heart Attack Jack Addie's roll."

Farrington burst into laughter. "Heart Attack Jack. That's a good one, Rosaleigh."

Vernel tore apart the warm roll and offered a hunk to Jack. The boy took the bread and slowly calmed down. "Addie's yeast rolls could calm an angry bear," Rosie mumbled to herself.

Once Jack settled down, Beauregard became engaged. I made the mistake of asking him about his job. He carried on and on, making it sound more important than it probably was. Once Beauregard was through bloviating, Farrington took the opportunity for a subtle dig. "It's his daddy's company," Farrington told me, knowing I would get his dismissive point. (I learned over our weekly Sunday dinners that Farrington wouldn't usually use the word "daddy.")

Regarding my line of work, Beauregard, the lumpy little prick, peppered me with backhanded compliments and demeaning musings about railroad work. I could tell by Farrington's expressions that he was getting about as sick of it as I was. I guess I had earned some respect from Rosie's dad over those weekly Sunday dinners. Right when I was ready to dress down Beauregard in front of everyone, Jack had another explosion, seemingly for no reason. His third explosion in less than an hour. Beauregard shifted into his useless blank stare mode, stuffing more meat into his mouth.

Farrington chuckled quietly to himself, "Heart Attack Jack."

Looking at Vernel, instead of contempt, I suddenly felt sorry for her. Her hand shook as she put down her fork. A look of shame, helplessness, and exhaustion weighed on her. Rosie excused herself, rounded the table, and lifted Jack from his high chair. Snot, drool, and tears covered his red face. This was not a spoiled brat crying tearlessly. Rosie tucked Jack's shaking hands and arms firmly between her breasts and cradled the back of his head, pushing his sloppy face between her neck and shoulder. Rosie and I exchanged a knowing look. There was something not right with this poor child, and his parents were not equipped to handle him. Rosie whisked Jack through the butler's pantry to the kitchen. After several minutes, Rosie returned to her seat with Jack asleep in her arms. Vernel looked across the table at Rosie holding her child and mouthed, "Thank you." I cut the remainder of Rosie's steak and green beans into bite-sized pieces, which she ate with her free hand.

After dinner, Rosie put Jack down on the couch in the formal living room and joined the rest of the family in the parlor for coffee, white cake, and the gift exchange.

In sorority girl fashion, Katherine had the handkerchiefs she gave me and Beauregard monogrammed. She also pointed out how the monogrammed stationery and wax seal kit she gifted Rosie would still be good should she ever take the Paxton name.

After the awkward gift exchange, Farrington and Katherine took their coffee and cake to their chairs by the fire. Rosie and Vernel talked intimately on a settee in the corner of the room. The sisters had a relationship breakthrough.

I was looking out the picture window, admiring all the fancy houses on the street, when Beauregard sidled up to me. "So, I guess you got the milk without buying the cow," Beauregard said like a redneck preacher passing judgment.

I'd had enough. I summoned my innermost Uncle Clem and quietly let the self-righteous little shit have it. "That's right. I get all the milk I can drink, and it's warm and creamy. You know, Beau-Re-Gard, once when Rosie and I were lying in bed, she brought up your wedding day, then Punkin's birthdate. She did the math and figured you bought your heifer right off the auction block without squeezing the dry udders first. You know, Beau-Re-Gard, Vernel seems like the type of woman who thinks sex is such ... well ... messy business. I'll bet there's no oral pleasuring happening in the Parcell house. I guess Punkin and Jack are proof you've been laid twice. Speaking of Jack, there's something wrong with your boy. You need to act like you've got a pair and help your fragile wife with him."

Beauregard probably wanted to cold-cock me, but I had him by at least six inches and a laborer's physique. Instead of taking a swing, he finished his cake and left the parlor without saying a word. He went up to the guest room and didn't even come down to say goodbye. I knew tearing Beauregard down was wrong, but I didn't regret putting the little shit in his place. It wasn't the Christian thing to do. I knew Rosie would not have approved of my characterizing any woman as a heifer. But through the grace of God, I knew I was forgiven.

Christmas at the Picketts may have been a little strange, but it had been a success in the end. The siblings made a connection. Rosie resolved to visit her sister in Nashville every month or two to help with Jack. Katherine's willingness to work around our family Christmas traditions validated the Paxtons' equal social status.

As she did most every night, Rosie descended into sleep with her head on my chest. She twitched, mumbled, and giggled while my mind drifted back to those Great Depression days in Chicago when I wasn't much bigger than a June bug. Back then, I prayed for the return of ice cream sundaes, picture show matinees, and the sun-drenched bleachers of Wrigley Field. I prayed hardest for Dad to find steady work. God's answer was "yes" to all but one prayer. Perhaps one day I'll find myself basking in the afternoon sun of the Friendly Confines with a cheese steak dog and a whiskey as my beloved Cubs lose another one.

Author's Notes

T hank you for reading *The Education of Asa Paxton.* If you enjoyed the novel, I hope you will write an online review and share with your friends.

Much has changed in the Heart of Dixie since this story's era, yet sights, smells, and personalities of an earlier time remain. Tufts of cotton blow across back roads during harvest season. The acrid scent of coal-fired home furnaces lingers over small towns. Four a.m. meetings of the minds around a spittoon still occur in old-school service stations. Irony rules the day in many small towns; streets named after Dr. Martin Luther King Jr. intersect with town squares boasting confederate monuments protected by Alabama's legislature and Gov. Kay Ivey's pen.

Juxtaposed to the remnants of yesteryear is the reckoning and reconciliation of Alabama's dark history. Civil rights trails meander through towns. In Montgomery's Lynching Memorial and The Legacy Museum, the soil collected from beneath strange fruit trees around the United States reminds all who visit that Alabama is not alone in its original sin. Sights, smells, and people of progress have emerged since the Great Depression. Automobile factories repurposed acres of farmland. Award-winning restaurants make use of local organic produce. Alabama universities produce titans of tech, space exploration, and medical miracles. A vibrant cultural arts community reflects the characteristics and customs of this place.

The best and worst of the Heart of Dixie is anchored by one of the most beautiful and diverse environments in the United States. From the Appalachian foothills in the northeast to Bayou La Batre in the southwest and the sugar sand beaches kissing the Gulf of Mexico—waterfalls, natural springs, and lakes abound. I encourage everyone reading this to explore what Alabama has to offer.

Peace,

Gary

ABOUT THE AUTHOR

After living in Ankara, Turkey, and Pittsburgh, GARY S. MINDER landed in Tuscaloosa, Alabama, at the beginning of school desegregation. He is one of nearly six hundred graduates from the powerhouse melting pot of Central High School. Over the years he has called Chicago, Boston, Seattle, and Portland home before returning to Tuscaloosa in 2006. *The Education of Asa Paxton* is his debut novel and the first installment of the Haint Blue Series.